Bram Sol

by

H. Pilkington

Grosvenor House
Publishing Limited

This book is published by
Grosvenor House Publishing Ltd
28-30 High Street, Guildford, Surrey, GU1 3HY.
www.grosvenorhousepublishing.co.uk

A CIP record for this book
is available from the British Library

ISBN 1-905529-54-6

For Ann - with love…

Thanks to Glen, Mark, Julie and Dave.

Not forgetting Damien, Kayleigh and Thomas.

Thanks to Joti Bryant.

Special thanks to Mr Chris Bem
& his team at Bradford Royal Infirmary.

1

Emma Dobson had come to the last day of her latest modelling assignment on a Costa del Sol beach.

The limousine, at her disposal for the week, was waiting on the roadside overlooking the beach. She kept her bikini on, slipped into her travelling clothes and climbed in the limo.

In less than fifteen minutes, the limo came to a halt a few paces from her accommodation, a luxurious motor yacht called Oliver, moored in a prominent spot close to the bars and restaurants of Marbella.

Omar, a bronzed-faced lad of twenty, dressed in a smart white uniform, gave her a broad smile and unhooked the brass ends of the two-inch thick, bright red rope that barred the gangway. 'Welcome aboard, Emma, day nice. You leave? Is a shame.'

She shook his hand. 'Yes, wish I could stay.' She walked up the gangway to the stern of the three hundred, forty-five foot vessel. She smiled and shook her head; when she'd arrived a week earlier it was to gasps of, 'Oh my God!' There was no mention of the size.

"You'll be staying on my yacht," Alistair Guinness had said, in a nonchalant manner. Well, it dwarfed everything in the harbour, and to call it a yacht was a huge understatement; it was a floating palace.

The vessel was used for spectacular parties, banquets and conferences. There was a swimming pool, beauty salon, gymnasium, sauna, disco, a hundred-seat conference room and forty luxury suites, each with a marble bathroom and Jacuzzi.

Normally there were up to eighty guests staying on board, celebrating whatever their company was launching, and firms paid £100,000 per day plus expenses for the privilege.

Charters Worldwide owned the vessel and Alistair Guinness owned the charter company, along with the Party Scene magazine that Emma had just done a photo shoot for.

It was no coincidence that she was in the master suite, complete with bathroom, dressing room, Jacuzzi and steam bath, sitting area, breakfast area, sixty-one inch plasma screen, and a commanding view. *And why not*, she thought, *seeing I was the only one on board all week.*

Not that she'd been lonely; each night, every yacht in the harbour seemed to have an invite to the dinner parties.

A crew of seventy manned the vessel and the highly trained staff had pampered her every moment of her stay. She drank champagne at breakfast and dined on exquisite meals prepared by world-famous chefs.

Emma checked through her suite to see if the porters had left anything, but no, it was as if a forensic team had gone through and removed all the evidence of anyone ever having stayed there.

A porter escorted her to the helipad where a helicopter was waiting to transfer her to Malaga airport for her flight in a private jet back to the UK. She climbed in the chopper and sat there thinking, *That was really great, a most enjoyable week. If Alistair Guinness was trying to impress me, he's done a good job, but I'm just an ordinary model, not the queen of England.*

Back home in Bromley, and after two days of continuous rain, the sun was out. Emma slipped into her casuals, poured a glass of wine, picked up her diary and went outside to the garden. A warm breeze blew from the South and the air was sweet with the smell of apple blossom.

Emma flicked through her diary, her agenda was simple; she spent a third of her time modelling, a third partying and a third sleeping, but not always in that order. She looked at the entry for that evening. *I might have known,* she thought.

At that moment, Pal, her huge Alsatian, came bounding from the potting shed, with part of a coat dangling from his mouth. He dropped it at her feet, cocked his head to one side and locked eyes on her as if to say, 'Come on then!'

Emma smiled. 'I'm not playing with that, Pal; it's mucky.'

He shook the thing and tossed it in the air. At that point, a letter dropped from a torn pocket; it was dated five years earlier, to the month, May 1995, and addressed to her husband, Gavin. She opened the letter.

Half way through the letter, she swore aloud. Pal licked her arms, one after the other. She stroked his head, 'Come on let's go for a damn walk; it's not your fault.'

At the nearby park, she sat on her usual bench next to the small lake where Pal normally swam; instead, he jumped on the bench beside her and sat licking the tears from her face. She hugged him.

'I'm okay, you go and play.' He gave her face one last lick, jumped off the bench and ran to the lake.

She ran her fingers through her long, wavy blonde hair and shook her head. *What other secret is he hiding? Well, I don't want to know, I don't care and I feel bloody sick.*

An hour later, she threw her casuals to the other end of the bathroom, showered, and transformed herself in a trice.

Ready for the inevitable cameras, she waited for her transport to Lockstock Hall, an imposing residence on the outskirts of London. Alistair Guinness, the owner, invited Emma to every party he threw; he also, reluctantly, invited Gavin. *You'd think running a cosmetic surgery clinic, Gavin would be a celebrity in his own right. Not so, far from it,* she thought.

At that point, the doorbell rang; her transportation had arrived.

'Hi, my lovely blue-eyed girl. Did you have a good day, Emma? Where's Gavin?' Ted, Alistair's chauffeur asked when she climbed in the Rolls.

'Amateur dramatics, you're to pick him up when you've dropped me off… and I've had a rough day, thanks.'

'Blimey, what's gone wrong then?' He turned a flirty face towards her, his brown eyes flashing.

Ted was a tall, good-humoured man in his mid-thirties; he had short, coal-black hair, a round nose and the whitest of teeth. He had a permanently happy-go-lucky expression, and was extremely good looking.

She forced a smile. 'It's a private matter.'

He started the engine, turned to her again and eyed her body as if she was about to become his next conquest. 'Not serious I hope.'

'I said, it's private.'

'Maybe I can help.'

'Ted give over, you make me laugh.' She'd no doubts about his ability to help; the girls didn't call him the 'baby machine' for nothing. He'd seven kids with his wife Ann and, reputedly, as many again elsewhere. He didn't pay maintenance; the pregnancies were intentional; being a sort of surrogate father, the women paid him.

'Emma, you're the party girl I respect the most. Is it the modelling?'

'Thanks Ted, but it's not the modelling.'

'The dog then?'

'Pal's fine.'

'Not Gavin by any chance?'

'Mind if I sit quiet, please?'

Emma Dobson had been a commodity since she was fourteen, though there had been snares along the way. She got caught in one eight years ago, and was still in it.

'They call him the pharmacist,' her friend Amy had said on Emma's seventeenth birthday, 'He's the main supplier on the drug scene. He's thirty-two, but a poor example, you'll see; he's coming over now.'

A poor example of what? Emma had wondered. *A drop-out, skid-row drunk, or a thirty-two-year-old trying to make himself look forty and lonely?* Emma watched as he made his way towards them. His dark hair was in a pigtail; he had a tight little mouth, sticking out ears, troubled eyes and a pained expression that seemed frozen on his face. He wore a dark suit, with a jet-black polo-necked jumper underneath, and, for some reason, black leather gloves; *maybe to complete the frozen look,* she thought at the time.

He peeled off a glove and held out his hand, it was red hot. 'Hello, gorgeous.' His lips moved just enough to let the sound come out. *Not exactly the type of guy you'd hang around with,* she thought. *Oh, yes, and boy did I get that wrong. Renting a room at his house, with access to heroin…yippee. Well, it seemed yippee at the time, but it rapidly went downhill.*

Two years later, Emma Dobson staggered into a registry office and married Gavin in a haze of drugs and booze. She spent her honeymoon in a rehab clinic and he went off to a health farm.

The next time she met Gavin, he'd transformed himself. 'I've finished with the drug scene and set up a cosmetic surgery business,' he told her. His frozen face had changed to a smile; his hair was short, neat and tidy and he had on a smart business suit. From then on he would say, 'I love you dearly,' with monotonous regularity. Emma knew they were just words.

Maybe things would have worked out okay, she thought, *but the letter I found earlier has put a damper on that. Worse, he's kept it to himself for five years and that hurts.*

At that moment, Emma fell asleep.

Ten minutes later, she woke to a sudden lurch forward.

'You okay, Emma?' Ted peered at her in the rear view mirror. 'I nearly hit a tree. You let out a hell of a scream.'

'Just watch the road, please.'

'Bad dream, eh? Sounded as though you were being tortured. What happened?'

A shiver ran down Emma's spine. 'It was no dream, it really happened.'

'That was a bleedin' painful scream.'

'I wish I could've screamed at the time.'

'Somebody prevent you from screaming?'

'Yes, a slob in a slum area of Manchester. What's so remarkable is the way everything has changed. Lockstock always reminds me of how far I've moved on.'

'Snap, I get that when I jump in the Rolls… Manchester… not Moss Side?'

'Worse, the Back of Little Hell; not far away though.'

'That was a 'no-go' area for us; it was a 'no-go' area for everybody, I think.'

'Ted, you never lived in Moss Side!'

'Two up, two down, a right shack, two houses to one outside loo.'

'I know, but at least, the orphanage had proper toilets and no tin baths.'

'Orphanage… not '*The*' orphanage?'

'Yes, there was only one in the area.'

'You mean you were living with interfering care-worker, 'Morphine Jack' who got jailed?'

'Ted…!'

There was a long pause.

Emma thought about what she had lost just after her fourteenth birthday. *When I prided myself on the attention from the boys, when I felt wanted for the first time in my life. Then that night, and before I could scream, he held a pad over my mouth…*

'Emma, you okay?'

'I was the one that reported him, need I go further?'

'No, you don't, the scream said it all. Anyway, it's over now, but if need be, counselling may help.'

'I've a strong constitution, thanks to my grandma.'

'Don't remind me; you're the most untouchable lass on the circuit.' He glanced at her through the mirror. *What a pity*, he thought, *long, wavy blonde hair, large ice-blue eyes, small nose, thick lips, soft and curvy six-foot body, skin like cream and so sexy.* 'Don't you ever let yourself go?'

Emma gave him a wry smile. 'No, I don't let myself go, in the way that you mean.'

'There's a lot of fun out there you know Emma.'

'Oh, right. Listen Ted, I don't do nude, I don't do topless, and I don't sleep with Arab sheikhs, no matter what they offer. Although, I'm not even sleeping with Gavin and after this afternoon I'm really pissed off.'

'Blimey… well, in that case—'

'Ted, you're the chauffeur, and we're in the grounds of Lockstock Hall, not chatting on some Moss Side embankment.'

'Sorry Emma, I thought we were.' He pulled up on the forecourt at Lockstock Hall, leaned over the seat and smiled. 'Good lass. And now you're more likely to see a crocodile than a cockroach.'

'I know; trouble is, there's a few around here walking about on two legs.'

'Now, now, Emma… By the way, what did Ian have to say?'

She locked eyes on him. 'Sorry?'

'Katie's son, Ian, I met him earlier in the week.'

'My sister Katie… her son Ian… I don't get it.'

'Said he'd call on you; you mean you haven't seen him?'

Emma fell silent for a moment.

'No… when?'

'Tuesday,' Ted continued, 'I flew Alistair in the chopper to a game fair in Lancashire. Ian came in the beer tent with another lad.

'He didn't recognize me and was surprised when I told him I was a friend of his Auntie Emma. We had a couple of beers together. I gave him your address and phone number; thought he'd ring you.'

'Sadly, he didn't…beer… Time flies; he'll have grown a few inches.'

'Six-foot now. Alistair said he had your looks and would make a male model. I thought nah, too shy to be one, only spoke if we spoke. When he did speak, he had the slightest trace of a Welsh accent and wore class country clothes.'

'Did he not mention Katie and Stewart?'

'When I asked where they were living, he just shrugged his shoulders. "I've been living with an aunt, but I'm with my mum and my step dad now," he said. I pressed him further. "They are both okay, but I'd rather not talk about them," he replied. Then they finished their drinks and left the tent.'

'Don't say you left it at that?'

'No way, I caught them outside, told Ian his parents owed my wife a monkey. They came back in the tent and stayed a while.'

Emma gave him a blank look. 'A monkey?'

'Five hundred quid. My wife had a necklace with animals on, the badger dropped off; she took it for repair to Stewart's jewellery shop in Knightsbridge. When she went back two weeks later, the place was a boutique. Katie and Stewart along with Ian, had disappeared.'

'Yes, I know they disappeared. But now, seven years later and by sheer chance, Ian strolls into a tent in Lancashire; then he vanishes without giving out his address… What did he say about the money?'

'He paid me. Stewart gave him some money to buy a shotgun; Ian gave it me instead. "My dad won't mind," he said. Alistair wasn't pleased, and peeled off five hundred quid from a roll in his pocket. "Here buy your father's gun," he said, but Ian turned away, he wouldn't take it.'

Emma wiped her eyes. 'Good lad Ian.'

'Strange business.' Ted jumped out and opened the back door.

'Your friend's still here, been here for over two weeks.'

'How is she?'

'A total wreck.' He jumped back in the Rolls, blew a kiss and drove off to pick up Gavin.

James the butler clocked Emma as soon as she strode into the Hall; he eyed her slowly from head to toe. 'Good afternoon madam.'

'Afternoon James.' She avoided eye contact but forced a smile. His dickey-bow outfit and ever-polite voice meant nothing to her, and hardly made him a butler. He had a shiny, clean-shaven head, cheerless hazel eyes, a flat nose and square cheeks. He was built like a heavy weight boxer and eyed her as if she was about to become his next victim. *No surprise he doubled as a doorman on party nights,* she thought.

She made for the rainbow room; he followed her, carrying his silver platter.

She ignored him and made for the swimming pool, a 'no-go' area for the platter; he retreated elsewhere. She could never understand the rule, because people ended up stoned and skinny-dipping anyway.

The full sized pool was a top-notch affair with chandeliers hanging from the high glass roof. Tropical trees and plants on all four sides, with ornate tables and chairs set back from the pool. Mingled scents of expensive perfumes and exotic plants hung in the air with not the slightest hint of chlorine. Soft classical music played in the background.

There were about twenty people in the pool and a few dozen sitting around the pool on plush loungers. Alistair Guinness was sitting at a large round table in a corner with a group of girls who seemed smitten by him. *Yes, well, isn't every girl smitten by him,* Emma thought.

Alistair was breathtakingly gorgeous. He had a charming smile with deep blue eyes that turned you on, no matter how well you thought you could resist him. He had a smooth, slightly tanned face, with flowing jet-black hair, resembling a swash-buckling pirate. He was six-foot-one with a physique tailor-made for a woman's desires, and an asset that was greater than his looks; he could entertain royalty or bin men with equal panache.

Emma spotted her friend Amy, a non-swimmer, in the shallow end of the pool. After slipping into her bikini in the changing room, she joined Amy, who was alone, and obviously not fit to be in the pool. Emma gave her a hug. 'I wish you'd go into rehab, Alistair will pay I'm sure.'

'Flippin' heck, there's nothing wrong, why go into rehab?'

'Okay, there's nothing wrong, it doesn't matter.'

'Never felt so good. I'm ok; it's everybody else that's not ok.'

'Forget it, just enjoy yourself.' Emma hitched her up onto her shoulders and waded further out.

Amy began laughing and pressed her on until the water was up to Emma's chin.

Suddenly, Amy began shaking uncontrollably. At the same time, someone pulled Emma's feet from under her. Amy, in a frenzy to keep above water, stood on Emma's back trapping her on the bottom of the pool.

The more she tried to push herself up, the more Amy kicked the strength out of her, and the more Emma's lungs emptied in tiny bubbles rising to the surface. She desperately tried to hold them back, but it became impossible. The last bubble forced its way out of the corner of her tightly pursed lips.

In the few seconds of consciousness before gulping in water and certain death, time seemed to stand still, she thought about Alistair. *The kiss he forced on me when I first met him, how I backed off when I felt myself responding, how I backed away from him ever since.*

Now, of all damn times, I'm thinking of Alistair, not Gavin, Pal, Katie or Ian...

She knew then, that she had become addicted to Alistair, the way she had once become addicted to drugs... *If I could only see him now I'd say, 'Alistair I love you', then kiss him for a long time, a very long time.*

Lungs bursting, she had no option other than inhale. *Please, God, let some air come in with the water!* She inhaled deeply, the water gushed in and she passed out instantly, as if she'd taken a large shot of anaesthetic.

When Gavin arrived home from the amateur dramatic class, he found a note on the kitchen table reminding him to feed Pal. 'As if I need reminding,' he muttered to himself. 'After all, I feed him every day.'

He gently opened the patio door, just enough to shove the dog bowl through. Pal snapped at his hand before he withdrew it. 'You sod. That hurt!' He quickly slammed the patio door. 'You won't ever do that again Pal!'

At that point the doorbell rang; Ted had arrived to pick him up.

Ten minutes later, Gavin, fiddling with a plaster on his finger, climbed in the Rolls next to Ted. 'Dog treats me like a burglar.'

Ted eyed the plaster. 'Grief; you don't get on then guv?'

'No, and no intention to, even if he'd let me.'

'Well, when you've a dog that's as big as yourself roaming the house I reckon the best way is to like them as much as possible.'

'Don't worry, he doesn't roam the house, unless Emma is in, then he just follows her from room to room and sleeps next to her bed at night.'

'Doesn't surprise me. I mean, Alsatians are known to be a one-person dog.'

'Yes, well, he has his own kennel he uses from time to time.'

'What an intelligent dog, thinking about you both like that.'

'Intelligent? The dog needs treatment.'

'He's okay with me, and Alistair plays with him, no problem.'

'Yes…I know. Love your dog, love you, type of play.'

'Bit risky don't you think? Considering his success rate with women.'

'Alistair flirts with her; Emma flirts with him, nothing serious; it comes with the job. If you can't flirt then you can't be a model, simple as that.' *They won't be flirting much longer, though.*

Ted pulled up on the forecourt at Lockstock. 'You'd better get in there before they do decide to get serious.'

He drove off, shaking his head in disbelief, muttering to himself. *Nothing serious in that; they're only flirting, who cares. Emma wouldn't dream of jumping into bed with Alistair. Well, we're only talking about a guy with raging hormones, six-foot-one, devastatingly handsome and the richest in the land.* He scratched his head, raised his eyebrows and laughed to himself. *Why would she be interested in Alistair when she has sexless Gavin?!*

James met Gavin in the hallway. 'I think Emma has gone for a swim; she ignored the platter altogether.'

'You must be doing something wrong, or you've upset her. You need to keep on the right side of her.'

'I can only do that if she'll let me.'

'That's stupid talk; don't keep pushing drugs at her.'

'I thought we were—'

'Well, don't think, please.'

'Listen, I'm the one who thinks around here.'

'Okay, okay; just don't keep pushing the platter at her; she's clean, I don't want her freaked out on dope.'

'She'd be more use to us that way don't you think?'

'Maybe, but she is my wife, I'm just about hanging on to her as it is. I've seen how their eyes sparkle and the way they smile. We don't need to drug her up.'

'Well, it worked before, only this time she won't be fallin' for you, will she?'

'No, and I think she already loves Alistair, and that hurts.'

'She's just a dolly bird that lives with you, that's how I see it. She'll stay in the suite for a couple of weeks. By the time the two weeks are up, Alistair will make an offer. You'll say yes to a divorce and he'll announce his plans to marry Emma.'

Gavin gave him a wry smile. 'So simple, eh?'

'Look, I've dropped enough hints about you being broke. I think he'll make a good offer... I'd like to see Emma on somethink, though.'

'She'd be in the abyss, that's no good to anybody.'

At that moment, a girl brushed past and collapsed, sobbing, on the doorstep.

'What's the matter?' James asked.

'Emma's dead!' she blurted out. 'She drowned in the pool!'

2 After passing out, Emma found herself floating six feet above the pool, *I'm fully conscious and not at all dead,* she thought. She saw two men pull her body from the water, she knew she'd left her body and tried to get back in, but couldn't. 'I'm okay,' she shouted to her friends, but it was as if they were deaf.

'Call the air ambulance!' someone shouted.

She floated, ghost-like, into the changing room and looked in the mirror, but there was no reflection. She looked down to her body, but there was nothing to see; it was translucent. Terrified, she stared at the blank mirror in disbelief. She hovered there thinking, *This is weird, I'm just floating like an invisible balloon.*

Then a wonderful feeling came over her. *I feel free like a bird, no cares and no worries,* she thought. She zoomed off at a fantastic speed in some type of capsule, as if going up a transparent elevator with no top. One minute she was looking down on London, the next, looking at craters on the moon. Earth became a dot.

She passed galaxy after galaxy, just zooming through space and thinking, *I don't know where I'm going and I don't care what's happened to my body. I feel euphoric; I'm going somewhere very special.*

Then other capsules, with ghostly apparitions inside, began flying past her as if in a hurry to go somewhere.

Suddenly she landed in a corridor, and saw the ghostly shapes that had passed her in the elevator, all floating towards a strange cubicle. She glanced over her shoulder; a queue had formed behind her, all moving at the same speed, as if on a conveyer belt, heading towards the cubicle.

On entering the cubicle, something clamped on her temples. She went rigid, lightning flashed behind her eyes like an electric storm inside her head. For a moment, her mind went completely blank.

Seconds later, the clamps came off.

She floated into a large, octagonal-shaped chamber. Drawn to one side of the chamber, away from the others, she stuck out her hand, but it was just a blur, her body was a blur, yet her body felt normal.

She gazed around the room for a good few minutes, but could see nothing to indicate the nature of the place; she'd seen nothing like it before. She couldn't see any form of lighting, yet a bright radiant glow filled the place. The floor and walls glistened like stainless steel. There was no furniture and no pictures on the walls.

The other shapes were queuing in three lines, waiting to enter three compartments at the far end of the room. *It's some type of high-tech morgue,* were her first thoughts.

The three compartments had distinctive names: Planet Duplico, Planet Ungad and Planet Extungad. She looked back to the cubicle, with Planet Earth on the sign above.

Then a shutter on the sidewall opened, exposing a porthole window. She floated over and peered through; three planets looked very close by.

Just then, a voice seemed to speak inside her head, making her jump.

'Hello, Emma, I'm Waldo Sultan a galaxy space flight captain. The nearest one, Duplico, is the premier planet. You are out of your earthly body, at an intersection of the spirit beam.' The voice was serene and talking to her from inside her own head; it had a hypnotic affect on her.

'I saw myself leave my body. What's going on?' *Strange, no words came out of my mouth,* she thought.

'The souls passing you are transmigrating to one of our planets; they are souls of the dead and cannot go back. You are not one of them. You are what we call a hitch-hiker; this occurs during a near-death experience or an out-of-body experience.'

She rested her elbow on a ledge, held her chin and stared through the porthole at Duplico. 'It's amazing, so what happens next?' *Hey, I didn't move my lips, just said the words in my head.*

'Do you want to cross over Emma? The computer selected you for the Duplico shuttle.'

Confused, she didn't reply and thought, *How can you have a conversation with somebody that's somehow inside your brain; that's like talking to yourself, surely?*

'Emma, calm down. Listen, you have a choice, Duplico or back to your soul-container or body-shell if you like. But the next few minutes are critical; you must choose now.'

She didn't answer. *I believe in the 'after-life' but not like this. If you're dead, then you go to the other side, or whatever; you just can't pick and choose. I mean, if you were executed you couldn't just stand up and walk off...*

'No you couldn't,' the voice interrupted, 'it doesn't work like that.'

'How can you know what I'm thinking?'

'When a soul enters the spirit cubicle, the computer scans the mind, the conscious to the subconscious; the mind is completely opened up and logged onto our computer. We are conversing via the computer; your thoughts are on a screen in front of me.'

'And your voice?'

'Transponder on a chip attached to your temple, but so tiny you won't feel it.'

'Tell me. Am I dead or alive?'

'You're certainly not dead, but the computer found a query; otherwise you wouldn't have a choice. You'd be on one of our planets or auto-rejected back to Earth, like ninety percent of the other out-of-body hitchhikers.'

'So, I'm in the ten percent.'

'Yes, and that's good. It's your choice, not the computer's.'

'Supposing I decide to cross over?'

'Then your mind will be de-fragmented and you'll be taken to your new home on Duplico.'

This man wants to de-fragment my mind then take me home; that's a new one. 'What do you mean, de-fragment my mind?'

'Your mind will be copied, saved on a special disc and kept under lock and key. All the cobwebs that have accumulated in your mind will be deleted, the rest you keep.'

'I don't have any cobwebs in my mind.'

'It's just a clean sweep of the old material that you don't need. Every event that has happened in your life is in a file in front of me. You don't need half of it.'

'Very funny, okay, my birth, what's it say about my birth?'

For a few moments, there was an eerie silence.

'Here's a quick overview… Aged eleven you were on your hands and knees scrubbing the flagstone floor in the kitchen. Your strict, handicapped grandmother was sitting in her rocking chair reading the paper. "When's mum coming home?" you asked, for the umpteenth time. Without taking her eyes off the paper, she blurted out "Your mum won't be coming home. You were born in a filthy, disgusting alley a couple of streets away. They found you crying next to your mother's heroin-overdosed, dead body. Your father is unknown." That must have been awful, Emma.'

'I know, they were the most heart-stopping words. I threw the scrubbing brush across the room and screamed the roof off. There was no compassion. She was as hard as nails and expected me to be the same. I hated the world I lived in. Rats played in the backyard and I'd to knock cockroaches from my shoes every morning.'

'Yes, you tried to exterminate them by stamping your foot on them. This created a mini explosion; white ooze came out in a loud crack, leaving a messy dead creature on the flagstone floor, which you had to clean up. The cockroaches made you throw up.'

'Huh! Thanks for the reminder.'

'Your grandmother died when you were twelve. You had a shocking experience in an orphanage, and then found out that you had an older sister, Katie, living with foster parents. You moved in with them, and started modelling teenage clothes when you were fourteen.'

Emma sank to the floor in disbelief; he was spot on. She sat with her back propped against the wall, wondering what to say next.

There was a time in her life that was now a complete blur. She stood up and looked at Duplico through the porthole.

'Okay, what does it say about my wedding day?'

There was a pause. 'Wedding?' There was another pause. 'Ah yes… tenth of April, nineteen-ninety-two, at eleven twenty, a registry office wedding. Your mind was in turmoil. You said to yourself, "Let's get this damn thing over; I need another fix."'

'Are you sure about that?'

'Yes, and here's why; when your mother died, she left you a legacy waiting to be ignited. You were addicted to heroin before you left the womb.'

'Never! No wonder I was hooked from the first fix.'

'Do you want to hear the rest Emma?'

'No I don't. The computer has a better memory of my life than me. How come?'

'Well, it's your memory, some of it lost in drugs no doubt, but the computer doesn't miss a thing; we're a little ahead of earthlings in this field… In just over five minutes you will be on Duplico, unless you choose your body-shell back on Earth.'

Emma peered out at Duplico again, wondering about her mother and her grandmother. *Would they be alive and living a happy life somewhere out there? Would they meet up if she crossed over?*

Waldo's voice broke in. 'Emma you are dithering, you're now at the critical 'yes or no' point.'

'I've no desire to go back.'

'Let me help before you finally decide. The computer has flashed up a question mark on Friday the nineteenth day of May, which is today, in Earth's time-frame. The computer has highlighted some points in your day. A letter you read concerning Gavin. Then you discover from Ted that long lost Ian turned up, without contacting you. And, when you were drowning, your last thoughts were on Alistair, not Gavin your husband.'

Emma raised her eyebrows and shook her head in disbelief. 'Okay, your clever computer is correct again. Anything on there about Katie and Ian? like where they are living?'

'That's outside of your mind, but I'm on my way to Earth and I have your DNA, I might just zoom in on them. Have you any other blood relatives alive?'

'Possibly my father, but I never knew him.'

'The DNA detector will trace Earth for the highest reading; that should be Ian and Katie, if they're in the same place. Once I'm past the moon the detector will pinpoint the exact spot, but there's no way that you'll ever know about it, not from me anyway.'

'Why?'

'You'll have started your new life on Duplico, or you'll be back in your body on Earth.'

'Pointless then, and if they are deleted from my mind, it'll be as if they never existed.'

'Fifty-six seconds remaining, I'm bound by the regulations to warn you, unfinished business on Earth cannot be deleted and may affect your new life in our galaxy. You must decide now.'

∾

Gavin ran towards the indoor pool.

The Rainbow room, normally full, was empty. He sat down and gathered his thoughts. *Emma could swim the Channel, how can she have drowned?*

He made his way to the swimming pool. People were around Emma's body on the poolside. Amy ran to him, slid to his feet and held on to his leg, sobbing. He prised her off and pushed through the group of party guests. Dr. Len was working on her lifeless body. Gavin took one look and covered his eyes with his hands, pushing the skin up and down on his forehead.

Someone hugged him. 'She's gone, dead when we pulled her out of the water. The air ambulance is on its way, but the doctor's pronounced her dead. I'm so sorry.'

Gavin turned away. 'I'll… go outside… meet the paramedics.' He sat on the steps and thought, *Shit, what a devastating setback. I don't like this; I don't like this one bit. What we going to do now? How can we replace her?*

∾

At Strathdale, a remote fishing village on the northern shores of Scotland, Ian arrived home at the farm, wondering what Stewart had said about the gun money.

His mum, Katie, met him at the door. 'You're home early, didn't expect you until tomorrow, is everything alright?'

He shrugged his shoulders and nodded. 'Yep, everything's okay. What did dad say after I rang you?'

'I haven't told him, I was going to tell him tonight.'

'Mother!'

'How was I to know you'd be home a day early?'

He raised his eyebrows and shook his head. 'Drat, now I'll have to break the news.'

14

'He won't mind — talking of news, wait until you see the caravan. The other night, Zoe slept in the caravan; she'd had too much booze, afraid to go home. She only let Sam sleep in there.'

'You're joking!'

'When she fell asleep, Sam climbed in with her... She woke up and kicked him out of bed, then went back to sleep. Sam woke her in the morning by slapping her face. That's when she saw the damage.'

'What damage?'

'We need new curtains and an electrician to fix the wall lights.'

'That bad?'

'It can be put right, but I'm not sure about Zoe.'

'Why?'

'She told me she'd talked to a man sat on the beach path bench, a strange-looking man. Well, if there was a stranger in the village, everyone would know.'

'Did she describe him?'

'One morning, she was feeding the animals before college, I was in the garden. She shouted over to me, "That's him Katie," and pointed to the bench. I felt goose-pimply; I could see nobody. She frightened me, and I wondered about her state of mind. Stress at college, too much drink, I can't say, but she should see a doctor.'

'Mum, if something's wrong she'll tell me, I'm sure... Dad in the Tav?'

'Ian it's past nine, where else?'

'I'll have a shower then go see him.'

Katie played with her necklace. 'Don't say anything to Zoe, she's already upset.'

Ian stared at the necklace; he felt his face flush and quickly looked away. 'I will...I mean, I won't, mother.'

Crossing the village to the Tavern, he felt nervous and wished he'd gone fishing instead. Most of the village would be there. *Every girl in the place will turn to look when I walk in; I just hate that.*

Then he heard loud music coming from the village hall, reminding him that it was Friday and disco night; the Tav would be quiet. He paused outside for a few minutes before entering.

'Hi Ian.' Zoe, the village fete queen, approached him before he reached the bar. She stood level with him, tossed her shiny, ebony hair back and flashed her twinkling brown eyes at him. 'Didn't expect to see you tonight. Katie's told you about Sam I suppose?'

'Yes, how stupid is that? Got a bit amorous, eh?'

'Ian!'

He laughed, thinking, *Why else would he jump into bed with her?* 'Why didn't you keep him on the chain?'

'Can't remember right; I just fell asleep. Sorry.'

'Good thing I bought a monkey and not a gorilla... 'You seen any strangers lately?'

'I couldn't wait to tell you, when you see this guy you'll be knocked over.'

He gave her an odd look. 'Mum wasn't exactly knocked over.'

'I've spoken to him.'

'Been on Alex's strong home-brew again then?'

'Ian, I'm serious, this guy is real.'

'You mean real one minute, unreal the next? You seen my dad?'

'Practicing darts, on his own. Everyone's at the disco or Mairloch, It's boring.'
Put your arms round me Ian and give me a big kiss.

'Yes, well, I've come to see dad. Going night fishing after; the sea trout are due in.'

'They are in, 'cos dad caught some in his net, said they were moving upriver.'

'Thanks, Zoe, that's good info; back in a few minutes.' He marched into the games room.

'Ian...you're a day early...you get the gun?' Stewart carried on throwing his darts.

There was a short pause.

'I didn't have enough money left.'

He held back and turned to Ian, a blank look on his face. 'What's that supposed to mean?'

'I bought a necklace instead.'

He threw his darts harder at the board. 'You've got to be kidding — a necklace?!'

'The one mum's wearing now; it belonged to Ted's wife.'

Throwing another dart, Stewart faltered and hit the fireplace, then slowly bent to pick it up. Keeping his back to Ian, he stared at the fireplace for a while then put his darts in a glass jar kept on a shelf for that purpose. Eventually he turned to Ian, with an expression of disbelief. 'Carry on.'

'I met a chap called Ted, a chauffeur; he knew me, and Emma—'

'Christ!' he cut in, rubbing his chin and staring at the dartboard. 'You haven't been to London!'

'No, honest; met him at the game fair, he'd brought his boss in a chopper.'

Stewart grabbed his darts from the glass and started practicing again. 'Did you get his boss's name?'

'Alistair, a nice guy, said I'd make big money under his wing... Do you know him?'

Stewart, about to throw another dart, held still and turned to Ian. 'No, but I knew of his parents before they died: they owned Lockstock Hall near London, and enough property and businesses elsewhere to make up a town.' He threw another dart. 'What did Ted say about the necklace?'

'Ted's wife took it to your jewellery shop for repair, two weeks later she returned to collect it but the place was closed. Ted wanted our address; I wouldn't tell him. He said you owed him five hundred quid for the necklace. I gave him the gun money. I rang mum and told her.'

'You did right son, it was among the items we managed to keep before they cleared us out.'

'Before who cleared you out?'

'A long story, we had to cut ourselves off from London, sadly, that included Emma. It was about drugs. I blew the whistle, but they didn't jail the big guys. We had to move fast or end up dead. That's why it's important that we safeguard our address.'

Ian went back to Zoe and pulled a small parcel from his inside pocket. 'A little present from the game fair.'

'A Swiss army knife. I've always fancied one of these, but they're so expensive. Thanks.'

'The best fishing knife around; a guy was selling two for one.'

'You staying for a drink?'

'No, I'm fishing soon as it goes dark.'

'I'll come with you; I want to learn night fishing.'

'You need to be competent in the day first. Another time maybe.'

3

At Lockstock Hall, Emma suddenly opened her eyes wide. She wondered why she was lying by the side of the swimming pool, her wet hair stuck in strands to the tiles. For a moment, she lay frozen. A group of worried party guests in various stages of undress gazed down at her.

Len, a doctor friend and a guest at the party, knelt beside her, checking his watch and her pulse. Startled, he let go of her wrist and glanced back at his watch. 'You were dead, Emma,' he blurted out, beads of sweat running down his face.

Moments earlier she was in a euphoric state, now, her head and chest felt as if she'd been in a boxing-ring, and her emotions were all over the place. She just wanted to cry and blurt everything out, but they'd think she'd gone loopy.

She tried to act normal. 'Are... are you sure I was dead Len?' She struggled to her feet, straightened her top and adjusted her thong. She looked round at the familiar faces and her friend Amy, slouched against the poolside window, sobbing out of control.

The guests started milling around, curious, agog in some cases, stunned in others.

Len stayed by her side, bewildered. 'Your heart stopped beating for fifteen minutes; you can't get much more dead than that.'

'I...I haven't been d...'

Len interrupted, 'I worked hard on you, but you'd gone.'

'Thanks, Len, but...' She shaded her eyes from the evening sun now reflected on the surface of the pool.

'Where's Gavin?'

'He's gone to meet the air ambulance.'

She patted him on the shoulder. 'Oh, yes, I'd forgotten.'

Len pulled out a handkerchief, wiped his still sweating brow and inspected her eyes.

'You'll need a check up, at least... What do you mean... forgotten?'

'It doesn't matter, some other time.'

Len was a regular on the party scene; he'd come in useful on a few occasions, but this time she wasn't ripped out of her head from drugs, or suffering from alcoholic poisoning. However, if collected by an ambulance from a party at Alistair's, you were treated as an addict, an alcoholic, or just insane. They'd take you away to some private drug rehab clinic and nobody would see you for a while.

Gavin rushed in with two paramedics. 'You're alive!'

'Thanks, Gavin, glad you've finally noticed.' He had such a worried look on his face; she forced herself to give him a smile.

He eyed her in disbelief, turned to the paramedics and scratched the back of his head. 'She was dead.'

One of the paramedics gave him an odd look. 'Well, she's lively enough now, sir.' He winked at her. 'Are you feeling okay?'

'Fine, thank you.'

'Nice outfit, if you don't mind me saying.' His eyes flicked curiously at the half-dressed guests, now dispersing, then over her body from head to toe. 'We finish at twelve, any chance of us calling back?'

'Ask the boss, he's coming over now.' She pointed to Alistair.

Alistair took the paramedics to one side and had a private word with them.

Gavin snuggled up to her and thought, *If she only knew what was coming, she'd have stayed at the bottom of the pool.* 'It's as if nothing's happened, fifteen minutes dead, then you're suddenly alive.'

She gave him a dirty look. 'I didn't have to be, some unfinished business; I came back because my time wasn't up.'

Gavin stared at her. 'What do you mean — back?'

'A tall glass please, quarter filled with brandy and topped up with water. I'll get dressed, see you in the ballroom.'

In the quiet of the poolside changing room, Emma slipped out of her wet swimwear, gave them a few minutes blast of hot air from the hair-dryer then dried her hair in front of the mirror.

This time she could see herself. She looked radiant, and had a feeling of inner peace that wasn't there before. The feeling was something else completely, as if the cobwebs had left her mind for real. Her previous fears about death had gone; her fears about everything had gone; other than that her mind was clear, alert and serene.

She knew she'd gone through a special experience, having left her body. *But you could only do that if you were dead, and then you'd have to come back from the dead.* She smiled at her image in the mirror. *Well, I've just done both, and boy hasn't it changed my outlook on life... and death,* she concluded.

Never wearing much at parties, she quickly dressed: just a tiny tight top and the shortest of skirts and high heels. She left the changing-room through a side door and along a passage that led to the great hall, used only for the big formal parties.

The hall was empty apart from a half-undressed couple in one corner. She knew it was impossible not to make a noise unless she took off her shoes, but she'd learned it was better to leave them on.

She flicked back her hair and strutted across the polished oak floor, sending echoes around the great hall. The couple froze, in what looked like the most uncomfortable position, until she'd passed. Emma smiled to herself, *At Lockstock there is never a dull moment.*

She stepped from the hall onto the thick carpet, where, if desperate, you could snort coke out of the pile.

A long passage led to the ballroom where they held the disco; a short passage led off to the unused nursery. She walked a little way towards the nursery, noticing a portrait of a woman with two girls hung on the wall.

She froze on the spot, thinking of her sister Katie, *Where is she? What's she doing?* She gave her head a good shake and took a last look at the portrait. *I won't be going down this passage again, unless I happen to be carrying a baby, which is highly unlikely…but who knows?*

As she passed the study, she heard the door open behind her. A finger trickled down her back and a voice whispered in her ear. 'Emma, what is the thing women most desire?'

She knew it was Alistair; each girl he met he asked the same question, and to most, he provided the answer. She turned and gave him a smile. 'In my case I'd say a good husband, two boys and two girls, but as you know, I'm already married and until now, too busy to have kids,' she lied.

He gave her a flirty look. 'You can use one of the bedrooms to recover if you like. Have a lie down for a while.' His eyes wandered over her body.

She looked up at the ceiling, shook her head and grinned. 'How thoughtful of you, but I'm fully recovered. Anyway, Gavin's waiting for me; he'll wonder where I am.'

Did this discourage him? She pulled away and stood back. Unperturbed, he came in close again, pressing his lips to her ear.

'What about when he's at work?'

'Oh, yes…just like that. Must go, I'm bursting for the loo,' she lied again.

She left him in limbo and carried on along the passage, sighing. *I wish I could bring myself to take him on. Gosh he's powerful, and at times tempting beyond endurance.*

She knew Alistair kept a notebook full of young starlets' phone numbers, who were willing to do anything and everything to get into show-business. According to them, Alistair was a sexual stuntman. She reckoned it was true, because the only thing missing at Lockstock was a gym.

She went in the powder room feeling rather overcome. Looking in the mirror, 'Gosh, whatever next?!' she said to her reflection.

Alistair had always flattered her, but he'd gradually moved in closer each time she'd seen him. She could hardly forget her first encounter with him; just a meeting of eyes and a stolen kiss that made her heart flutter.

Today, aged twenty-seven, the same age as she, he'd gone through enough celebrity girlfriends to fill a function room on their own. However, it was no secret that he wanted her. She smiled at the mirror, *But it's a big secret that I want him!*

Emma knew that Gavin despised Alistair, but he wouldn't dream of letting it show and never missed a chance to party at Alistair's place. Of course, they met Alistair at other functions; they never stayed in.

At the ballroom, Gavin was sitting on a barstool in deep conversation with James the butler. Her drink was on the bar top in the middle of a tray. 'Sorry madam, the waiter looked everywhere for you,' James said.

Gavin pointed to the side of the room. 'Trish is over there,' he said, as if she'd interrupted at a bad time. 'Give me ten minutes, I'll be over,' he added, without glancing at her.

She left them with their heads together and ambled over to Trish, thinking, *Why is James the only person that Gavin ever talks with, the one person I've come to hate? Is it because they are two of a kind?*

She sat next to Trish. 'No boyfriend tonight?'

Trish was looking in the other direction and almost knocked her drink over. 'Hi… I wondered when I'd bump into you. I've moved back to London.'

'You've met Alistair then?'

Her eyes widened. 'Don't ask… what a guy… Yes, I've met him. What is the thing that women most desire? I told him he'd be high on my list.'

'That's his chat-up line, seems to work.'

'It worked for you then?'

'Almost.'

'Tell me about him.'

Emma took a sip of brandy, inspected the ceiling and smiled.

'He's not short of a few quid.'

'Yeah, well, I've seen furniture here worth more than my house. I mean, where did he spring up from?'

Remember when you left London, well, that's when he blew in. Just taken over his father's business empire, and he went crazy.

Trish sighed. 'I wish I'd stayed, but he fancies you, you know.' She spoke as if imparting secrets from her mother's diary. 'I take it you haven't slept with him?'

'Only in my dreams… Trish, he's a good friend, okay.'

'Last Friday I spent some time with him here. He wanted to talk over a photo-shoot for the Party Scene magazine.'

'I guess you got past the talking stage.'

21

'He's overpowering.' She took a sip of wine, a twinkle in her eye.

Emma raised her eyebrows. 'And very persuasive.'

Trish took another sip of wine, staring across the table. 'And very good looking.'

'Extremely.'

'And like sleeping with five different guys.'

'Well, well, well, what do you know?' *More than me obviously,* Emma thought. *I can't believe he has slept with her. She was the bike behind the bike-shed at school and the best little liar around.*

'He invited me back tonight.'

'You're privileged. You like Lockstock then?'

'Yeah, it's excellent. They have a strange butler, offering anything you like on a silver platter. He came in the bedroom. "Champagne, or anything, madam, breakfast is in the dining room when you're ready, madam," he said.'

Emma glanced round the guests in the room. 'James caters for all tastes, whatever takes your fancy.'

Trish grinned, sipping her wine robot-fashion. 'All the pleasures in life at a snap of the fingers. I'd never get dressed.'

'Well, if you did get dressed, you could order the butler, one of the gardeners, or the sexy chauffeur to help you. Then there's a choice of foreign chefs in the kitchen, they could help you undress later.'

'Nothing wrong with your imagination then, thing is, you could have it all for real. Not considered it?'

'It had crossed my mind, but I'm still with Gavin.'

'Oh, I thought you'd split up on your wedding night. Leave him, he probably wouldn't notice.'

'On the contrary; I've replaced his pen-pal in Australia.'

'Oh, it's like that then.'

'Gavin is the most timid person you could meet. Whatever I say to him, he just says, "Sorry love, what do you want me to do love?" It blows me away. Yet, if I left him, there'd be a double murder.'

Trish played with her glass and frowned. 'Possessive then?'

'He accepts guys flirting with me, but secretly jealous. Unless James the butler is around, then I might as well not be there. There's something going on, I can't work it out.'

Trish went quiet and looked at the ceiling. 'Is Gavin still into drugs then?'

'No, he runs a respectable cosmetic surgery clinic, hasn't touched drugs for ages. At least I don't think so. I don't know who supplies James though, but it isn't Alistair.'

'Just a thought… Anyway… when I climbed out of Alistair's bed…'

'You went down to the massive dining room with the huge mahogany table that seats forty. You sat at the head of the big table where some of the most influential business people from around the world have dined. The butler brought you the ice bucket with a bottle of crystal champagne and rhymed off the breakfast menu.'

Trish interrupted, scratching her head. 'Has it been taped or something?'

'Alistair strolled in, with the Financial Times, and sat at the opposite end of the table. Took a mouthful of grapefruit, laid down his spoon, wiped his mouth with his napkin, then finished with a mouthful of champagne. Then took his eyes off the paper and looked at you.'

'Emma, that's scary. What happened next then?'

'I don't know; up to that point the tale is the same, from then on the girls have a conversation with him, but mostly they keep that part to themselves.'

'I'll fill you in on mine then…Gosh, look who's coming.'

'Another drink girls? Or anything?' The young waiter asked.

Trish eyed him seductively. 'Have you a long one?'

Emma put both hands over her face and coughed.

He turned away and blew his nose. 'Sorry about that.' He put his handkerchief away. 'I beg your pardon?'

'I want a long drink this time, in a tall glass. Think you can provide that?'

'Yes, no problem.'

'Well, it was a simple yes or no question in the first place.' She gave him a serious look. 'Have you got a long one or not?'

He looked from side to side, his face had changed colour.

'Yes, sorry if I misunderstood.'

'That's lovely, what time do you finish work, I'll—'

'Trish, leave the lad alone. A white wine and lemonade in a tall glass and a double brandy topped with water, please.'

He gave out a sigh of relief and headed to the bar.

Her eyes followed him. 'Nothing like having one or two reserves.'

'Look Trish, you've probably had more sex in a week than I've had since I married.'

'Got the picture; doesn't know how to use his dick. How the hell did you get off with Gavin in the first place?'

'My friend was into drugs; he was her supplier and soon had me hooked. Two years later, I married him in a haze; it was foggy outside the house, foggy inside the house and foggy in my brain. Before I leave you Trish, finish off the Alistair story.'

'Yes well, for some reason, he seemed to be in a bad mood, scattered his paper on the floor and went on about you, saying you'd have nothing to do with him. He said Gavin should be sweeping the streets.'

'Well, Alistair suffered pain last week at Gavin's clinic. Had his ear rebuilt after a girl bit part of it off. He called the doctor brutal and blamed Gavin for employing him… Carry on.'

'He opened a magazine and brought it to my side of the table. "You must admit, Trish, she's beautiful," he said, and went on about you for ages.'

'Interesting.'

'Don't tell anyone I've told you, will you?' Trish picked up her glass. 'I'm off to mix with the guys.'

Gavin suddenly appeared. 'A top-up, love?'

'No, I want to go home.'

'Whatever, I'll tell James to sort the Roller.'

An hour later, they were at home and in the kitchen.

'Any brandy left?' she asked.

'Plenty of wine, what's with the sudden change to brandy?'

'Kills the pain!'

'A full bottle in the lounge… What pain?'

'Nothing.' She went to the lounge and poured a neat brandy; it was three o'clock in the morning, but sleep was the last thing on her mind.

She pulled out the letter she'd found earlier in the day and read it again. It made no difference; the words hadn't changed, they just hurt more.

She stormed into the kitchen. Gavin was engrossed in the Party Scene magazine. Startled, he closed the page and spun round. 'What's wrong Emma?'

'Alistair thinks you should be sweeping the streets.'

'Who cares about Alistair? I have something he cannot have. Everything all right love, you had a good night?'

'What do you own that's so precious?'

'You of course.'

'How do you work that out? Escort me to a party then dump me. Something sadly wrong.'

'Like what?'

'Like the children issue, our pledge: we had an agreement, remember? I was to break off modelling on my thirtieth birthday; then we'd start a family.'

'Yes…well, that's a while off, love.'

'Get lost, that's a load of shit. I saw the hospital letter confirming that you're sterile. Why didn't you tell me?'

'I meant to; didn't want to upset you.'

'The letter's dated May, nineteen ninety-five. Five years ago.'

'Sorry love.'

'We made the pledge in June, nineteen ninety-five, how pathetic is that? Then you decided we should sleep in separate beds, another pathetic idea. In fact, everything you've done or not done since has been pathetic.'

'You were all over the place modelling. I got used to sleeping on my own, and the physical side didn't matter.'

'Well, it matters even less now.'

'What can I say? Apart from sorry, and it's not the end of the world love.'

'Might as well be, because you're not my husband, you're just somebody that lives here, trapped in a stupid world of amateur dramatics.'

'Thanks Emma, what's your world?'

'Reality.'

'What's real about it? Prance in front of a camera with next to nothing on, and let Alistair flirt with you.'

'I'm told he's quite a considerate lover, makes it last and always pleasures the girls first. Then, according to Trish, he pleasures them again for as many times as they like.'

'There's something wrong with him, it's not natural.'

'Sounds okay to me.'

'Try him then, he's been after you for long enough.'

'I might, if you keep treating me like a lump of meat.'

'Okay, I've a personal problem.'

'Your personal problem involves me. The letter you forgot to mention shows how distant we are. We don't discuss anything. You're obsessed with something and I don't exist.'

'That's your view.'

'If I come home with green hair, bright shocking green hair, you wouldn't make one comment. You wouldn't notice.'

'Am I noticing you now?'

'I don't know, are you? You never say I look all right, I'd rather you said I look horrible.'

'I'm too polite.'

'Why don't you say I'm going to bed goodnight? Is that being polite?'

'Okay love, I'll start saying goodnight then.'

'Just because I've told you to; frig off.'

'Love, you've been off the rails since we came home.'

'Well, the letter didn't exactly say you were the most fertile guy in London.'

'I know, but what can I do, love…? I'm off to bed. Don't worry about the kids; we'll adopt some… Where's Pal?'

'In my room, I'm not stupid.' .

'Good. I'm going to bed now, goodnight, love.'

'Yes, goodnight Gavin!'

Emma took Pal to the park, sat on her usual bench and stayed to watch the sun come up. *Don't worry about babies, don't worry about sleeping together, don't worry about sex. Well, you speak for yourself, Gavin, I have other plans.*

Five hours later, the bedside phone woke her. 'You left a handbag in the ballroom, madam.' She slammed the phone down, *Damn, and I was sober.*

She was about to leave for Lockstock, when Len pulled alongside her car in the drive. He leaned out of the car window. 'Mind if I ask a few questions?'

'Depends.'

'The swimming pool?'

She invited him in.

'At the hospital we keep a file on near-death and out-of-body experiences. You were dead for fifteen minutes; remember anything?'

'Yes, everything, but you won't believe me.'

'Well, I'm here to listen.' He pulled a notepad from his briefcase and sat pen in hand like a reporter. 'Start from when you drowned.'

'I passed out, then drifted out of my body.'

'You were dead Emma. Anything else?'

'I zoomed off at a fantastic speed in some type of beam. One second I was looking over the Earth, then the moon, then the end of the universe. I ended up in a space station.'

Len raised his eyebrows. 'A space station?'

'Yes, I could see three planets close up.'

He looked up from his pad with narrowed eyes.

'Anyone in the space station?'

'I guess so, but I saw no one, apart from ghostlike people floating into three capsules. When each capsule was full, it zoomed off to one of the planets.'

'Some nightmare eh?'

'The opposite, I felt serene.'

'You make it seem real.'

'Look Len, it was real. Where else would I get the info, I knew you wouldn't believe me. I don't do drugs any more. I know the difference from reality and hallucinating.'

'It's most unusual; of the NDE files I've seen, only one mentions a space station. Anything else?'

'A voice came into my head. 'I'm Waldo Sultan, a galaxy space flight captain. You are almost at the point of no return.' I had to make a choice, Duplico or back to my body-shell on Earth. I wanted to continue to the planet, but the computer put me off in the last few seconds. "It's not your time," Waldo said.'

Len raised his head and smiled. 'Normally, people come back because there's a strong urge to stay with loved ones.'

'Maybe Gavin…maybe somebody else…I don't know.'

Len rubbed his chin and locked his eyes on hers. 'Doesn't sound like a strong urge to return?'

'I'm not here to divulge my marital status, and you don't believe a word I've said.'

Len shook his head. 'On the contrary.' He put the pen in his top pocket and the notepad back in his briefcase. 'Your story echoes the other NDE space station story, almost word for word. He also came back, and I'm sure glad that you did.'

'Waldo Sultan wished me a safe return to Earth and said I'd be welcome in their universe when the time came.'

Len made for the door, then suddenly turned around. 'But then you'd be dead for sure, or at least on this planet.'

4

Emma went to collect her bag, fifteen miles from her home in Bromley. A right-turn took her past a church and half a dozen quaint little cottages, then over a cattle grid and past the two lodges at the entrance to the grounds. She never failed to be amazed at the tranquil setting of Lockstock.

The private road meandered for one and a half miles; passing by a lake, and through glades and open fields where racehorses grazed. The only other signs of life were the pheasants, rabbits and deer. At the hall, peacocks strutted amongst Alistair's collection of fine cars on the forecourt.

She was about to raise the heavy knocker on the sturdy entrance door, but robbed of the opportunity when James pulled the door open, and startled her.

'Lovely morning. A drink or anything, madam?'

'Fresh orange please.'

'Take a seat with the fish if you like, madam.'

A side door in the entrance hall led to her favourite room; they called it the Rainbow Room. The floor was wall-to-wall, thick plate-glass. Underneath, tropical fish swam through weed beds and over the pebbles. A fountain sprang from the centre and small waterfalls cascaded over rocks in each corner. Three ornate bronze benches with marble-topped tables lined each side among exotic plants. She watched the fish swimming below her feet, thinking: *I could sit here every morning after breakfast. Gavin would be a memory, and I'd be pregnant.*

James placed a napkin on the table and carefully lowered her or-ange juice. 'Sorry about the delay madam; Alistair rang from the office, asking if you had been to collect your bag.'

'What did you say?'

'I told him there was a dust-covered Ford Escort between the Rolls and the Lamborghini, madam.'

'That's bloody awful. Why didn't you just say I was here?'

'Sorry, madam, but you should have the thing cleaned before entering the grounds.'

'Stop calling me madam. I'm surprised he didn't sack you.'

'He wouldn't do that. I'm an important person here at Lockstock; you underestimate me, madam.'

'Just give me my bag; then I can climb into my unimportant, dirty Ford, and get it out of your sight.' *I don't like him, but he doesn't know how much. One day, I'll completely blow my top. That's if I haven't already sacked him first.*

Before leaving the grounds, she pulled in by the lake and opened her bag. There was a note inside with just two words written on it: *Love you.*

She looked across the lake at the deer and the racehorses shining in the sun. Then her eyes lingered on Lockstock Hall. *How could an orphan from the slums be offered all this and not take it?* She tore up the note with a tear in her eye, started the engine and set off back to Bromley. 'James would be on his bike that's for sure,' she said, to a curious deer that was staring at her.

At Strathdale, Zoe had lain awake for a long time, thinking about the stranger. The man seemed sinister, as if he were a ghost. *I wish I'd seen him close up. Then I would've known for sure.*

It was Saturday and therefore no college; she decided to go look for him.

A slight breeze blew off the sea, the early morning air was quite chilly, but a sunny day was in store. That was good because later she'd be out on her father's speedboat, water-skiing.

She went down the harbour road and checked out the boats, noticing that there were no visitors in the marina. She took the track to the cove beach. No small boats beached up and no footprints in the sand…

Pointless going to the Cathedral Cavern, she thought, *nobody can get in there without going to the Tav for the master key, and the other is in my pocket.*

Suddenly, she spotted him on the bench at the top of the hill. *That's strange, he wasn't there when I walked through the village.*

She paused at the bottom of the path and shivered, Maybe it wasn't such a good idea to meet him close up, but she couldn't stave off her curiosity and pressed on until she was beside him. The man sat rigid like a corpse, oblivious to her presence; he seemed dead. She waved her hand inches from his eyes. 'Excuse me.'

For a moment, the only sound was that of the waves, amplified by the breeze. She cringed and raised her voice. 'You all right?'

'Flight Captain Waldo Sultan… I'm fine thank you,' he said, in a regimental-type voice.

'Sorry, for waking you,' she said, and briskly strode off.

At the edge of the village, her two friends Jodie and Carl stood watching.

Jodie confronted her. 'Zoe, what you up to? We went over to see that oddball; gave me the creeps.'

Zoe puckered her nose. 'I'm not surprised, the milkman scares you.'

'Oh, sod off, Zoe—'

Carl interrupted. 'Yeah, I clocked him. Seen some odd tourists around here, but he's a real weirdo.'

'Maybe, but at least you could see him. Well, no time now for my doc's appointment. I'm off to the farm; see what Ian says while the guy's still there.'

Zoe crossed the village green practicing her singing voice, and feeling much better now others had seen the strange man. *Okay, he had hair like straw, leathery skin and clothes that were in danger of falling to dust, but his eyes made up for all that, the most stunning I've ever seen: a crystal-clear deep blue; they were captivating.*

At the farm, she noticed Ian's fly rod wasn't on the caravan hooks, indicating he was out fishing. *He's like the elusive butterfly; can't get him in the Tav, can't get him in the speedboat, can't catch him in the caravan and he'd never go near the barn if he thought I was in there. Why is he so bloody shy when other lads throw themselves at me?*

At that moment, Katie came out of the menagerie shed. 'Hi Zoe, thought you weren't coming. They're all fed. You alright?'

Zoe glanced back to the bench; Waldo was still there. 'I'm fine. Do you know Katie, if I could paint, then this is where I'd stand my easel. The beach top bench would be a focal point.'

'Not now though, much better when somebody is sat on the thing, it's a dead picture otherwise. I have photos of both, and I know which is the best.'

'Katie, please don't be offended; how many fingers am I holding up?'

'Three, why do you ask?'

'How many now?'

'Five... Have you been to the doctor's yet?'

'Don't know what to do.'

'Just walk in and see him; he's sat in that fancy big house doing nothing, he must be bored stiff.'

'It's like, what do I say?'

'Don't say anything; let him do the talking, you'll just answer his questions. You'll be there for a while, but not today; you'll have to go on Monday. Or catch him in the tavern; he won't mind speaking to you in there, that's where he dishes out most prescriptions.'

'I'll see... Ian gone fishing for the day?'

'Who knows, he helped with the milking then cleared off. Try his mobile.'

'Pointless, never has it switched on. If he's back before twelve, tell him to come to the harbour; we're taking the speedboat out.'

'I will, but don't build your hopes up.'

Zoe left the farm and immediately made for the bench and Captain Waldo. She wanted answers to a few questions, but the nearer she got to him, the more she felt like turning back.

She practiced her humming, pressed on and plonked herself down next to him. He completely ignored her, his eyes fixed somewhere out to sea.

She stopped humming.

Suddenly, he turned to her. 'Carry on with the tune, Zoe.'

'How come you know my name?'

'Your friend happened to shout it out.'

'Ian's mum said she couldn't see you, when I pointed you out.'

'Correct, nobody can see me apart from you and your friends; better if you keep it to yourselves, otherwise they'll have you in a psychiatric clinic.'

Zoe scratched her head. 'I don't understand.'

'I'm not a ghost, but you may as well look at it that way. Let's say I've found what I was looking for and will be leaving shortly.'

'What were you looking for?'

'Katie and Ian, a DNA search I was interested in. But I picked up on something while I was here; you and your friends are good candidates for our research and we need samples from remote places like Strathdale.'

'Who's we, and what sort of samples?'

'I live in another world, on planet Duplico. We borrow earthlings to help in our research.'

Zoe tried to keep a straight face. 'You're having me on. Trying to scare me.'

He turned and locked his deep blue eyes on hers. She melted into them, mesmerized by their beauty, so innocent they reminded her of a baby's eyes. They were hypnotic and she fell under their influence.

'The harmless tests take up one hour of Earth time; you and your friends will enjoy the experience. There's nothing to fear and you'll be helping your planet. Do you understand?'

Her eyes were still locked on his. 'Yes, we'll be helping our planet.'

'Good, and you'll forget this conversation, but you'll do your utmost to ensure that your friends all attend a meeting with me, details of time and place will be posted later… In one Earth minute, I'm leaving.' He held out his hand. 'Hold onto my arm. You'll remember this, but don't try explaining it to anyone.'

She gently rested her hand on his arm and, feeling it might drop off, put the other underneath just in case. At that moment, he vanished in a cloud of dust. She was left with a small piece of rag in her hand that looked more like an ancient bandage than a coat sleeve. Terrified, she dropped it to the ground. She stared at the thing, unable to believe what had happened. Shaking, she eventually picked it up and shoved it in her side pocket. *Jesus, what's happening to me…?*

∾

In Bromley, Emma arrived home after a photo-shoot and went to the kitchen for a coffee, but the jar was empty. 'Drat!' She grabbed a teabag, threw it in a cup and opened the fridge door for the milk; there was none. She scratched her head and looked around the kitchen. Unwashed plates were on the sink from the day before. She stormed out of the kitchen and found Gavin in the lounge. She stood in the doorway, but he didn't notice her as he rummaged through some papers.

She entered the room. 'Something wrong?'

'Emma, you made me jump.' He quickly put the papers in his briefcase and closed it. 'Nothing's wrong, things couldn't be better.'

'You forgot the coffee, the milk, left the plates out, not to mention that you're shaking. That tells me something's wrong.'

'Just the excitement, but the business is in trouble. I can't say why or how, only that I'm pulling out and we'll be moving house.'

'Thanks for keeping me informed. What's all this about then?'

'Be patient, I've struck a good deal. We'll be rich.'

She pressed him for details, but he skirted round every question. She got nothing sensible from him, but no longer cared - she had her own plans.

That night they sat in a corner of the function room at the Starlight club. Alistair was nowhere in sight. Gavin sat silent, twiddling his thumbs. She sat patiently like a blind dog with its owner, but feeling nowhere near as faithful.

She ran her fingers along the buttons on the inside of the recently re-covered chair. The chair she'd first sat in when they opened the club ten years earlier.

Now it had the same new leather smell, the same feel, and the same seventeen buttons that matched her birthday at that time; the night of her introduction to drugs.

Within two months, she'd moved in with her supplier, who was now sitting next to her staring into oblivion. At least she had enjoyed the hassle-free company; she'd had her hopes, but never realistically thought the friendship would ever become intimate. *Well, I got that bit right.*

She turned to Gavin. He'd stopped twiddling his thumbs, holding his half-empty glass of lager up to the light. Watching invisible fish swim around, as if it was a fancy aquarium. She broke the silence: 'Wonder what's happened to Alistair?'

He kept his eyes fixed on the glass. 'He'll be here before long no doubt. Unless he's already been, and gone out for a quickie, seeing that he beds every new face that comes along.'

'According to the girls, there'll be nothing quick about it…' As she spoke, Alistair came in with Trish on one side of him, and an actress on the other.

When he saw Emma, he left Trish with the actress and made straight for their table.

'They could teach you a few tricks Gavin, I'll introduce you if you like?'

'No thanks; I've finished with amateur dramatics. I've been offered a good role when we move.'

'Moving… One party too many?' He slapped Gavin's back.

'It's our last; we're moving out of London, thank goodness.'

'Promoted then?'

'We're pulling out; the house has gone, repossessed. Emma is moving to another agency in Yorkshire, I'm starting up a new clinic in Harrogate. I'm going tomorrow to sort out some digs.'

'What about you Emma, when are you going?' He had a saucy look on his face, unconcerned that Gavin was by her side.

'According to Gavin I'll have to find somewhere to stay for a couple of weeks, until I've completed some modelling assignments.'

'I thought you were doing okay. House repossessed – it can't be that bad, surely?'

'Afraid so, times are hard, that's how it is,' Gavin answered for her.

Alistair put his hand on Emma's shoulder. 'Look, you can stay at Lockstock, in the self-contained suite. Bring Pal with you. Gavin can stay in my other mansion near Harrogate.'

Emma gave him a grateful look. 'Thanks ever so much Alistair, you are too kind.' Gavin then took a quick drink of lager, which came back down his nose. 'Drat,' he said, rubbing himself off with his hands.

Alistair laughed and called the waiter. 'Put their drinks on my bill.' He gave Emma a wink, and without a care, went back to the bar.

'Let me get out of his sight.' Gavin thumped his empty glass on the table. 'You stay if you like, but I'm going.' At that, he stood up and stormed off.

Emma stayed in her chair, feeling that was the best option. *House repossessed; business in trouble, times are hard; but we're going to be rich. What the hell is he playing at? Whatever, he'll be living on his own.*

Within minutes of Gavin leaving, Amy plonked herself in the chair that he'd vacated. 'Hi Emma, Gavin just jumped in the taxi I came in. Something wrong?'

'I think he's gone home, but to be honest, I don't care where he's gone and I'm glad you've taken his place; I fancy a mad night for a change.'

'Great, I've enough gear for the two of us and more.'

☙

Two days later, Gavin helped Emma move into the suite at Lockstock. She spent most of the time having a go at him and asking questions, but she got no answers; he just grinned and said, 'Don't worry.'

He took the last case into the bedroom and smiling, said, 'Right, I'm away, don't worry, everything's okay; you'll see.'

She flopped on the settee, sobbing. 'I'm not the least bit worried, just heartbroken. Not only are you a rat, but a lying rat with too many secrets for my liking.'

'Okay, I'll change my ways then.' He left her sitting on the settee and headed off to Alistair's estate in Yorkshire.

She gave out a long sigh. *I never want to see him again.*

The following morning, while eating breakfast, she wondered how long it would take Alistair to make a move. *How will I ward him off? What am I talking about? I don't want to ward him off...do I?*

She reminded herself however that there was the small problem of her morals, ingrained by her strict grandmother as a child. *Will I be able to throw my principles aside? I'm sick of Gavin and it hasn't been a real marriage from day one. But why should I bother about ethics, when Gavin hasn't any?*

The door opened before she'd swallowed the first mouthful of cereal.

Alistair came in and paused by the door, eyes searching the room. 'Where's Pal?'

She looked away. 'Dead. Gavin said he was too ferocious.'

'You're joking... He was timid, and the best Alsatian I've seen.'

'Absolutely. I'm devastated.'

Alistair looked at the floor and shook his head. 'That's awful, bloody awful.'

Emma pushed her cornflakes to one side, picked up a napkin and wiped her eyes. She turned to Alistair, she'd seen how he'd played with Pal, and she knew he cared more about Pal than some of the girls he entertained. 'Sorry, but Gavin always wanted rid of Pal and now he's done it.'

Alistair kicked the door shut. 'Bastard!'

She stared up at the ceiling, wondering if Pal had made it to Duplico. 'I don't think he's really dead though.'

He gave her an odd look and frowned. 'You'd better be joking; you just said he was dead.'

'Well, he's not on Earth anymore, but I'm pretty sure he's on another planet.'

'A nice thought, but dead is dead don't you think?'

'No, I believe there is no such thing as death, the mind and soul vacate the body, then reincarnate on another planet; it's just the same for the animals.'

Alistair smiled. 'Death is the end: ashes to ashes, dust to dust, the end.'

Emma took a long drink of her fruit juice, she didn't reply. *It would be pointless to go any further. I couldn't tell him that I'd flown beyond the moon and arrived back fifteen minutes later, not to mention the space station, and that I'd seen three planets with unheard of names. I'm not about to make a fool of myself by trying to convince him that there is an afterlife.*

Alistair stood by the window; he didn't look out, but stared at Emma's perfectly formed body. He moved to her side of the table and brought with him a whiff of something exotic. He stood behind her and began slowly massaging her shoulders. 'How much money do you owe?' he whispered in her ear.

Stunned, she paused for a few moments. *I certainly don't owe any money and I've plenty stashed away, but that's my business.* Nevertheless, she decided to pluck a figure out of the air just to hear his reaction. 'Gavin reckons a few hundred thousand,' she whispered back to him.

'Supposing I clear your debt and make sure you get to the top with your modelling career, or better still, start a family?' He carried on with the gentle shoulder massage.

'The second option sounds nice… And…?'

His hands slowed to a halt. 'You divorce Gavin, and we get married. He'll get a cheque, for say, half a million.'

'Alistair, you cannot buy me. I'm not for sale.'

'Gavin might think you are; he seems interested in money.' The massage struck up again along with more charm in his voice. 'You'll live in luxury for the rest of your life.' His hands suddenly stopped, he went to the other side of the table and sat facing her. He looked her in the eye, then, dwelled on her breasts then her hair. He smiled confidently, as though she was now his, and she'd soon be in bed with him. 'You remind me of Marilyn Monroe; you could be her double.'

She gave him a wry smile. 'You knew her then?'

'Very funny; I've seen a few of her films though.'

'So have I, and I can't help it if we've similar looks, but that's where the comparison ends.'

'True, because you're sexier than she was.' He peered under the table. 'And longer legs.'

'Oh yes, and you won't be happy until you've tested the goods.'

He smiled and nodded. 'Correct.'

Emma widened her eyes. *His charming smile, deep blue eyes, smooth, slightly tanned face and flowing jet-black hair make me feel weak.*

'I'll say one thing Alistair, both you and your offer are tempting, but you underestimate Gavin, he might kill you.'

She may as well have said he'd get his face slapped.

He grinned, shrugged his shoulders. 'No way, he's too soft. He'll let go for half a million, especially when he's losing you anyway.'

'I think he might've killed before, that's how soft he is.'

The charm left his face; he held his chin in thought, his eyes opened wide. 'Gavin, a murderer?'

'Did a spell in prison, for tax evasion. His cellmate had a fatal accident with drugs; I think he got in the way. Gavin once warned me; "If anybody takes up with you they won't see another sunrise," and I believe him.'

'Meaning, you'd leave him if it was safe to do so?' He moved to her side of the table, put his arms around her and gave her a lingering kiss… 'You'd take up my offer?'

'That's a plus in your favour; you know how to kiss.' *It was a huge understatement; the kiss affected every part of my body.*

He ran his fingers through her hair. 'Let's go to bed now.' He made it seem as if it was something they did every day.

There was a long silence.

He caught her off balance. *I can't jump into bed just like that; it needs to be with breathless expectation. Alistair has throwaway sex on a regular basis; I'm used to having no sex whatsoever. That could be a problem, but seems it won't be too long before I find out.*

His hands left her hair and slowly drifted towards her breasts.

At that moment, she placed her hands on his and held them still. 'You haven't paid the bill yet, and there's no free sample,' she joked.

He didn't see it as a joke; he pulled away, strutted around the room with an expression of disbelief, then made a sudden departure.

She covered her face with her hands. *I hate myself for what I just said.* Her tears dripped on the table. She loved Alistair but she didn't know how to handle him. She dried her eyes, wiped the table and prepared herself to leave.

Just then, Alistair burst back in. 'I'll pay the bill now.' He had with him a plastic supermarket bag stuffed with notes. He threw the bag on the floor as if it contained scrap bits of paper, but his expression said it meant power.

'There's a hundred grand to clear the debt and a few grand for some shopping,' he said, ever so nonchalantly.

Speechless, she crossed over to the window, rested her chin in the palm of her hand and stared over the grounds. 'I wish you hadn't done that; you're embarrassing me. I don't want any money, I don't need any money!'

'In the Starlight Club you said you were broke.'

She turned to him, frowned, and shook her head from side to side. 'No, it was Gavin that said we were broke, not me. Unknown to him, I only put half my earnings in our joint account.'

'Good for you, I like your style, but I honestly thought you were broke, didn't mean to offend.'

'It's okay.'

'Tell you what, take the money, buy a nice engagement ring, then sort out what you need for the nursery; it needs a complete makeover.'

'Really, and my divorce, don't you think we should get that out of the way first?'

He went to her, placed a hand on each of her shoulders and locked eyes on her. 'It's already out of the way.'

She pulled away from him and inspected her fingernails, first on one hand, then the other. 'Alistair, there's the procedures to deal with first; you're ahead of yourself. What about Gavin?'

'I've spoken to him and transferred half a million quid to his account; he seemed pleased. I told him I was in love with you and you were in love with me and we planned to get married.'

There was a good minute's silence.

Then she turned and gave him a furious look. 'Alistair, that's just not on; I'm the one to tell him, not you. Also, you're taking a big risk telling him before he's heard it from me.'

'You won't see or hear from him again… Now, can we go to bed?' He spoke as if he'd just cancelled the milkman, and had a wicked grin, full of sexual possibilities.

'Sorry, Alistair; I'm off to the salon, then the agency.' *I dearly wanted to say yes, but I was more nervous than aroused.*

He lifted her off her feet and carried her into the bedroom. 'Take the day off…the week off… Forget the bloody agency, please.' He plonked her on the bed and began undressing himself; his face took on a look of the pleasure about to unfold.

She tried to put on a serious face. 'It's an important assignment. You can unwrap your present tonight.' She jumped up and made for the door. *Damn, I've never felt so nervous.*

'I love you. Honest.'

'I believe you, just be patient.' She made it to the door before he grabbed her. As she opened the door, James the butler almost stumbled in.

'I was just about to knock. Ted is waiting outside madam.'

Thank God for Ted, she thought. James escorted her to the Rolls without saying another word.

Ted greeted her and opened the door. 'Thanks, Ted.' She settled on the back seat, feeling upset on one hand but delighted on the other. Now, she just hoped not to disappoint Alistair.

She thought about the orphanage. *Would the past affect me? I'm not sure; but one thing I am sure about, I've never had sex voluntarily. On each occasion, I was drunk, drugged up, or both, and thankfully, I vaguely remember the sex. I still feel like a virgin.*

'Emma, you're quiet.' Ted peered at her in the rear-view mirror.

'Just thinking.'

'Past, present or future?'

'All three.'

'Just live for present, have some fun; the past has gone and the future hasn't arrived.'

'Oh, right, just forget everything that's happened in the past, which was the present at the time, and just live for the minute?'

'Why clutter up brain space with something you cannot change?'

'I know where you're coming from, but demons from the past can affect the present.'

'You can't live in slums and expect to come out unscathed. I was glad to get out alive. But the slums had their advantages.'

'Like?'

'Everybody had nothing, expected nothing, and if you went with a girl it was pure and simple, almost animalistic.'

Emma glared at him through the mirror. 'Yes I know, the girls called it rape.'

'Maybe, but it didn't stop them coming back for more… or so I was told.'

'So you were told? Come off it Ted, you've already given out your track record.'

He burst out laughing. 'No, you got it wrong; the girls were doing the raping. They enjoyed overpowering guys like me. They went about in pairs, they were strong girls.'

'Oh, so strong you couldn't escape them?'

'I tried once, after that, I put up with it.'

'Yes, I'm sure you did, but that's in the past and taking up brain-space. I thought the past had gone?'

'The point is, if you dwell on the past, then make sure it's on the good times.'

'Suppose there were no good times or you can't remember any for the bad times?'

He pulled into the picnic area by the lake, cut the engine and turned to her. 'Then the past can creep into the present and ruin the future, and I think we're talking about your future here?'

Emma bowed her head and played with her empty ring finger. 'I know.'

'What's happened to the ring?'

'Gone.'

'Blimey, divorce pending?'

'Yep.'

'A new geezer in your life?'

'Yep, from today.'

Ted started the engine and pulled away. 'So I won't be running Gavin about anymore?'

'You seem pleased.'

'Course I'm pleased, you'll be chuffed with Alistair.'

'Maybe, but I never said who it was.'

'No matter, I've felt the vibes. What took you so long?'

'Scared of his reputation, scared of letting him down and scared of letting myself down.'

'And now?'

'I'm terrified.'

'Well, if he loves you and you love him, what's so terrifying about that?'

'All the girls he's had.'

'He can't help having a reputation, but it's mostly unfounded; if he'd slept with every girl that gave him the come-on, he'd be dead for sure.'

She gave him a questioning look in the mirror.

'How come you're still alive then?'

'Now, now, Emma.' He pulled up at the private salon that she used, in the heart of Knightsbridge. 'What time do I pick you up?'

'Don't worry; I'm going to the agency after, they'll send someone.'

Before going in the salon, she took a stroll along a side street trying to clear her head. She wondered about Gavin. *How would he take it?* She felt awful about what Alistair had done without first consulting her.

At that moment, she glanced at her watch and realized that an hour and half had passed since Alistair had phoned Gavin. Why hadn't Gavin phoned her? She checked her phone to see if it was on.

After a while, and feeling rather nervous, she phoned him. 'You okay, Gavin?'

'Don't worry, I know him inside out, if he wants something, he pays for it, trouble is, he wants you, and he says you love him. Well, if he's stupid enough to think that, he has a problem.'

'I know…' She was lost for words and couldn't bring herself to tell him it was true. 'Why… why didn't you phone me?'

'I was checking out my new bank account, I've half a million to play around with.'

'So… so what do you think?'

For a moment, the phone went quiet. 'Alistair's tried it on already I suppose?'

'Sorry Gavin, but that's how it is.'

'He's playing with fire. Tell him that!'

'I already 'have. As far as he's concerned you no longer exist.'

'Well, I'm still here. Otherwise, I wouldn't be talking to you, would I?'

'If…if half a million's not enough, he may up the stakes.'

There was a long pause.

'It would have to be a much bigger slice of his money and the mansion here in Yorkshire.'

'Really…well, I suppose you could put me on E-bay; a well sought after article like me, who knows what I might fetch.'

'Alistair would still outbid them all, may as well keep it private; tell him I want two million and the mansion. Nothing to stop us getting back together later, is there?'

'You bloody tell him!' Emma switched off and almost threw the phone across the road.

5 It was early evening when Emma arrived back at Lockstock. In the suite she found a note on the coffee table: *Meet you at Isabella's at seven-thirty.*

That should turn a few heads, she thought, *and why not?*

Meanwhile, she sorted a few things in the suite, then showered and spent the rest of the time dressing. First, in her sexiest underwear, then her slinky, new black dress that left her classy red bra on show.

At that point, James knocked on the suite door. She grabbed her bag and stepped out, feeling ready for a good party. Without a second look, James escorted her to the Rolls as if she'd done something wrong.

Apparently, James had worked for Alistair's parents; he came with the hall and seemed aloof to the present-day use. Yet, he seemed to be doing okay out of the place. He had staff quarters at the hall and it was rumoured that he had a wife and family in the country. One of the girls had seen them in a village pub having a slap-up meal; then they drove off in a top-of-the-range Mercedes.

Ted dropped her off at Isabella's. 'Have a good time.' He had a big grin on his face.

Inside, the place was already buzzing with celebrity party girls dressed in as little as they dared, and the men were arriving in droves.

She met Alistair at the bar. Nobody seemed to notice that Gavin wasn't with her, though the same crowd attended every party. Eyes shining, he put his arm around her and kissed her on the lips. 'My future wife. Gavin has dumped her, silly fool him.'

'Well, who cares about Gavin; I bloody don't.' Amy was drinking some concoction and plainly ripped out of her skull.

Emma hugged her. 'Are you okay?'

'I think my head's gone.'

'Emma's taken over my body, sorry girls.' He took her head in his hands and gave her a long kiss. 'Let's celebrate,' he said.

He did, for the rest of the night, leaving Emma with Jane and Clare, while he made the rounds. He ended up more than a little tipsy and invited a few friends to Lockstock.

His 'few friends' turned up in thirty taxis. People began arriving from different clubs; bodies were spilling into every room, including the swimming pool. James was strolling around with his silver platter, serving cocaine and Ecstasy and looking like he needed some himself. Emma unintentionally caught his eye. He came over and held out the platter. 'Interested madam?'

'No, just disappear James.' At that, she left and headed for the suite and some sleep.

The following morning, she went around the hall looking for Alistair; everyone had gone and housemaids were cleaning up the mess. Mary, one of the housemaids, told her that Alistair was at the races.

On her way back to the suite, she met James. 'You having breakfast madam?'

'Yes please, in the suite.'

'What time madam?'

'Soon as it's ready…and James, from now on…' She suddenly held herself back. 'It doesn't matter, carry on.'

Pointless, she thought; *he'll find out soon enough that he has a new boss.*

Just as she entered the suite her mobile rang, it was Gavin.

'Remember John C, my prison friend,' he said, 'I bumped into him in the estate grounds early this morning.'

She hadn't a clue what he was talking about, but pretended she knew. 'What's he doing there?'

'He's on a job here, interesting, isn't it?' he laughed.

'Is it? Since when has John C been interesting?'

'Since he first became a friend. However, you've never met him.' He laughed again.

'You've never even mentioned the guy before. Is this another of your secrets? Well, I'm not laughing, it's not at all funny.'

'We thought it was funny. We're having a get-together drink tonight.'

'Yes, to discuss a drugs deal I guess; you make me shudder.'

'By the way, I've got my hands on Alistair's diaries from when he was seventeen, makes interesting reading… Must push off, some work to do at the clinic.' He rang off, before she'd finished the conversation.

As soon as she put the phone down, it rang again. 'Meet me at Nancy's, at seven thirty, I've booked dinner; then we're going to Jane's thirtieth,' said Alistair.

'Okay, I'll see you at Nancy's.' She knew she couldn't do the party after dinner though; she had an evening appointment with her sponsors.

At Nancy's, some well-known celebrities were dining. Alistair was propping up the posh bar with a skimpily-dressed girl chatting to him. 'Emma's my fiancé, we've booked dinner,' he said.

They left her chatting up the barman while a waitress escorted them to a table. 'The usual sir?'

'Champagne, Emma love?'

'Fine by me.'

'Yes, carry on Carol.'

'You look stunning love,' he said, as the waitress came to pour the champagne.

'Thank you, sir.' The waitress smiled and blushed.

How cheeky is that? She just stole my compliment, Emma thought.

Alistair grinned. 'You're miles away, are you okay?'

He reached over and put his hand on hers. Emma noticed the ring on his finger: a copper coin in a gold setting.

'I'm alright Alistair…' *I wanted to say, 'Alistair love,' but it stuck my throat.* 'What an unusual ring.'

'Yes, you won't see another like it. An eighteen-forty-four half-farthing; the gold came from father's mine in Wales.'

'I've noticed it before, it's beautiful.'

'I was conceived one foot above the coin, my father once told me, when on a brief visit back home. From this single coin his business empire grew.'

'Interesting, how did that work out then?'

'Father was fishing on the River Ribble in Lancashire, when my future mother came along the opposite bank and started sunbathing, flaunting herself. He said she was doing her best to distract him from fishing. The more he tried to concentrate on fishing, the more clothes she took off, until she was sunning in just bra and panties.'

Emma tried to hold back her giggles. 'Carry on, it sounds funny.'

'She went topless and started rubbing sun cream on her boobs, but he carried on fishing, not knowing what to make of it.'

'I bet he packed in fishing.'

'No he didn't; he tried to ignore her. Then she dressed and strolled down to a bridge in the next field. Next thing she was standing on the bank behind him.'

'I guess he packed in fishing at that point surely?'

'You'll never guess what he said.'

'No, but you're going to tell me.'

'He said to her, "What's wrong miss, haven't you seen a fisherman before?"'

Emma almost choked on her champagne. 'I bet you take after your mum.'

'Well, I'll give dad his due, he made love to her on the river bank and never went fishing again.'

'Good for him, so where does the coin fit in then?'

'He took up metal detecting and scoured the riverbanks for rings and coins. He came across the half farthing in exactly the same place he'd made love to mum, he reckoned that's where I was conceived.'

'What an odd story.'

'After that, he found thousands of Roman coins in a field. He became a million-aire overnight. By the time I was old enough to know him, he was a multi-billionaire.'

'I bet you had a cushy childhood.'

'It was horrendous; I spent all my time crying in somebody else's arms. I hardly knew my parents; they were travelling all over the world. I only knew the au pairs, then it was boarding school; I spent half my time crying there. My parents died in a car crash, a year before I took over Lockstock.'

'What a sad tale; so you decided to bed every girl in London until you found what you wanted, is that it?'

'Is that what you think? Well, I like a kiss and a frolic now and again.'

'Oooh… pull the other one. They talk you know.'

'I breakfast with every girl that stays here.'

'Yes… I believe Trish was latest.'

He burst out laughing. 'Out of her tree; I passed her on to Ted.'

Emma smiled, looking into his eyes. 'I'll give you the bad news first; I can't go to the party, I'm going to Birmingham for a night photo-shoot.'

'You're not serious!' He shook his head and spun his glass on the table.

'The photographer is flying to Germany in the morning. Sorry love, can't wriggle out of it.'

'And the good news?'

'You stay in bed tomorrow; I'll join you at nine.'

He moved to her side of the table, kissed her and picked her up. 'Come on let's go now.' He carried her across the room to the door.

'I can't, but I'll be thinking of nine o'clock. I have to do the shoot tonight.'

'In that case, ring the chap, tell him to do the shoot at Lockstock.'

'The background's no good. We're using a Mercedes showroom. It's the last shoot in my contract, can't let them down. Better hang on until tomorrow.'

The following morning, heading back from Birmingham, *One thing's for sure,* Emma thought, *he won't ever get my bikini bum on a car bonnet again.*

When she arrived at Lockstock, James took her to Alistair, who was fully dressed and eating a bowl of mixed fruit in the empty dining room. 'Breakfast, madam?' James asked in a tired voice.

'Just coffee please, call me Emma, and I'd rather you didn't bow.'

'Very good, madam.' He gave a slight bow and went for the coffee.

'You won't stop him,' Alistair said.

'So, you're off to the office then? What happened to the lie-in?'

'Spoil the effect if I were in bed. Better if we start from scratch. There's two bottles of champagne on ice in the bedroom and one next to the Jacuzzi; we'll start in the Jacuzzi.' His face was a charm, his voice slow and sexy.

He told James to drink the coffee, led her upstairs to the Jacuzzi room and poured two glasses of champagne. 'You're so desirable, Emma...' He began kissing her; his hands were in her hair, stroking her neck and shoulders, pulling her closer. Then he began kissing her through her clothes, undoing her buttons at the same time.

She emptied her glass. 'I'm feeling slightly nervous Alistair. Pour me another glass please, while I go to the suite for my dressing gown.'

'It's okay love, no rush... Why are you crying?'

'Because I'm so happy.'

It was twenty minutes to ten when she put on her dressing gown and headed back. Alistair's technique intrigued her.

She felt light-headed; the glass of champagne, coupled with her expectations, added a spring to her step. *Hell, I feel naughty; this is definitely my first man.*

When she entered the Jacuzzi, he was naked and drying himself off. 'Don't worry, it's bigger than it looks at present... Here, drink it down, settles the nerves.' He passed her the glass.

No wonder the girls called him Adonis, he had the most well formed body.

He gently held her hand and led her into the bedroom.

'You still nervous?'

'New ground, understand, but I'm okay.' *It's a lie; my tummy's fluttering like mad.*

He pulled a bottle of oil from the bedside cabinet.

Emma let her dressing gown slip to the floor, lay naked on the bed and closed her eyes.

Her heart pounded between her ears, her breath came in gasps.

Something will explode soon, she thought.

The oil dripped onto her hard nipples in tune with the grandfather clock, striking the hour on the landing. He played the oil over each nipple with his fingers. Her hands explored his body with closed eyes as if in a dream; afraid it would end if she opened them. *God, Alistair I'm ready now... now... right now!!*

As if to keep her on the edge, oil began dripping on her nipples again.

At that moment, Alistair's mobile rang in the dressing room.

'Bloody thing.'

'Pleeeease, don't answer it.'

The oil drips stopped along with the last chimes of the clock striking ten. She opened her eyes; he was heading into the dressing room.

'Sorry love, no choice, expecting an important message.'

When he returned, his face had dropped.

'I'm going to the estate immediately. Ted will take me in the chopper, be back this evening; we can take up where we left off.'

'Alistair, you can't do this to me. Surely it can wait half an hour?'

'We either go the whole hog, or nothing.'

'Hell… Somebody dying or what?'

'Worse, somebody is dead. That was my gamekeeper, accidentally shot a poacher. I need to be there before the police are involved.'

'That poacher, it wouldn't be Gavin by any chance?'

'Not unless he's taken up poaching; I'll see you when I return, meantime grab some sleep.' He threw on his clothes, kissed her and left.

Only when Alistair had gone did she realize how near she'd come to sexual fulfilment. Now she hungered for him. She lay on the bed, closed her eyes, and carried on with the oil where Alistair had left off. She let her hands run freely as if they were his, until she fell asleep.

The grandfather clock woke her at twelve noon; no drips of oil just the chimes. Alistair would nearly be in Yorkshire by now, she reasoned.

She rang Gavin's mobile. 'Are you okay?'

'Apart from a sore nose, I'm fine, but I can't hang about.'

'Alistair's on his way in the helicopter… What about the shooting?'

'Shooting? Oh, the poacher, it's nothing… must go—'

'Hang on…!' The phone went dead. *What the hell's going on now?* she wondered. She rang Alistair, but his phone was switched off and she didn't have Ted's number. She rang Gavin again; no reply.

Shaking her head in frustration, she threw the phone on the bed. She finished off the champagne then climbed back in bed.

That evening she prepared for Alistair's return.

She asked James for three more bottles of champagne, she put two in the bedroom and one in the Jacuzzi. Then she showered in the huge shower cubicle; big enough for a large family to wash together.

It made her think of her grandma and the tin bath. *Sunday nights were for boiling kettles and pans to fill the bath. The soap was more likely to remove your skin than clean it. A huge block of ragged-edged soap, that never seemed to reduce in size, and felt like sandpaper. When you'd finished there were no blackheads or pimples, just bright new skin, and one hundred percent of all known germs were dead. The chemical smell stayed with you for a week. Then you went through the process again.*

Emma had never seen the soap since, nor a tin bath, but wondered if these things were still around. She inspected the array of soaps and perfumes that were scattered on the shelves around the shower room; *I think not,* she concluded.

She went down to the lounge in her dressing gown, switched the main lights out and went over to the bar.

She'd just poured a drink, when she heard someone open the door; she spun round. 'Alistair; you startled me.'

'Just make sure you keep calling me Alistair,' he said.

She went cold, her breath came in gulps, and she fought to get her head together.

Then it clicked; his job... the clinic... amateur dramatics. She tried to compose herself. 'For a moment, I really thought it was Alistair. You've almost got the voice, and you definitely look like him.'

'Good, I'll polish the voice before the next party. You're married to a billionaire,' he laughed.

There was a long silence; she stared at the floor, wondering what to say. *This is ridiculous, what's he playing at? Must have planned this for ages, no wonder he wanted to be sociable with Alistair, when he really hated him. I need to think, I need to stall him.*

'There's two bottles of champagne on ice in the bedroom, and one next to the Jacuzzi. I've also found some sexy body oil.'

He looked puzzled. 'What's all that in aid of, then?'

'From a good sex guide I once read.'

'Funny you should say that. It was Alistair's favourite with the women. It's all in his diaries.' His eyes were wide open. 'Plus a lot more sexual stuff.'

She led him upstairs, thinking, *I'll get him drunk, then drown him in the bloody Jacuzzi.* She poured two glasses of champagne.

His hands shaking, he began fumbling with his shirt buttons; pausing for a good sip of champagne.

'Think you can make it last?' She knocked her champagne back and waited for his next move - knowing there wouldn't be one.

'Well...' He stepped back and drank from the bottle. 'According to this...' He put the bottle down and pulled a diary from his back pocket. 'We are only on the first exercise, and we've another twenty to go; that should take a while...'

She stood there with a frozen soul while he sat on the edge of the Jacuzzi reading the diary. She nudged him. 'By the way, where is Alistair?'

'John C's taken him to Loch Ness, some sort of diving expedition, says he'll make a good anchor when they reach the deepest part.'

She pushed him in the Jacuzzi and ran screaming to the bathroom, spewing up on the way. She retched in the sink until her throat was sore and her eyes were stinging.

A noise behind her made her spin round. 'Gavin, don't creep up on me like that.' He stood dripping in the doorway; he resembled a voodoo rag-doll image of Alistair. She turned back to the sink, retching.

'What's wrong with you Emma?'

She felt his hand patting her on the back. She couldn't remember the last time he'd touched her, but now, it was the last thing she needed. 'Get your hands off me! I can't take this in, I'm going back to the suite.'

'Okay, but I'm sure you'll come to in the morning.' He walked her to the suite and, taking the key from her hand, shut the door behind her and locked her in.

She tried to scream but nothing came out. She rested her back against the door to hold herself up. She put all her effort into screaming, but no sound left her lips. *A living nightmare,* she thought, *and worse than any sleeping nightmare.*

No longer able to keep on her feet, she slid to the floor, trembling; it was as if her vital organs were having major problems and about to give up on her.

Instinct told her to take deep, long breaths. After a while, she felt her strength returning, but her heart was beating faster than she'd ever known. She wanted to take a pulse count, but she probably wouldn't believe it.

Her eyes settled on the phone, she pushed herself up off the floor and made for the phone. When she picked it up the line was dead.

Then she realized she'd left her mobile in the main lounge.

She dropped down onto the sofa. The keyhole in the French window glared at her; the key had gone, and that could only be James.

She pondered for a while; the more she thought about the situation, the more frightened she felt. *Would Gavin say I was involved? Yes, he would. Could I prove my innocence? With great difficulty. I'd be the one that set up Alistair; he announced we were to marry. Now I'm back with Gavin, taking over Alistair's business empire. How would I get out of that?*

At that point, her mind turned to Alistair. She felt her body go weak and shaky. She went to the drinks cabinet and poured a large brandy, it seemed an effort. She made it back to the sofa, her heart thumping as if it were about to stop any second. She took a large gulp of brandy. Shortly her heart eased to a less frightening pace. She emptied the glass and, still shaking, went to the cabinet and grabbed the bottle, determined to finish it off.

The shakes faded and her heart stopped thumping, but the brandy didn't remove her feeling of deep sadness, sorrow and hate.

In tears, she fell asleep on the sofa.

The next morning she woke with a startle and a thumping headache.

'Coffee? Coffee love?'

'Gavin, you made me jump… Just leave it there…and don't lock the door.'

'How do you feel?'

'Frig off!'

He raised his eyebrows. 'Diving accidents happen, no need to shove me in the Jacuzzi, screaming your head off.'

There was a long pause.

She sat bolt upright, stared him in the eye and smirked. 'What a pity – another hour and we could have been trying to have sex.'

'There's no hurry love, we can—'

'Can what…? Hundreds of stage plays you've done, and you can't remember a few simple lines from act one in a diary.'

'We never did sex scenes.'

'Oh, I wonder why. Piss off, you're not Gavin anymore and you certainly aren't Alistair.'

'You didn't give me the chance love, my first attempt at steamy seduction.'

'And the last!'

'Emma, I love you more than you know. You love me, don't you? You've never said otherwise.'

'Well, I'll say it now; I don't love you and never have. You hooked me with drugs…remember… and you knew exactly what you were doing. Principles…my stupid principles said stick it out; obviously, you never had any.'

'That was before I became a billionaire, I don't need any now — you know, like Alistair.'

'Fat lot of good it did him. Anyway, everybody knew Alistair's principles, and if he had been with the person he wanted in the first place; he wouldn't have been a womaniser.'

'Meaning you…? I put up with his flirting for years; I never went on about it.'

'No, you just let it eat you up. All the time, murder was on your mind. First, take up acting, then run a cosmetic surgery clinic purposely for your own makeover. Not only did you want to kill him, you wanted to be him. Alistair would be no further threat and you'd step into his shoes. That's one hell of a murder plot.'

'Let's say a nasty accident plot. Not bad eh, you played the carrot he was the donkey. In the end, the donkey bit the carrot.'

'You're sick.'

'I'm the director, you played the leading lady; you were good, so much so that you're in the next scene. John C is one of the leading men, and James the butler is the other. They're partners in our business empire.'

'I'm leaving; the police will sort you out.'

'Only if you tell them, and you were the leading lady.'

'I want no part in it.'

'The police will think you played a big part.'

'Piss off.'

'Listen, everything will be all right love.'

'Why are you calling me love when you haven't a clue what it means?'

'I'm Alistair now; don't forget.' He tried to kiss her lips but she gave him her cheek then pushed him away. He screwed his face.

'Okay, but it's the lips in future; if we're to be convincing. See you in the dining room.'

I'd rather kiss a skunk's bum, she thought, as he left the room. *I'll play the next scene though, until I find a way out. I can put on a good act but I won't be kissing the leading man, to say the least.*

'Morning, Emma,' Mary the maid said, greeting her in the main dining room. 'You're sticking it out I see.'

Emma took in a deep breath and inspected her fingernails. 'We plan to marry, Gavin has left me.'

'Well, I'm not surprised; all the staff expected you'd get together sooner or later. Pity about Gavin though, but then, he never seemed the right chap for a nice girl like you.'

She smiled. 'Really? Thanks for that Mary.'

Gavin eyed the ceiling, a look of disgust on his face. 'I thought Gavin was a nice guy, a bit quiet maybe but otherwise okay.'

Mary gave him an odd look. 'You got a sore throat Alistair? Too many late nights chatting up girls, that's what it is.'

'Better if you don't talk to me then. One last thing, when you see James, wherever he is, tell him breakfast is for four tomorrow.'

'No problem.'

'Can you clear your things from the suite Emma? John and his wife Lucy will be staying there. I'm picking them up at the airfield at one.' He opened Alistair's appointment book. 'According to this we're at Annabel's tonight, its Amy's thirtieth.'

'Well, gosh, that should be interesting.'

'You okay? Changed your mind about me then?'

'I suppose I can stand a bit of luxury.' *That's if I don't kill you first.*

'Great, I put a lot into this venture for both of us.'

When he'd left for the airfield, she asked Mary to move her things from the suite to the master bedroom while she went to have her hair done at the salon.

Outside, Ted was cleaning the rolls on the forecourt. 'Hello darling, going somewhere, I hope.'

He raised her spirits instantly. *If only he knew what was going on.* 'Knightsbridge please, Ted.'

'The salon then?'

'Yes.'

'James never said.'

'Who needs James, don't you think it's better this way? I certainly do.'

'The worst thing is, James worked for his mum and dad. Alistair thinks that's good enough for him, and lets him run the place.'

'I know.'

After the salon, a friend drove her back to Lockstock. Alistair's Lamborghini - now Gavin's - was back in its usual place on the gravel forecourt. Laughter and the sound of clinking glasses drifted from the lounge as she passed the billiard room.

She strolled into the lounge. 'What you having, love?' Gavin asked from the corner bar. John and Lucy stood up to greet her.

John was frightening: well over six feet tall and built like a bull. A horrendous old injury took up one side of his face, a rugged appearance on the other side. A shock of red curly hair covered his head. He held out a massive hand and smiled. 'I've only one eye but it's a good one; it's my shooting eye,' he said.

She'd expected a vice-like grip, but it was gentle and his smile made you forget his facial disfigurement. She wondered how he managed to smile at all with such a hideous injury. He seemed a gentleman and his wife, Lucy, was quite pleasant, not someone you'd expect to marry a gangster.

Emma sat down sipping her brandy and let them do the talking while her thoughts, frightening thoughts, ebbed and flowed.

Big John smiled at her as though he could see the turmoil and was trying to ease it. 'You have the look of a film star,' he said.

'She's a model,' Gavin said.

'I've left something in the suite…back in minute.' Emma headed along the passage. John followed and intercepted her at the door; he held her arm. 'You all right?'

She couldn't believe how gentle he was for such a giant of a man. 'I'm okay, be back shortly.' She closed the door behind her. *Sure looks like a killer,* she thought, *why doesn't he act like one? Yet he's so placid, and his face has you feeling sorry for him, but you wouldn't want to meet him on a dark night.* She shivered.

6 Emma had a horrible trembling inside her; she did some breathing exercises to calm herself. Just then, the sitting room door opened and Big John walked in. 'Emma, is something wrong?'

'Everything's wrong, I wish you wouldn't pretend that you care. Like it's a nice sunny day and everybody's on top of the world. When it couldn't be much further from the truth.'

'I understand, splitting up is never easy. At least Gavin's got the mansion, he's okay.'

'I suppose so.'

'Tell me Emma; what is he like as a person? You see, he's my new boss now.'

'Your boss?'

'Yes, be handy if I knew a bit about him beforehand. I don't just work for anybody. Alistair's been good to me, but now he's given the place over to Gavin.'

'Gavin… Alistair… Alistair… Gavin… It's doing my head in!' She jumped up, ran in the bathroom, locked the door behind her and paced the floor sobbing.

Five minutes later, Gavin knocked on the door. 'Emma, it's time to get ready for the party!' he shouted.

'Give me ten minutes!' she shouted back. *Some party,* she thought, *if he thinks I'm going to enjoy a damn party with all that's gone on he can frig off.*

She returned to the main lounge.

'Alistair's getting ready. Okay if I use the suite now, Emma?' Lucy asked.

'Help yourself.'

'Sorry if I upset you Emma,' Big John said. 'Still having feelings for Gavin?'

'I don't have any feelings for him.'

'What's the problem then, you love Alistair, don't you?'

'That is the problem, you know very well, and it's no good pretending you don't know Gavin. You had a few drinks together for old time's sake. Said he was surprised to see you.'

'I was surprised when I saw a stranger on the land, thought he was a poacher. I'd just come off a week's leave when I saw this character entering a wood. I trained my telescopic sights on him and presumed it was my new boss. He disappeared through the wood and off the estate.'

'You didn't shoot him then?'

He laughed. 'I'm a good shot and proud of it. Only in self-defence would I pull the trigger. I never saw the chap again, but it wasn't Gavin, because, a few minutes later my mobile rang. It was Gavin. "I'm your new boss," he said, "Come to the estate office." That was the first time I'd met him.'

'Describe him, please.'

'Your husband…describe him?'

'Just making sure you haven't mixed him up with someone else, that's all.'

'You'll be seeing him later; he came with us in the chopper to the airfield. He's meeting you at Annabel's tonight.'

Confused, Emma played the game. 'Why would Gavin want to come here when we've separated? You sure it was Gavin?'

'He had a boxer-nose, enquiring brown eyes, dark hair, a thin moustache and goatee-beard. A tattoo on the back of each hand, not your usual gentry type.'

Shocked, she thought for a while. 'Not the usual Gavin either, and impossible to be true.'

John gave her a funny look and raised his one eyebrow. 'Pardon?'

'Must have grown a beard since I last saw him, that's all.'

'Right, I'd better get changed, see you later Emma.' He made for the suite.

She went to confront Gavin in the bedroom. 'Who's the mystery pilot called Gavin that came down with John and Lucy then?'

'John C.'

'Oh…yes! Now you tell me. I've been in a right mess.'

'I meant to tell you, I didn't expect Big John talking to you first.'

'Well, you'd better fill me in on the missing bits, if it's not too much trouble.'

'Sorry love, I meant to take you to the bedroom and explain things, but you went in the suite and Big John followed you.'

'I could've slipped up, Big John knows nothing then?'

'Not unless he's got it from you.'

'I thought he was the killer, I let him do the talking.'

'John C is the hit man, but he's now called Gavin; he's taken my identity.'

'According to Big John's description he looks nothing like you.'

'Doesn't matter, he'll be at the mansion in Yorkshire, running things from there as Gavin. When he's in London, he'll revert to John C… Okay, I'm ready, you'd better look sharp.'

Now at least, with Big John, she felt she could breathe easily, glad he wasn't the murderer and glad he was around.

After changing for the party, she joined the others in the main lounge. Gavin rang for James then went to meet him in the passage.

'You look stunning,' Lucy said, 'I like the dress. What do you think John?'

John gave her the once-over, smiling. 'I prefer the filling.'

'Well, she is a model, that's how they look,' Lucy said.

'First time I've seen one outside a magazine. We could do with a few dotted around the estate, a change from pheasants.'

'John, we know you're good at plucking pheasants. Models though…'

He grinned. 'A new challenge.'

Emma had a fit of the giggles. 'Could be interesting.'

'Yes, him trying to pluck you? Well, best for him to practice on one first, I suppose. Otherwise, he could be plucking about all day.'

John nodded his head in agreement.

Can't be true, Emma thought, *Yorkshire folk aren't this dim, surely?*

At that moment, Gavin entered the lounge. 'Taxi's outside folks.'

John and Lucy, made for the door, Emma followed.

'Right we'll see you later, or in the morning, hope the party goes well,' Big John said.

'Have a good night; enjoy yourself.' Gavin shut the door behind them. 'Ted's taking us,' he said.

'Where've they gone, I thought they were coming to the party?'

'The theatre, that's why they're here; it's a birthday treat for Lucy. Alistair promised them a night out in London. I couldn't let them down. We've to keep to his plans. Thankfully, he had everything meticulously laid out. A day-planner for business and another for his social life, plus his personal diary.'

'Not as carefree as we thought, eh?' Emma felt sick.

'Far from it, he had a good brain.'

'Are you ready?' James interrupted. 'Ted's waiting; you'd better jump to it.'

Emma, startled at James's attitude change, glowered at him and purposely took her time. *So this is his real vocabulary, it suits him better,* she thought.

James left them to make their own way.

'What the hell's going on?' she whispered, as they made their way to the front door.

'James is now in charge of Alistair's entire business empire. Our role is to run Lockstock. We carry on as though nothing's changed. We keep the Hall and Alistair's personal wealth; they keep the business side. How does that sound?'

'Bloody awful, nothing will ever be the same, it won't work.'

'Emma, you know nothing; years of planning have gone into this, we know what we are doing.'

She didn't answer. Tears were dripping from her cheeks. She slid to the floor in the passageway. Gavin grabbed her by the arm and tried to pull her up.

'Don't touch me!'

'The girls tantalised him and satisfied his sexual stamina, but we knew he'd soon want more than that. You were perfect. Remember the oil sheikh that offered you the world to go live with him?'

'How could I forget that?'

'Well, we arranged it, and you passed the test. After that, we knew we could dangle you in front of Alistair until he was bursting at the seams to have you.'

She shook her head from side to side. 'Gavin, he loved me. Frig off, please.'

'No, I won't frig off; and neither will you, if you want to keep breathing.'

She picked herself up and said nothing. *As if I'm bothered about breathing… But I'll be breathing long enough to see you lot off.*

Since her encounter in the swimming pool, she had completely changed her perspective on life; death was no longer something to be feared. If need be she'd take them out one by one, then kill herself.

When they arrived at Annabel's, a man on the pavement outside fit the description of John C. He wore a smart black suit, white frilly shirt and dickey-bow tie, but it did nothing for him, he looked ridiculous.

He opened the car door and offered his hand; it was a cold hand, though the night was warm. She forced a smile; he didn't return one, nor did he speak.

'You little, murdering bastard,' she uttered under her breath.

'Let's go in then,' Gavin said.

On entering, Amy spotted her and came over to greet her.

'Glad you could make it Emma… Who's the bodyguard?'

'John C, Alistair's friend.' She took a seat with Amy. 'You look well.'

'Thanks.' Amy passed her a note. 'You've to ring this number soon as poss. Dad had a call at work; it's about your sister.'

She borrowed Amy's mobile and went to the loo. When she returned, Amy was talking to Gavin at the bar.

He played the part better than she'd expected. He had the patter off, the stance and all the little nuances that Alistair had; the resemblance was painful. She walked towards them, trembling, her heart pounded against her chest.

'All ok Emma?' Amy asked.

'I'm going back to Lockstock.'

'Why?' Gavin gave her a funny look.

'I don't feel too good I need an early night. Sorry everybody.'

'Pity about that; you don't mind if I stay here?'

'No problem.'

Amy walked her to the foyer. 'Bad news, eh?'

'Wouldn't tell me while I was at a party. I'm to phone him when I leave, which is quite depressing. Can I keep your phone until tomorrow?'

'Yes, anything.'

She was about to climb in the taxi when in jumped John C.

'Where're you going?' she asked.

'Lockstock.'

'I don't need an escort, please stay out of my way.'

She went back in the club. John C followed her.

'Gavin, I'm not having him chase me around.'

'He's looking after you.'

'No way, either we're partners or not. You get him off my back, or we're finished.'

'He doesn't trust you.'

'Well he can buzz off, he's nothing without us.'

'Okay, leave it to me.' He went over to John C, who was propping up the exit door, patted his back and took him to the bar.

In the taxi, her mind was in turmoil. *Why would Stewart phone after all this time? Why did he say, tell nobody he had phoned? What's wrong with Katie?*

At Lockstock, she went straight to the suite. She poured a drink, took a deep breath and rang Stewart's number.

Fifteen minutes later, she crashed on the settee, sobbing.

At that moment, Big John and Lucy disturbed her. 'We've had a wonderful time, a brilliant show,' Lucy said.

'You're home early,' John said. 'Are you okay?'

'I left the party; my brother-in-law rang with some bad news. My sister's dead; a tractor rolled over on her and killed her instantly.'

There was a long silence.

Big John hugged her. 'I don't know what to say; you're having a rough time.'

'I lost my sister,' Lucy said softly, 'it'll be hard going for while.'

'I've to fly up there tomorrow. Stewart's arranged to have me picked up at Leeds airport,' she lied.

'Alistair will take you in the chopper, surely?' John suggested.

'No, he won't, Stewart hates him; he can't go to the funeral.'

'He could just drop you somewhere near.'

'You don't understand; it's a long story. They'd kill Stewart if they found him. I don't even know where he lives until I get there. I haven't seen him or my sister since I was nineteen.'

'Well, we are flying to Leeds in the morning; if you like, we can go to the airport together.'

'Thanks John, I'll see you in the morning.'

Emma broke the news to Gavin before breakfast.

'When's the funeral?' he asked with his back to her. *I didn't expect him to cry, but he could've stopped what he was doing,* she thought.

'Tuesday, I'm flying to Leeds in the morning,' she lied.

He turned round. 'John C will take you in the chopper.'

'Very funny, do you seriously think I'd let him take me?'

'He'll drop you on the doorstep.'

'Yes, from a great height. Right, I need to pack a few things if you don't mind.'

Sunday morning, everything that was precious to her went in the suitcase. The only photograph of Gavin that she put in the case was the best photo she had of Pal, Gavin just happened to be in the background.

Yes, well, that's all he's ever been, a background man. Well, he will be truly in the background before long, because I won't be returning to London. A call to the police will put him even further in the background, out of my life completely. Not that he's ever been in my life; he just made a good job of destroying it.

When she'd packed; she sat on the edge of the bed wondering how she'd crammed so much inside one case. Even so, she was leaving ten years of gear behind and that would normally hurt, but it was just a pinprick amongst the wounds.

'Are you ready Emma?' John asked when she entered the lounge.

'What do you mean, is she ready?' Gavin asked in a raised voice.

'We're sharing a taxi to the airport,' she answered for John.

Gavin raised his eyebrows. 'Oh, I didn't realize.'

'Taxi's waiting,' James announced.

'Thanks, Alistair; the show was fantastic.' Big John shook his hand.

'Yes, thanks, I've really enjoyed your hospitality,' Lucy said, 'hope to see you at the mansion before I depart.'

'Yes, take care,' Gavin replied, while scanning through some papers. 'You'll be back Wednesday then Emma?'

She glared at his back, hoping he wouldn't turn round.

'In the evening, I'll ring you,' she said, as pleasantly as she could.

He put down the papers, turned, and locked eyes on her. 'Make it as early as possible; we have a party to attend.'

She held his eyes for a long moment, only now, when it was too late, could she see what was behind them. She wasn't about to smirk. She looked at his feet then back to his face and gave him a lingering smile. 'Do my best, see you.'

He followed them to the forecourt and waved to her as they drove off. Holding back her tears, she turned the other way and let the others wave for her.

John touched her shoulder. 'Didn't you see him wave?'

'No!'

'You okay Emma? You seem agitated.'

She turned to him. 'Two reasons, I'm not coming back and I don't want them to find me or Stewart.'

'Never? I thought you were marrying Alistair. Who's Stewart?'

'No marriage for me, I'm having a clean break. Stewart's my brother-in-law; he left London in a hurry a few years ago. I found out why when I phoned him last night. Stewart shopped some drug barons; he's on their hit list. I might be followed, I'm not going to Leeds; I'm flying to Glasgow.'

They pulled in at the airport departures.

'Going to the loo, back in a minute,' John said.

He caught them up in the waiting area; John put his arms round her and gently shook her. 'Look, we can fly to Glasgow with you if you like, then fly back to Leeds from there.'

She melted in his arms feeling safe, feeling warm and protected. She closed her eyes feeling she could sleep for a week. 'You sure?'

'Positive; I've just changed our tickets. You've enough on your mind.'

'Delighted to have your company a bit longer,' Lucy smiled.

'Thanks, Lucy.'

John tweaked her nose. 'Don't fall asleep, that's our boarding call.'

Once on board the plane, John sat next to the window, Lucy sat between them. Within five minutes, Lucy had fallen asleep, snoring deeply. John leaned across and said quietly. 'She's terminally ill, only a few weeks left. We're doing as much as possible together during the time we have left.'

'Oh, dear, you'd never know, she seems so jolly and happy,' Emma whispered.

'She doesn't let it affect her; I'm dreading the day...'

His eyes glazed over, he turned away and peered out of the window. She watched him, expecting him to look down at the landscape, but he just stared, totally engrossed, in the empty sky above the plane. Then, 'I wonder if she'll go to Duplico?' he said softly to himself.

Emma's heart thumped. She listened intently, wondering if she was hearing things.

John, still transfixed on the sky above the plane, quietly muttered, 'She might meet Waldo Sultan.'

How could he know about Waldo Sultan? She reached over Lucy and touched him lightly on the shoulder. He spun round as if she'd stuck a gun in him, a vague expression on his face.

She gave him an enquiring look. 'Just then, you mentioned a name...'

He gave her a blank look. 'It's been a nice flight. We must be due to land soon.'

She reached over and shook his shoulder. 'Come on John; you've been talking out loud, I happened to hear. You said some things that intrigued me, like Duplico, and Waldo Sultan.'

He gave her an odd look. 'Why should Waldo Sultan intrigue you?'

'I almost met him in a space station; he said he would meet me one day. At the time, I was out of my Earthly body... a near-death experience.'

John took his eyes off her and stared out the window. 'He told me the same; then I woke up in the hospital intensive-care unit. A doctor pronounced me dead after a shooting accident.'

'So, what did the doctor think?'

'He was a bit dogmatic; he'd signed a death certificate, told me they didn't put live bodies in the morgue. I said to him, well I'm living proof that you do put live bodies in the morgue. He apologised profusely, but to his knowledge, it had never happened before and insisted that I'd been dead from the moment I was shot.'

'What did you say?'

'I told him that by signing the certificate he'd nearly killed me. "Thanks," he said, "I spent half an hour trying to revive you, I must have done some good, otherwise you wouldn't be talking to me now."'

Emma reached over Lucy and patted his shoulder. 'I once spoke to an undertaker about death certificates. You've no chance if the doctor signs a death certificate; then you're in the undertaker's hands, he's paid to bury you, come what may. They won't stop the funeral even if you're knocking the hell out of the inside of the coffin.'

John gave her a serious look. 'I know, and if you're just having an 'out-of-body' experience and you come back to your body, you can't get out of the coffin from six foot under. Same with cremations, you wouldn't even find your body.'

'In both cases, I don't think it works like that John. From what I saw, only a few get the chance to return to Earth, but your body has to be available, a sort of vacant possession. All the rest go straight to the other side. So if you're pronounced dead and leave your body, you must return to the body in time.'

He stared out of the window. 'Even then, it's only if you choose to come back.'

She held his massive hand as best she could. 'Well, we know that, but the doctors say they saved your life and you can't tell them otherwise.'

'I think they play a big part, but when it comes to the crunch, the decision is yours. Incidentally, they sent a chap to interview me. I told him where I'd been while my empty shell was gathering frost in the morgue. A space station doesn't fit in, but he'd put it on file with the rest, he said.'

She gave him a reassuring look. 'I know about the NDE file. There was only one other out of thousands that mentioned a space station; it must have been you?'

'I guess so. Someone meeting you at Glasgow?'

'Yes, Stewart's sending a light aircraft to pick me up at a nearby gliding club.'

'I'll shadow you while you swap planes, just in case things go wrong.'

'And if something does go wrong?'

'Don't worry.' He patted the side of his coat. 'I'm prepared. Never go without it, not since I lost half my face in an encounter with a shotgun hoodlum.'

'I wondered how your injury came about.'

'A supposedly *safe job* I was on when I was in the SAS. We couldn't take guns, but everything went wrong.'

'Sounds horrible.'

'My brother came to identify me in the morgue and saw me move. Never felt a thing until I came round in Intensive Care, then it was hell on earth. I ended up wishing I'd gone to Duplico when Waldo gave me a choice.'

'That's how I feel right now.'

John smiled. 'Things will improve for you, I'm sure. I chose to come back for Lucy's sake.'

'Well, I chose to come back to hopefully marry Alistair, but… Your face still looks painful.'

'But what?'

'I'll phone you after the funeral and tell you everything that's going on… We're descending.'

In the airport, John looked round the faces.

'There's my man,' Emma said, pointing to a man with dark hair, wearing a blue blazer and holding a brown leather briefcase.

'I'll follow you closely until you board your plane.'

They swapped mobile numbers. John hugged her; Lucy hugged her for ages.

Emma went to the taxi rank with the pilot. As they pulled away, she saw John and Lucy jump in a cab behind them. They followed her to the gliding club, a couple of miles north of Glasgow and stayed until she was airborne. She waved until they were two dots.

7

Mindful of Lucy's illness, it occurred to Emma that if she blew the whistle on Gavin, Lucy would have a miserable last few weeks. There would be police interviews; the mansion in Yorkshire would be shut down, and Lockstock. Moreover, who would take over Alistair's business empire? He'd no relatives as far as she was aware. Then she thought of one. Ted's wife had a baby by Alistair before marrying Ted. *That could be interesting,* she thought.

Until Lucy passes on, things could stay put, she decided.

Staring out of the plane window, she could see Loch Ness, where she once had a camping holiday with Katie and their foster parents. She wondered if the campsite would still be there, but her eyes glazed over and she could see nothing apart from Katie's face.

An hour later, the plane touched down on a small airstrip on the edge of a moor.

She could see Stewart, standing next to a parked Range Rover. Steve carried her case. Stewart ran to her; they hugged for ages without speaking.

She thanked Steve and climbed in the Rover and they set off.

'How did the journey go?' Stewart's eyes and nose were running.

'A nightmare, everything's a nightmare. I'm shattered. How much further?'

'Fourteen miles, about fifteen minutes.'

'Can we stop for a drink somewhere?'

'We're at the wrong side of Mairloch; you won't see a house, never mind a pub. Open the glove compartment; there's a couple of glasses, a bottle of whisky and a bottle of water.'

'Katie... what happened?'

'I was a short distance away, she was showing off her driving skills with the tractor, but it went off the edge of the old quarry. She ended up crushed underneath the tractor. She never shouted or anything, one minute full of the joys of life, the next dead. Pass me the whisky Emma. Let's talk about you.'

'For a start, I'm not going back to Gavin; he's changed so much you won't believe it.'

'Try me. I knew Gavin before you did remember? He's one of the reasons I ended up here.'

'One of the drug dealers you were involved with, I guess?'

'I had a steady business going. One day Gavin came walking into my jewellery shop and asked to borrow twenty grand.'

'Why would he do that?'

'He wouldn't tell me, but I refused. The next day two men walked in and threatened to shoot me. They escorted me to the bank. I drew twenty grand out and handed it over. When I rang Gavin he just said, "Thanks, you got me out of a hole, I'll see you right."'

'Stewart, I've been conned by Gavin all along and it's getting worse. I guess he didn't pay you back?'

'I never received a penny, then early one morning they frog-marched me to the shop, cleared all my stock. I had to close down. I reported them to the police. They didn't find enough evidence to charge Gavin and they never caught the other men. Gavin warned me if I didn't disappear I'd be dead.'

'I hadn't a clue; I buried my head in modelling, totally blind to anything else. We were never a proper married couple, but he'll look for me; he needs me.'

'Listen Emma, drugs had a stranglehold on him.'

'I had a lovely dog, but he had it put to sleep. I'll never forget it.'

'More likely shot it. What's happened to your house?'

'Gone – repossessed, according to Gavin.'

'What's Gavin doing now?'

'Good question… Tell me, the men that robbed you, can you describe them?'

'Yes, the little scumbag who wanted to shoot me was small, about five-eight, dark hair, piercing brown eyes, goatee-beard and a dragon tattooed on the back of each hand. The other, who waited in the car, was dressed like a spiff and talked with marbles in his mouth, sir this and sir that… Why do you ask?'

'That sounds like James, the butler at Lockstock Hall. The tattooed guy was with Gavin the night before I left, wanted to escort me everywhere. He's called John C.'

'That guy is regretting not pulling the trigger on me and won't be happy until he does.'

'Stewart!'

'So, you see, Emma, that's why you've never heard from us.'

'It's also why you only know half the story. Wait until you hear the rest. I mentioned you a few times; Gavin just shrugged his shoulders, saying he would like to bump into you. "If Katie ever phones, just let me know," he used to say.'

'It broke her heart when we first moved up here, but now it's breaking mine.'

'And mine… hope you can find a place for me; I'm not going back to London.'

'You can stay in the cottage. We rent it out to fishermen, but we're keeping it vacant now.'

'That sounds okay.'

'Remember little Ian? He went to live with my sister in Wales when Katie and me left London. He came up here three months ago and works on the farm; you won't recognise him.'

'Remember him, how could I forget him? I got a description of him from a friend who happened to bump into him at a game fair. Now I understand why Ian didn't call on me. It's been horrible, losing contact with you all.'

Stewart dabbed his eyes with his handkerchief. 'Yes, well, it's not been easy.'

'Tell me about the farm.'

'Not much to tell really, we have a salmon river running through the farm, a small loch a few fields away, and more sea that you'd ever want a few strides away, with a nice beach.'

'Sounds good; anything else?'

Stewart looked her over and laughed. 'Nothing, it's a fishing village. Of course, the people are nice and there's plenty of fresh air. It's a far cry from London you know.'

'I'm not surprised; I've not seen a car for ages.'

'If we see a strange car in the village we take the number.'

'You're joking.'

'The sheep outnumber the people by about twenty to one. We have one road in and one road out, any visitors normally come by boat and they can be from anywhere in the world. The Three Fishes Tavern can take eight visitors, but it's never full, even in the summer months. Each morning the bus calls and takes the kids to school and a couple to college.'

'What about work?'

'Sixteen miles away at Mairloch, and at the power station twenty miles away. Otherwise, it's fishing or farming, but with your looks, I don't think you need worry about work.'

'I've quit modelling and everything that goes with it. So there's just you and Ian. Any farm hands?'

'We had a couple, but they left for the power station, I'm on the look out for replacements. Carl, Zoe and Jodie - a pleasant trio of eighteen-year olds, and nineteen-year old Alex, the village poacher come rat-catcher, sometimes helps out.'

Emma thought about Big John.

What would happen to him when she rang the police? Better to ring him first and offer him a job on the farm, she decided. 'I might know someone.'

'Well, sound him out, I'm desperate.'

Just then, they passed a sign for Strathdale, and immediately entered the heart of the village. *The whole place would fit in the grounds of Lockstock Hall,* she thought.

Stewart turned up a gently sloping track where a fine stone-built farm over-looked the village and the sea.

'What a magnificent view!'

'Yes, you'd be hard pushed to beat it.'

At the entrance porch, Ian opened a fine old oak door to greet her. He had a sad face, but raised a smile. She'd last seen him as a twelve-year old boy with long locks of golden blond hair. Now, he had short-cropped hair, around six-foot tall, and terribly good-looking with clear blue eyes, a round nose and a fresh-air complexion. She hugged him and held on.

They went through to the huge kitchen. A large bare wood table dominated the centre of the room. Home-baked bread and pastries were on a worktop next to an oven, baked by Katie she presumed, and left untouched. She could smell something cooking in the oven, and realized she was famished.

She went to admire a salmon that lay in the stone sink. 'Seven-pounder, Ian caught it this morning, it's our dinner tomorrow.' He made towards the door. 'Come on I'll show you the digs.'

At the side of the farmhouse, a fine old caravan stood against a barn wall, with a long shed adjacent. A cottage, in its own grounds, stood at the other side of the barn. 'Open the door,' Stewart said, 'it's not locked.'

She opened the cottage door and entered. 'Excellent.'

'Mains water, electric, double bedroom, three single bedrooms, bathroom, kitchen and this is the lounge with television.' They entered a cosy room with wooden beams and an extraordinary fireplace that would grace a mansion.

She went to the sliding patio doors that took up three-quarters of a wall, over-looking the village and the sea. Quaint cottages lined the main street, a church stood at the top end. She could see a store at the edge of the village green and the Three Fishes Tavern with a beer garden at the front.

A road led down to a little fishing harbour with a sandy cove further on. A curving harbour wall protected a small fishing fleet, where the river entered the sea. The harbour and the sandy cove sat cradled between two rock promontories, giving a pond-like stillness to the place. She shook her head from side to side. 'It's spectacular.'

'Every village has boats in the harbour.' Stewart led her out of the back door and opened a gate to an enclosure. A large black and white goat nudged Emma and made an almighty fuss over her. 'That's Bill and the white one is Nancy, they were Katie's; just make sure they stay in the enclosure or there'll be hell to pay in the village.'

Emma kissed Bill on the nose then she kissed Nancy and put her arms around them both. 'My, aren't you big softies.'

At that, Bill sank his teeth into her skirt and proceeded to eat it, while Nancy started on her blouse.

Stewart intervened and sent them packing. 'Watch 'em or they'll have your knickers.'

'What's in the long shed?'

He took her over to the shed. 'Only a few pets.' He opened the door. 'Fred the parrot was Katie's; Sam the spider monkey and the guinea pigs, four doves and the rabbits belong to Zoe. Ian's just bought Jaws, the python. Zoe feeds them twice a day. She'll be here before college in the morning.'

After a meal that matched the best, though Emma hadn't a clue what she'd eaten, Stewart poured her another glass of nameless though excellent wine. Then Ian fumbled about with something in an old rag he'd pulled out of a boiling pan.

'Are you okay?' Stewart asked.

'Yes, fine, that was delicious.'

'Rabbit pie.'

Ian interrupted and shoved a bowl in front of her filled with jam roll and custard.

'Rabbit pie! Don't tell me I've eaten a pet.'

Stewart laughed, 'Don't worry; it was wild.'

Later, at the cottage, Emma sat outside at a picnic table on the patio and eyed the strange-looking bottle she'd found in the fridge. It contained lager, according to the handwritten label. She unscrewed the cap, it smelled as if it could be lager, she was no connoisseur, but poured a glassful anyway.

She watched the daylight fading. *What a change from the bright lights of London,* she thought, *a fishing village on the loneliest coast of Scotland. I'll have to get used to that.*

The caravan door opened and Ian came out, wearing waders up to his armpits, and unhooked a long fishing rod from the side of the caravan. Then he pulled a large net from under the caravan and strung it over his shoulder.

He wore a deerstalker hat and had a torch and other gadgets dangling from his waders. He seemed oblivious to her presence. Emma sat chuckling to herself. 'Going somewhere Ian?!' she shouted.

Ian dropped his bag and spun round. Emma, you scared me to death!'

'Come and sit with me Ian, it's been so long.'

'I know, but I was just... okay Auntie Emma.' He leant his rod against the caravan and joined her.

'Glass of lager?'

'No, thanks, I need a clear head. We call that stuff loony juice. Alex brews three strengths: normal, double and, the one you're drinking, triple strength.'

'How can you tell?'

'Green bottle.'

'Stewart said you'd been living in Wales with his sister, were you okay with that?'

There was a long pause.

'Yeah, but it wasn't his sister, it was his first wife, I got used to it though. Mum drove down every other Friday and stayed until Sunday. Anyway, the fishing was good in Wales and I was close to the university at Aberystwyth where I studied agriculture.'

'That's good, but with your looks you could make serious money.'

There was another long pause.

'Yes, as a stupid male model.'

'If people enjoy looking at you, then it's not stupid, it's a compliment.'

He stared at the caravan for a few moments. 'I call it staring, and I hate people staring at me.'

'Never thought they might be admiring your body?'

He didn't answer, and seemed to be thinking about it.

'If they want to go around admiring people's bodies, that's their thing; I'd rather watch salmon in the river.'

Emma changed the subject. 'What are the people like around here?'

He shrugged his shoulders without replying.

It soon became apparent that Ian wouldn't answer a question unless he put some thought into it. She asked him again.

'Don't know, but I'm told you can go into anyone's house without knocking… Must go; I like to be on the river bank just before dark.'

Monday morning, Emma heard a girl singing a folk song in the sweetest voice. She went outside to meet her.

'Hello Emma, I'm Zoe, sorry about the sad news. Stewart rang mum and told her about you arriving in the village.' She spoke in a warm cheerful voice. She had shoulder-length, shiny ebony hair, twinkling brown eyes and a healthy open smile in a riveting face. She was close to six-foot tall with a figure fit to grace the modelling scene, looking like a young goddess. 'I've come to feed the animals.'

Emma followed Zoe into the shed and watched her give some mixed fruit to Sam the spider monkey. Sam gave Emma a dirty look. She smiled at him. 'He's cute, can I hold him?'

'If he likes you, he'll smile back, but he can be awkward.'

Sam gave Emma another dirty look; she backed off, 'Okay, you know him better than me.'

Zoe put Sam back in his huge cage. 'Sorry I can't stay longer or I'll miss the bus, it leaves in five minutes.'

'No worries.'

Zoe left, whistling her way across the village.

Emma watched her reach the single-decker bus, thinking, *She's the most pleasant and the most beautiful girl I've seen in a long time, but so plainly dressed… Which reminds me, I need some new clothes for the funeral.*

                                 ∽

On the school bus, Zoe sat alone on the back seat. Jodie was late again, but the bus driver waited.

Zoe sat thinking about Ian. *Why doesn't he say, you look nice Zoe, or I like your hair, or just any compliment? Then I could say, Fancy going to Tizzy's restaurant at Mairloch for a meal? And he'd say, I'm glad you asked. Then I could play hard-to-get, pretend I wasn't falling in love. Later, he'd chase me in the barn, hold me down on the hay and force a kiss on me. Then we'd do things and he'd say, I love you Zoe, and I'd say, I love you too, Ian.*

'Hi, you'll never guess who I've just seen, Zoe,' Jodie blurted out before she was halfway along the bus.

'You mean Katie's sister; she's dazzling. She's coming to the Tav tonight; I reckon she'll fill the place.'

Jodie gasped. 'A top model in the village, wait till word gets out, they'll be comin' from Mairloch.'

Zoe smiled and winked. 'And they'll all be lads.'

'Yeah, let them come here for a change.'

After college, Zoe rushed home and chucked off her college clothes, then threw on her combat trousers, hiking boots and a lumberjack shirt. She let down her hair, and then ran across the village, hoping to catch Ian. Instead, she met Emma coming out of the shed.

'Hello Zoe, I've stocked the fridge with fresh fruit.'

'Like your clothes Emma, wish we dare wear them around here... Ian in the caravan?'

'No, he's fishing.'

'Blast, any idea when he'll be home?'

'When he's hungry I suppose, did you want him?'

'Just wondered if he'd like to meet up at the Tav tonight.'

'Good idea, I'll tell him when he returns.'

'Drag him out please; he's been here three months, nobody's seen him 'cept me.'

'Good for you Zoe. You his girlfriend?'

'Planning to be, but he doesn't know.'

'Tell him; he might be thinking the same about you.'

'Oh, gosh, that'd be great.'

'Zoe, it's a big might.'

'Think you could find out? In a roundabout way, sort of?'

'I'll see, but don't hide your assets too much; entice him.'

'Ha ha, he'd turn and run.'

'Try it, then he will have you naked if you're not careful.'

'No worries, I'll make sure I'm not careful... I mean, I know when not to be careful.'

'Think I know what you mean, Zoe.'

Zoe left the farm and sat beside the big oak tree in the middle of the village green. *I'm confused; I was brought up not to flaunt my body. Now Emma says flaunt it. Well, if you lived in London, suppose you'd do what they do; try it here and you're called a tart.*

That night, before entering the Tavern, Zoe undid three top buttons, hoping her dad didn't decide to come out early.

'Going somewhere Zoe?' Pete, the owner asked, as if there was a choice. *I can tell he likes my new look, but he makes me feel over-exposed; better button up until Ian arrives.*

Jodie and Carl were in the games-room playing pool. Carl was limping round the table in agony.

'What's happened this time?' Zoe asked.

'Pulled a muscle at work. It's better than this aft', I could nay move.'

Jodie stood behind him smiling. 'They took him to hospital at Mairloch. They were expecting him, seeing they hadn't seen him for a while… My, look who's come in; you were dead right, he's gorgeous.'

Zoe went over to him. 'Hi Ian, come to join the youth of Strathdale? Where's Emma?'

'Tryin' on some gear for the funeral… I caught a twenty-pound salmon today, put up a hell of a fight; a bar of silver straight in from t' sea.'

Zoe smiled at him. 'Well, don't go jumping about; I caught a twenty-pounder when I was twelve, and another fifty under twenty-pounds since—'

'Yeah,' Carl butted in, 'not wi' a rod.'

'Have to go, some work at home,' Jodie said, 'See you at the funeral tomorrow.'

'So what else do you guys get up to?' Ian asked.

'More than you'd think. Odd parties, disco at Mairloch, golf, water skiing and snorkelling. Not much in winter, just shooting and the disco if we can get there. I'm thinking of taking up modelling; Emma says I've got what it takes and she should know. What you think, Ian?'

'I'm gob-smacked, a twenty-pound salmon at twelve years old.'

Carl burst in. 'Wi' help from her dad's boat an' a big net, that's all, an' salmon jump in your boat around here.'

'You ever tried the rod Zoe?' Ian asked.

'A little bit, I know the casting terms and different fly lines, but it's tough learning on your own, I hoped you'd give me some lessons. I'd hold your rod while you stood behind holding my arm and showing the movements. That's how you learn; I've watched them being tutored.'

'Yep, best to have lessons; it's not just a case of grabbing any old rod and sitting on a riverbank with it in your hand all day… Okay, can't stay.' He stood up and marched out.

Zoe detected a tear in his eye. 'Poor Ian, he's upset, and so am I; I'm going home Carl. Since Ian came on the scene I don't know what's come over me, I can't concentrate on anything.'

Carl took a sip of his beer. 'Yeah, I've noticed.'

Tuesday morning, along with most of the village, Zoe went to the funeral service with her mum and dad. Stewart, Emma and Ian were at the front on their own, there were no other relatives.

Maybe there are none, Zoe thought, *but they have plenty of friends. I've never seen so many solemn faces together; that's really upsetting. I won't see Katie again, the best friend you could have; encouraged me to sing, bought Sam when I said that I liked monkeys... And now she's gone...*

8

After the funeral, Zoe didn't see Ian for over a week; according to Emma he was always either working somewhere in the fields, or fishing.

Then one morning she found him sat on the caravan steps, crashed out, head in his hands. 'You okay Ian? You look awful.' He flashed his alluring blue eyes at her in a way that gave her palpitations. 'Actually, you look okay now; it was just the way you were sitting.'

'Been fishing all night. I'm off to bed. I want to ask you about the man you saw on the bench last week, but later. I'll meet you in the Tav tonight.'

'Want me to make a coffee while you get ready for bed? You could tell me at the same time.'

'No, you'll be late for college.'

'I can go in at lunchtime.'

'It takes a couple of minutes to make a coffee, then what you going to do, watch me snoring?'

'Probably.'

'Put the kettle on then.'

She filled the kettle. *I spend half my time at college brushing lads off. Ian is something else; I haven't a clue what's going on in his head.*

Ian fell asleep in the chair before the kettle boiled.

She sat opposite him drinking her coffee and watched as he slumbered; he fell into the deepest sleep.

This fascinated her. She put her elbow on the chair arm, propping up her head with her hand, as she watched every inhale and out breath.

He was breathing deeply through his nose; his lips looked ever so inviting. *The lips I'd wanted to kiss since I first set eyes on him.*

She went over to him and gently played with his hand, expecting him to wake, but he never flinched; she squeezed it and whispered in his ear; it made no difference.

She was so close to him that she was inhaling his breath. *Dare I kiss him?* She gave him a gentle peck then looked for a reaction, there was none. *He's unconscious,* she thought, now she was lost in the moment and wondering what else she could get

69

away with. She wasn't going to stop now, and climbed on top of him, put her hands behind his head and gave him a long lingering kiss. He began to perspire and his eyes were twitching. She quickly went back to her chair.

He jumped up. 'Zoe, you still here?'

'You look warm, shall I open the door?'

'No, I'm off to bed… what a frightening dream I've had. A girl tied me up in the barn and started kissing me; then she began undressing me.'

Zoe burst out laughing. 'And then what?'

'I woke up, and it's not funny.'

He had such a serious look on his face it made her laugh more. 'You didn't like the kissing then?'

'Actually, I did, she sent me dizzy. It was the undressing bit that scared me; she turned into an animal, frothing at the mouth and ripping my shirt off; I couldn't get away.'

'Well, it was only a dream; glad you enjoyed the kissing though, it made me dizzy too.'

He scratched his head. 'Pardon?'

'It made me dizzy… just watching you dreaming.'

'Yeah, well I'm off to bed, let yourself out Zoe.'

That night, Zoe went to the Tavern early and played pool with Jodie and Carl.

'The weirdo seems to have gone,' Jodie said.

'Probably an old tramp,' Carl said.

Jodie looked at him. 'Strange; we don't normally see tramps around here.'

'He wasn't a tramp,' Zoe butted in, 'more like a ghost.'

Carl scratched his head. 'Yeah, that'd explain why nobody's seen him. The bench is visible from the Tav and half the village drink here; not t' mention people walkin' their dogs.'

'We need to tell harbour-watcher Rob, just in case he comes back.' Jodie ruffled the back of her shoulder-length blond hair. A sure sign that she was worried, but it didn't show on her face, which wouldn't look out of place in a sentry box.

Zoe laughed. 'Yes, old Rob, why hasn't he seen him?'

'Because he's half drunk all the time,' Carl said.

'Nothing to do with Rob being drunk, only four people in the village could see Waldo, us three and Ian. He's due back and wants to see you both, maybe tomorrow.' Zoe watched for their reaction.

'Count me out, I'm off back t' the doctors; my leg's not right.'

Zoe gave him a wry smile. 'Your mother told mine that when the doctor's a bit quiet he rings to see if you need anything doing.'

'So what, he looks after me.'

Zoe smiled, thinking, *Carl watches his body like an athlete, but so accident-prone: he runs into accidents meant for someone else and catches their infections before they did.*

'Ian just walked into the bar,' Jodie said.

'Yes, we've arranged to meet here.'

Jodie's face flushed up. 'Well, golly gosh; you've done well there.'

Ian walked in the poolroom carrying a glass of lager. He sat down in the corner without speaking.

There was a long uncomfortable silence, as if the mafia had just walked in.

'Jodie and Carl, my friends,' Zoe broke the silence. 'We do everything together. So what happened last night?'

'I was fishing for sea trout when I felt a presence behind me, making my skin crawl.'

'Sounds scary.'

'When I turned round, I shone my torch on a guy sitting on the bank. I thought he was a local fisherman, but when I got back at milking time I described him to my dad; he said nobody around here fit the description.'

'Sounds like a chap called Captain Waldo Sultan. Ancient face, wrinkly skin?'

'Yeah. And he gave me something.' He pulled out a brown envelope with a computerised drawing inside. 'Where's this place? It says meet me here with Carl, Jodie and Zoe next Friday at eight.'

'It's a map of the cavern,' Zoe answered.

Jodie played with her hair. 'Some hopes of me going.'

'No hope,' Carl said.

'What's the cavern like?'

'It's an underground seawater lake in a cathedral-like cavern, about two hundred feet long, a hundred feet wide and a hundred feet high. There's about a twenty-foot gap in the roof covered with a thick plastic dome; it's almost daylight inside.'

'When did you last go there?'

'We go every Sunday, snorkel, have a few drinks, but last Sunday we had to wait till the whales left before we snorkelled.'

'Whales!'

'There's an opening out to sea in the bottom of the cavern; they swim through. We only see them at certain times of the year.'

'How do you get in the place?'

'Through a chamber, an' down some steps,' Carl answered. 'Jodie an' Zoe have a key; supposed t' keep the place tidy for Pete at the Tav.'

'It was used for storing food in the Iron-Age,' Jodie added.

'Ever seen anyone else in there?'

'Tourists, but they have to come here first for the key. It's two pounds for one hour.'

'What about the other Sunday, anyone in there then?'

Zoe shrugged her shoulders. 'Nope, nobody.'

'Well, the old guy saw you, knew all your names and said you were drinking home brew. Is that right?'

'Ian, pack it in, you're frightening me…Yes!'

'Let's sit outside Zoe; it's stuffy in here. Put the envelope in your pocket.'

They left Carl and Jodie playing pool and took their drinks to a picnic table in the beer garden.

Zoe pointed up the road. 'Brewery Boy Alex is coming, with his ferrets and snappy little terrier friend.'

'He's been out ratting, look, there's two hanging from his belt.' Ian said.

'Looks a bit fresh.' Zoe turned away as he entered the beer garden.

'What're you two toe-rags up t'? Want a rat in your shirt Zoe?'

'No, you're drunk.'

'Well, that's tuff, coz tha goin' ta get one.' He grabbed her and tried to shove one of the rats in her shirt.

'Get off! Stop him Ian!'

Before Ian had a chance to move, she thumped Alex in the face with her fist. At the same time, the envelope fell out of her pocket.

'I felt that…! Aye, what's this?' Alex held his face with one hand and grabbed the envelope with the other.

She tried to wrestle the envelope from him and, at the same time, shake off his terrier from her heel.

'Get lost.' He pulled away, pushing the envelope in his pocket and smirking, he threw the rat in Ian's face. 'Come on Lassie, let's go.'

'I guess he's been on the strong stuff.'

'He certainly has.' Ian took her hand and led her towards the doorway. 'He could do with some work.'

She wasn't listening; her mind was elsewhere. *He's holding my hand as if we're a natural couple;* she tingled inside. 'That's a nice feeling Ian.' She stopped on the doorstep, half expecting a kiss.

'Just a thought, that's all, work wouldn't harm him.'

'You'll be agog to know, I'd forgotten about Alex, but since you're interested, he hasn't worked since leaving school three years ago. He gets by with what he can make off the land and selling his dad's home-brewed beer. Trouble is he makes some triple strength.'

Zoe went to a corner of the room and sat with her elbows on the table, chin resting on her hands.

'What's wrong with Zoe?' Jodie asked.

'Its Alex, he was drunk. She gave him a right cracker, but the envelope fell from her pocket, he's gone off with it.'

'He's a bully,' Jodie said.

Ian grinned. 'He'll think twice before tackling Zoe again.'

Jodie looked at her watch. 'Time I left, see you.'

'Okay, I'm also going,' Ian said.

Carl held his glass up to the light. 'Do you fancy a walk on the beach Zoe?' He had a Casanova look on his face.

She burst out laughing. 'Thanks for the invitation Carl. Soon as you get a glass in your hand, you think you're a Roman conqueror.'

'Well, lasses around here think they're Cleopatra.'

'And I'm going home to my palace.'

Closing her bedroom curtains, she saw Waldo's silhouette on the bench.

∽

Friday morning, Emma woke to the sound of the cockerel. Now, Wellingtons and jeans were her normal dress.

I'm getting up now at the time I was just going to bed a month ago. Here the pure air alone gives you a high.

She really felt the benefit, but yearned for a night out. She knew Stewart went out every night, but he hadn't been in the Tavern since the funeral. She could only think that he went to Mairloch.

At breakfast, she turned to Stewart. 'Fancy a look in the Tavern tonight?'

He gave her an odd look. 'Thanks, Emma, I'm overdue a visit.'

'Dad you can't go in the Tav yet,' Ian interrupted.

'I know what you mean, but with Katie's sister, how can that be wrong? No matter, we'll go to Mairloch.'

Emma left them to it and went for the morning paper. An old man walking towards her stopped and looked up at the sky.

'Lovely morning, make the best of it. Be raining by eleven, but you'll be able to catch the sun again by mid afternoon.'

In London, the weather meant nothing to her. Here it meant everything, it was like some form of therapy; everybody talked about the weather. They certainly didn't let much else clutter up their minds. She found it fascinating.

At the store, the headlines of the Daily Mail shouted out at her:

Model killed. Trish Noble and party girl, Amy Johnson, murdered in a drive-by shooting outside top London nightclub.

Devastated, she read the story while sitting outside the store. According to the police, the shootings were drug-related. Emma's eyes became so blurred she couldn't finish reading the story. She went back to the farm.

'I'm going to the cottage for a lie down,' she told Stewart.

'Yes, you look a bit pale.'

She decided to make a couple of phone calls before showing Stewart the paper. First, she called Jane. 'What in hell is going on?'

'Trish became an item with Alistair soon after you left,' she said. 'Amy took up with Alistair's new tattooed side-kick and started supplying drugs.'

'Trish with Gav...' Emma corrected herself. 'Trish with Alistair? You're joking.'

'No, and she was about to move in with him. Amy had already moved in the suite with John C.'

'So what's happening now?'

'Police are questioning everybody; they questioned me for ages. I told them I was with Trish and Amy at Lockstock the night before the shooting. Amy went off to the suite with John C before the party ended.'

'No surprise there, she was brain dead almost.'

'After Amy left, I sat talking with Trish. You know what she was like; sex was a five course meal.'

'I know, and she liked to describe the meal in detail.'

'Yes, and Trish said she'd slept with Alistair the previous night, and a waste of time. Not only that, his body had changed dramatically.'

'So, she told you about the non-performance?'

'She said she'd had sex with him once before and it was like being with five different guys. The second time, she said it was the other way round and nothing at all happened.'

'She'd be sick about that.'

'She wasn't really worried, she could get sex anywhere, but not the sort of money Alistair was sitting on. She said she'd persevere, but, as you know, she never had the chance. Killed for nothing, seemingly.'

'I'm sure the killers will be found. Even so, I can't believe they've been murdered.'

'I have to serve someone, ring me later.'

This needs some thinking about. Emma went back to the beginning... *Met Gavin and became a drug addict, married him, went into rehab and came out clean. Everything was going fine, but Gavin, instead of being delighted, preferred the drugged-up me. That way I'd go along with his plans and he could hide his personal problem. Gavin must have been planning the take-over before he met me. First, he or they killed Alistair's mum and dad, and then used me to seduce Alistair.*

Gavin didn't care if I fell in love with Alistair; he'd just eliminate him, step into his shoes and still have me. Trouble is, I did fall in love with Alistair, and now he's dead. Well, I'll just ring the police and tell them everything.

She was about to pick up the phone when it struck her that she couldn't call them just yet. She rang Big John at the mansion in Yorkshire and found out that Lucy had died. Then he asked if she'd heard about the shootings in London.

'Yes, and worried, very worried,' she told him. 'I know who the murderers are and I'm about to blow the whistle on them. Better if you left the mansion.'

'I'm leaving anyway, don't get on with the new boss.'

'What will you do?'

'Nothing for while.'

'We have a vacancy on the farm if you fancy it.'

'I'd be delighted to help out,' he replied, without hesitating.

'Excellent, I'll make arrangements for Steve to pick you up at Glasgow Airport. I'll ring you back as soon as I've confirmed it with him.'

With an extra spring in her step, she went to tell Stewart.

'So, you reckon this Big John chap will take to it here?'

'Yes, and he'll be an asset I'm sure, especially with everything that's going on.'

She unfolded the front page of The Mail. 'Friends of mine.'

'You're kidding.'

'I'm hundred percent sure it's Gavin and company. They killed Alistair's parents then infiltrated the business empire. They planted a man at Lockstock Hall and the mansion in Yorkshire then murdered Alistair. Gavin's had plastic surgery, a complete make over; he's taken Alistair's place.'

'And you suspected nothing?!'

'Not a thing; Gavin played the game well, somehow managing to keep it from me until the day he took over Alistair's role. Running the cosmetic clinic solely as a cover for his own makeover, acting in his spare time, he impersonated Alistair, right down to the voice.'

'Where did the two girls fit in then?'

'Trish must have said something. She'd slept with Alistair in the past and recently went to bed with Gavin, but he didn't have the moves that Alistair did; she was sure to notice the difference.'

'You'd think Gavin would have known that.'

'Trish was a nymphomaniac. I guess she dragged him to bed. I wouldn't expect Gavin to go on his own free will.'

Stewart raised his eyebrows. 'What about Amy?'

'She moved in with your friend the bank escort (the dragon man. I'm worried she might have given something away; I used her mobile to ring you. What can we do?'

'Not a lot by the look of things, but you said Big John had been a member of the SAS, perhaps he could advise. Talking of John, do you want to move into the farm? Then he can have the cottage.'

'No, he can move in the cottage, there's plenty of room. I don't mind at all, he's very easy to get along with.'

'You're my sister-in-law, no need to be embarrassed, you just take over the other double bedroom at the end of the landing.'

'Stewart, I like the cottage.'

'Maybe, but will you still like it when you're sharing it with a stranger?'

Her first thought was: *Stewart seems eager for me to move into the farm, a bit too eager. And Katie was his second wife.* She brushed the thought aside. 'I happen to like John, he's good company. We'll just have to wait and see.'

'Okay, but when we get the second farmhand you won't have a choice; they'll share the cottage. You wouldn't want pestering by two farmhands when they come home from the pub. Would you?'

'You underestimate me, Stewart, I've been round the block; I know how to handle myself.'

Later, Stewart arranged for his friend Steve, to collect Big John at Glasgow airport on Sunday, and they'd wait for him to arrive before informing on Gavin.

9

Saturday morning, Zoe woke to a commotion outside. Her mum shouted upstairs, 'Zoe, get up!'

She threw on her dressing gown and ran downstairs. 'What's happening?'

'I'm not sure, but it must be serious; the Mairloch police are here, they want to see everybody in the village hall at midday.'

'Police in Strathdale, must be a murder.'

Her mum gave her a questioning look. 'We'll soon find out.'

Later, everyone gathered in the village hall. The four friends stood together at the front with parents behind. Alex stood on the next row, sporting a black eye.

'Good morning, I'm Sergeant Brown from Mairloch. Last night, after the village hall dance, Mr Samuel and his partner were, for some reason, strolling along the beach top path, when they came across a corpse sat upright on the bench that over-looks the sea. I must stress this is not a murder inquiry, more an enquiry into how the corpse got there. Anyone seen anything suspicious in the last few days?'

Everyone looked blankly at each other, shaking their heads.

'What about you young man with the black eye, been fighting have you?'

'A guy hit me.'

'Point him out please.'

'He's not in here, 'cos it happened in a pub at Mairloch last night.'

Alex's father interrupted. 'They're a right bunch of thugs in Mairloch; every time he goes there, they rough him up.'

'What's your date of birth son?'

'December the fifteenth.'

'What year?'

'Every year.'

'Forget your date of birth, just tell me your age.'

'Nineteen.'

'What did the man say before he hit you?'

'I'm goin' ta kill ye, ye bastard.'

'And did he kill you?'

'Na!'

'In that case, you could say he saved your life!'

Zoe giggled inside. *What a tale.*

Alex's father interrupted again. 'If he'd a killed him, I'd a done every thug in Mairloch.'

'Well, yes, but Mairloch is my patch, I'd have intercepted you before you crossed the boundary line.'

'Think your bike would move that fast?'

'If you took notice when you came in, I've moved on a bit, didn't you see a lump of white metal twelve foot long and six foot wide, with blue flashing lights, parked outside?'

'No, but I remember thinking it was a bit early for the disco.'

'Don't talk to him Sarge,' Jodie's mother cut in, 'you'll have to catch him sober, and no one in the village has ever done that. He's been found asleep on everyone's lawn.'

'Funny you should say that. I've come across the same problem in Mairloch, but mostly they're just enjoying their hobby of star-watching. After observing these star gazers, mainly after the nightclub had closed, I made inquiries, and found that we have more astronomers in Mairloch than in the rest of Scotland.'

'Thanks, Sarge, nobody believed me.' Alex's father shouted.

'Right folks, I'll ask again, does anyone know anything about the corpse?'

'He's not from the village,' the vicar said, 'everyone's here.'

'I walk that path every day on my way to the harbour and back, I've seen nothing, and certainly no corpse,' Zoe's dad said.

'Well, the corpse didn't drop from the sky. Somebody in this room must have seen something. Unless you all drink like Alex's father?'

'Hang on, seeing you've brought me into it again, how do you know it didn't drop from the sky?'

'You saw it sky-diving in, no doubt. Somebody take him home please.'

Jodie began to speak… but at that moment, Alex held up his hand. 'Can you hang on while I go to the loo?'

'Excuse me too.' Ian said.

'Yes, but don't be long. Now, young lady what have you to say?'

Alex and Ian came back and took up their places again.

Ian whispered to Zoe, 'I've got the envelope.'

'So, your name is Jodie,' Brown continued. 'What's your date of birth? No, forget that. How old are you?'

'Eighteen.'

'What were you going to say?'

'I know him; he was on the bench for a few days.'

This caused quite a stir around the hall.

'Don't be silly, Jodie,' her father said.

Brown cut in, raising his voice. 'Now Jodie, you know that's not true, Zoe's father passed that spot twice every day and didn't see him.'

'He was on the bench,' Ian interrupted.

'Yeah, he was there,' Carl added.

'Yes he was,' Zoe confirmed.

Zoe's mother interrupted, 'Take no notice, Lord knows what's going on.'

Zoe stood her ground. 'He's called Captain Waldo Sultan.' Zoe heard a sigh coming from directly behind her; she turned and saw Emma, mouth and eyes wide open in an expression of disbelief.

Her father went red in the face. 'This is ridiculous, we're going.'

'Hang on, I've not finished yet. What did he say Zoe?'

'He just mumbled in a weird voice.'

'I've doubts about that. I've also no doubt that you're all lying. I think you saw the corpse while everyone was at the dance, and then dreamed up this cock-and-bull story in the Tavern. Not too much to drink by any chance?'

'They might have the occasional drink,' Ian's father said, 'but they don't usually get drunk.'

'Well, I'm sorry, but, they were either drunk, hallucinating or telling a load of lies. Probably all three.'

'No, and we hadn't been drinking,' Jodie said.

'Well, well. The innocent gang of four caught out lying in front of the entire village. For a start, if, as we are led to believe, the corpse was sitting on the beach-top bench for days, someone else would have seen it, especially Zoe's father who walked by twice a day—'

Carl interrupted. 'I definitely saw him.'

'Furthermore, Zoe claims to have conversed with the corpse. That, however, would be impossible, because the corpse has been dead for three thousand years.'

Commotion spread through the hall; the four were spellbound; only Alex seemed to find it funny. Villagers began edging their way out of the hall.

'Before you leave! This is a serious matter; our investigation will be ongoing until we find the person responsible for bringing the corpse here. How did a three thousand year old Egyptian mummy arrive here? That's what I'd like to know—'

Ian's father broke in. 'Yes, and so would the rest of us.'

'And just as important, where did it come from? One thing's for sure, a detective from London's Scotland Yard will be coming. So, expect a visit. Meanwhile should anyone need me, I'm staying at the Tavern.'

Outside the hall, groups of villagers were talking about the big event.

The parents had their heads together in serious conversation. Emma stared at Zoe with an astonished look on her face. 'Waldo Sultan?'

'Yes.'

'Can't be true; where did you hear the name?'

'Why… you know him?'

'I know of him, but where did you hear the name? And don't say it was the old man on the bench; there's not been anyone on the bench all week. I can see clearly from the farm cottage.'

Zoe pondered for a moment. 'Remember when you fell asleep in the Tav, after the funeral?'

'Yes?'

'Well, I was chatting to Carl nearby. You were talking in your sleep, repeating the name Waldo Sultan. In court, it just came in my head.'

'Thank goodness for that, you had me worried.'

'Why?'

'Not just now Zoe; I'm tired and it's a long story.'

Zoe moved over to her mother's group and stood behind them.

'Alex's father is going downhill fast,' her mother said, 'he seems to live off nothing but home-brewed beer. Mind you, Sergeant Brown was a bit off-key.'

Stewart laughed. 'He won't do himself any favours staying at the Tavern.'

'He must have run out of stock,' Carl's father quipped.

Sergeant Brown, due to retire shortly, over the years had set a few tongues wagging in Mairloch, Stewart recalled. He had this exceptional ability to arrive at the local whisky distillery within minutes of them reporting a crime.

Even more baffling, at one crime he attended, a few eyebrows raised much further away, he remembered. A gang of villains had stolen a lorry-load of whisky from the distillery compound.

Sergeant Brown apprehended the driver on a country road five miles outside Mairloch, and arranged for the return of the lorry.

Curiously, when they opened the lorry at the compound, three tons of whisky had gone missing.

At the time, Brown said the gang's accomplices must have transferred it to another wagon before he arrived at the scene. Yet, a farmer working in a nearby field had seen nothing pass by him that day, apart from every police car in Scotland.

Ian beckoned Zoe away. 'We've a few minutes; we must come up with something and pretty quick.' Ian looked at the others for an answer.

'We're already in trouble,' Jodie ruffled her hair.

'Just say we were drunk,' Ian suggested.

'Yeah, might as well, they don't believe us anyway,' Carl answered.

'Oh, yes, your parents might not mind, but mine would go crazy,' Jodie said

'Don't fuss,' Zoe said, 'seeing everything's taboo in your house; we'll keep you out of the drinking bit.'

Just then, Sergeant Brown came out of the hall and approached the parents. 'We'd better have a talk; can you come back in the hall. We need to tidy one or two things up.'

Ten minutes later, they were back in the hall.

'Hello again,' Sergeant Brown said, 'the adults can take a seat; the gang can stand by my table. Your names, please.'

After giving their names, Ian apologised for all four, saying the drink was too strong.

'That's okay; the blame lies with whoever brought the mummy here in the first place. Now, what's been going on?'

'They've explained everything,' Zoe's father said, 'Apparently they saw an old man on the bench while everyone was at the dance. Although at the time, they didn't know it was a corpse. Then they made a story up in the caravan. Unfortunately it's backfired on them, and of course they didn't know that there would be a police enquiry.'

'Yes, very unfortunate indeed, and now I've Scotland Yard on my back. Right, that's all for now.'

'Like the black eye you gave Alex,' Jodie said, 'he tells a good lie, though.'

'Well, he couldn't exactly own up to me sticking one on him, could he?'

Jodie fiddled with strands of hair. 'This corpse thing is a bit out of hand. I'm having dreams. I keep looking to see if he's back.'

'Oh, yeah, a dead mummy and you expect him back. I don't think so; 'cos the police have him now.' Carl pointed out.

'It was no mummy who gave me the map,' Ian said.

'And it was no mummy that I spoke to.' Zoe pulled out the bit of rag she'd kept in her pocket. 'I tried to get this analysed at college. Their equipment couldn't date it, they said.'

'Maybe things will come to a head Friday in the cavern,' Ian said.

Jodie ruffled her hair again. 'I won't be out for a few days; I'll be stuck at home doing chores.'

Carl smiled. 'I've arranged to go fishing with Ian for a few days.'

Zoe gave him an envious glance. 'On the river or the loch?'

'Both, I expect.'

'If it's a nice day, I might skip college, and find you.' *Well, I've already decided, I'll definitely be skipping college.*

⟜

Sunday morning, Stewart came in from the field cursing Alex's dogs. 'That's the second sheep killed this week and what a gory mess. It wasn't Butch this time it was Rambo; I saw him running off. He'll have to get rid of the dog.'

Emma frowned. 'What a shame, couldn't you have him muzzle the dog instead?'

'I'll see, but I have to leave now to pick up Big John at the airfield, I'll call on Alex for sure when I return, maybe we can sort it out.'

When Stewart had left, Ian stared at Emma. 'Who's Big John?'

'New farm-hand, he's got a terrible injury on one side of his face, don't let it put you off him though.'

'Where's he from?'

'His last job was a gamekeeper in Yorkshire, but he's well travelled, ex SAS.'

'Is that how he came to be injured?'

'Yes, he'd half his face blown off and was certified dead, but he's built like a bull, he pulled through.'

'What's he like?'

'The nicest bloke you could meet, don't worry, you'll get on with him.'

'Hope so.'

Later, Emma watched the Range Rover come up the drive and went out to greet Big John. He threw his huge arms around her and lifted her off her feet. 'Nice to see you again Emma.' He put her down and took in the surroundings. 'Stunning view you have here, I like it.'

Stewart carried his bags and two rifle cases into the cottage. Emma stared at the rifle cases.

'Don't worry they're licensed,' he patted his side, 'and so is this.'

They showed John his digs and, after a coffee, gave him a tour of the farm.

In the barn, John raised his one eyebrow. 'What happened here?'

'Alsatian.'

'Must be a huge dog.'

'It is huge.'

'Good, that fits into my plan perfectly… You rang the police on Gavin yet?'

'No, we were waiting for your take on it first,' Emma answered.

'Obviously, the gang haven't arrived here yet?'

'Why would they? Nobody knows we are here,' Stewart gave him an odd look.

'Put it this way, you'd be dead by now if I'd been looking for you. I reckon; if they aren't already here, they soon will be. I found you on my computer.'

'How come?'

'Newspaper obituaries, four Katie's died that week: Wales, Birmingham, Lancaster and here, Strath Farm. Luckily, your address must be the last on their list, so we'd better act fast. Do you know how big the moor is?'

Stewart scratched his head. 'Good question, how big is the north of Scotland?'

'Yes, well, let's stick to the immediate moor between here and Mairloch, about twenty miles by twenty. We know they have a chopper, so they'll land within walking distance; that cuts it down to five square miles, and they won't land near the road or the farm.'

Emma gave him a look of terror. 'Where do you think they'll land then?'

'At Loch Strath, then it's an easy walk down the bridleway and straight into the farmyard.'

'Yes, but they won't know that. Anyway, how did you know?'

Ian butted in. 'I know, Emma, anybody can find it if they have your address or post code.'

John pulled out an aerial view of the farm in close up and two further aerial views of the entire moor and surrounding area. 'Wherever I go I like to know the terrain before I get there. I'm quite happy with the layout, apart from one blip. What's this cavern above the beach cove?'

'It's a tourist site; nobody else goes in there apart from Zoe and her friends. You need to ask her; she has a key for the steel door.

The Tavern owns the place and charge to go in there.' Stewart said.

'Okay, I'll suss it out.'

'So what's the plan?'

'Steve the friendly pilot has gone to Wick. I left some gear in a friend's garage there two years ago; he's taking it to the airport for Steve to pick up.' John eyed Stewart's shotgun propped up in a corner. 'Is it loaded?'

'Yes, always.'

'Good keep it with you. First, you need to ring the police. Tell them there's a loose tiger on the moor and show them the dead sheep. I'll take over from there.'

'The police are already here, a Sergeant Brown is staying at the Tavern. I'll go over and tell him.'

'No, stay here, just ring the Tavern.'

'He'll laugh.'

'That happened at Wick, until I came up with a dead tiger that was loose in the hills. I'll ask the local police to ring Wick; they know I'm no pigeon. The police will need to put warning signs on the road advising the moor's temporarily closed.'

'Anything else?' Stewart asked.

'Do you have a Land Rover?'

'Yes, Ian will show you where it is.'

'I need a few sandwiches; I'll camp on the moor tonight and stay there as long as necessary.'

Emma made him a dozen sandwiches and put them in a cool-bag, adding some fruit, two bottles of beer, and a flask of coffee.

'Thanks, Emma, don't phone me; I'll phone you if need be.'

John went for his rifle, and Ian took him to the Land Rover at the back of the farm and gave him the keys.

By late afternoon the following day, Emma was on her eighth cup of coffee and her twentieth lap round the farmhouse. 'Why hasn't he phoned? Something must be wrong…'

'Fancy a brandy?' Stewart propped his shotgun against the kitchen table.

'A large one please; I feel awful, I don't want to see anybody hurt.'

He poured two large brandies and sat by his gun. 'Well, if they come to the farm, it won't be to say hello.'

She sipped her brandy and sighed. 'I know; they're out to kill us.'

'Precisely; we'd be dead and they wouldn't give it a second thought.'

She took another sip and fixed her eyes on him. 'I believe in the afterlife, do you?'

'No.' He patted his shotgun, 'If you get your head blasted with one of these then it's the end—'

The kitchen door opened; Stewart grabbed his gun and spun round. 'John, how did you get in here?'

Ian popped his head round the door. 'I let him in.'

'I was attracted by the smell. I'm famished,' John said.

'Oh the smell; it's lamb stew with dumplings. We saved you some, hope it's still okay,' Emma said.

Stewart stared at John. 'Well?'

He sat down, rested his elbow on the table, cradled his chin with his hand and smiled, but gave no reply.

Emma gave him an odd look. 'Get his dinner out Ian.'

He passed his knife and fork back to Ian. 'Get me a spoon, good lad.'

'So what happened?' Stewart asked.

'They can reopen the moor.' He shovelled the food in his mouth as if he'd be shot before he had chance to swallow it. He then laid down his spoon and wiped his mouth with the back of his hand. He glanced at the wine rack, leaned back in the chair and inspected the ceiling.

'Glass of wine?' Emma asked.

'Please… Ted the chauffeur from Lockstock Hall was sitting in a helicopter near Lock Strath. Pretended he'd brought three prospective buyers for a holiday cottage and waiting for their return.'

Emma almost dropped the glass. 'You've seen Ted?!'

'Yes, had a long talk with him. Told him he could go, as they wouldn't be returning and he wouldn't be seeing them again.'

'How did he react? What did he say?'

'Seemed pleased. "Thank God for that," he said. He started the motor and before he took off, told me to give you a message.'

'Oh, right, and?'

'He said, "Give blue eyes my love. If only we'd met on that embankment in Moss Side, Manchester."'

The message brought tears to her eyes. 'Poor Ted.'

Big John patted her shoulder. 'Well, he's not poor anymore. Shortly, he'll be running Lockstock Hall, and Alistair's business empire with his stepson, Oliver.'

She raised her eyebrows and dabbed her eyes, thinking, *Well, if Oliver has half the looks of Alistair, and teams up with Ted, the future of Lockstock should be okay.*

'Did you know Alistair had a son, Emma?'

'Yes… I knew… and he was about to have—'

'And the thugs?' Stewart interrupted.

A long silence followed.

John took a sip wine, looked at the ceiling again and watched a spider. He kept his eyes on the spider until it disappeared into a web in the corner.

Stewart dabbed his forehead and drank the last of his brandy. John took his eyes off the web and looked over at Emma. 'That's a mighty big spider.'

'Yes, but it doesn't scare me; you are scaring me though. What happened on the moor?'

'There were four dead animals in the traps. Three I recognised, but the other I hadn't seen before.'

Stewart poured another brandy. 'Where are they?'

'One's in the barn, the others are in the incinerator.'

They all rushed out to the barn, John sauntered in behind them.

'Huge isn't he?'

'It's one of Alex's Alsatians,' Ian said.

Emma turned away, ran back to the farm, and sat, head in arms on the kitchen table, sobbing.

The others returned. Stewart put his arm around her. 'It was to be put down anyway.'

'Yes, but what about Gavin and the others?'

'Well, if some animals are out to kill you and they end up dead themselves, so be it. What matters is that we're still alive.'

Big John sat opposite her and held her hand across the table. 'I came here to look after the farm and protect you Emma, that's all. I had the police close down the moors, signs and cones advertised the fact, so if anybody decided to ignore that, then they were up to no good.'

'Yes, but you knew they'd come in a helicopter.'

'Nevertheless, I didn't kill them. They accidentally killed themselves; they walked into the traps I'd put out for the tiger. Otherwise, we'd probably be dead by now; they had enough artillery to kill the whole village.'

Emma raised her head. 'You're joking.'

'I don't joke about things that make me sick.'

'Sorry John, I appreciate your help.'

He turned to Stewart. 'When the police arrive show them the dog; tell them the early morning mist blurred your vision. They didn't believe there was a tiger on the moor in the first place, we can expect a ribbing.'

'We're free to go back to London,' Stewart said. 'Anybody want to buy a farm?'

'That's stupid talk,' Ian said.

'No, I'm serious.'

Emma shook her head from side to side and laughed. 'Stewart, you're having us on.'

'I'm not. I've always wanted to go back, jewellery is my trade, and London is my home.'

Ian walked out in disgust. Emma and John followed him to the caravan. Ian, tears in his eyes, sat on his bed. Emma sat next to him and put her arm round him. 'Come on let's go to the Tavern, I'll buy the farm if he's serious.'

'Honest?'

'Sure — if John stays.'

'I'm not going anywhere, Emma, I'd love to stay here.'

'Oliver will inherit everything. Once things are back in full swing they may want you at the mansion.'

'This is a wonderful place. I'll run the farm for you, Emma, until you sack me.'

'Okay, let's drink on it.'

As they sat down in the Tavern, the door opened and in walked Stewart. 'You sure you want to buy the farm, Emma?'

'Positive.'

'How about half share, you pay half the value, the other half is Ian's; it'll be in your joint names. That will give me enough to get started.'

'No... you misunderstood me; I want to buy the farm for Ian and the cottage for myself.'

'Oh...well...I'll have them valued separately then.'

'Whatever, but you need to reconsider where you set up your jewellery business, because this farm won't buy you a parking space in London today.'

'She's right,' John said, 'you could have a new bathroom suite installed around here, for what London plumbers charge for a new tap.'

'Yes, I know, but I have some savings put aside.'

10

Late on Tuesday afternoon, Zoe met Ian and Carl coming down the bridleway from Loch Strath.

'Surprised at your dad thinking Alex's dog was a tiger. Saw the vet taking it away; what a mess, but nothing like a tiger.'

'Needed sorting, or it would've carried on killing, and the trap was for a tiger, bound to be a mess.'

'Zoe, change the subject,' Carl said.

'Okay, how did the fishing go?'

'I've a bag full of trout. How much you think we'll get for them, Ian?' Carl almost fell over as he turned his head.

'I don't know.'

'We've caught fourteen trout today and two salmon yesterday.'

'Yes, we have, haven't I?'

'A twelve pound salmon, a ten pound salmon, that's forty-four quid. Fourteen quid for the trout, that's twenty eight quid each.'

'You ruin the pleasure of it Carl.'

'How do you work that out? I sat quiet and landed your fish?'

'It's when you put them in the bag. "That's another quid," fourteen times you've said that today.'

'Well, it's good money, Alex even makes a living out of it.'

'I know, from poaching... My dad wants the small salmon, sell the rest and keep the money.'

'Thanks Ian.'

Zoe smiled at Carl. 'We can have a free night at the Tav then?'

'How's Jodie?'

Trust him to change the subject. 'He's giving her a hard time, she spilt some sugar on the table at breakfast and he flew into a rage. How could you live with that?'

'I couldn't, I'd knock it out of her pocket money.'

'Oh, yes, you mean to say you'd let her have some sugar in the first place? I don't think so.'

'You don't know; I might do.'

'Carl, I've seen Christmas presents from when you were five, still in their original boxes. What's that all about then?'

'You'll see, when I come to sell them.'

Zoe examined each fingernail wearily. 'Oh dear, I've thrown all mine away.'

'Serves you right, you'll never have any money.'

'Well, when I do, it will be from my own making, not from umpteen relatives leaving me thousands in their wills.'

'What's up, you jealous or wot?'

'Thing is Carl, everybody in the village thinks you're poor and gives you stuff, people buy you drinks, give you fags, shoes, clothes and God knows what.'

'That's their fault.'

'Okay,' Ian butted in, 'let it drop. I'm going, see you tomorrow.' He hooked his rod on the caravan and opened the door.

'Any coffee left?' Zoe asked.

'Plenty, but I've some serious work to do on my computer, sorry.'

'You in the Tav tonight?'

'Can't, see you here after college tomorrow, bring Jodie.' He shut the door.

When she turned round, Carl was half way across the village. *Great, that's really great.* She went home to practice her modelling. *I'm sick of this wardrobe of thick chunky clothes. How can you practice like this? I want some skimpy outfits, even if I don't wear them outside; wonder if Emma has any spare.*

The following day, Zoe met the others at the caravan.

'Last night, dad were talking to Brown an' two detectives from Lundun, they think the corpse was washed in by the tide an' dumped on the bench by us.' Carl said, taking a drink from the bottle of home-brew in his hand.

Zoe laughed, 'It was no corpse; my dad was in the Tav. When they peeled the bandages off the mummy it was just straw. Now they want to see us.'

'Yeah, well, if I were a detective, Alex would be my suspect.'

Ian nodded, 'We'll just point a finger in Alex's direction.'

Zoe grinned. 'Yes, all done in a drunken stupor that he can't even remember.'

'I'll find it hard lying to the detectives,' Jodie said, despairingly.

Zoe gave her a wry smile and shrugged her shoulders, 'Just keep your normal straight face.'

'It's okay for you lot.'

Carl patted her shoulder. 'It'll be ok. They might not even see you, they'll see Ian first.'

'Sorted then, you'd better go Jodie, if you've to be in for six,' Ian said.

'What about us?' Zoe asked.

'Same for you; I've some work to finish in the field.'

∞

Thursday morning, the dogs alerted Alex to the detectives coming up the path; he opened the front door before they knocked. His German shepherd bolted out, landed with its two front paws on the nearest detective's shoulders and growled, just inches from his face.

At the same time, his two terriers kept the other detective hopping.

Serves you right, Alex thought. 'Sorry chaps, sit Butch! Heel Lassie, heel Peggy… Can I help?'

'CID. Is this the dogs' home for the protection of criminals? Put them somewhere safe, please. We're here about the corpse, can we come in?'

'I'll put them in the back garden.'

They entered the stone flagged front room and weighed up the extent of his dad's home-brewing paraphernalia.

'All the village alcoholics then, or just you and your large family?'

'Like a sample?'

'I'll try a half, seeing that your dog talked me into it,' said the first detective.

'I'll try a drop. Is there somewhere to sit?' asked the other.

'Aye, come through, can you pay for the drinks first? It's a quid.'

'You're not allowed to sell it.'

'I know, that's why it's a quid a tip.'

The detectives ignored him and looked around, scanning the area, first the flagstone floor, then the rest of the room, inch by inch. The kitchen-dining room was crammed with nets, snares and miscellaneous poaching gear.

Two salmon, a rabbit and a number of trout lay next to the stone sink…

Alex stood there pondering. *They don't seem too bothered. If they'd been gamekeepers, I'd have been buggered… Though I canna see poaching on the crime list at Scotland Yard, more a country pastime.*

'Quite a good catch, nice little earner you're running here… Right, we want to know where you got the bandages from to make up the corpse.'

Alex burst out laughing. 'Don't look at me; I've better things t' do.'

'We can see that, but we are looking at you.'

'Well, ye can go milk a cow. I wanna report Stewart for killing my other Alsatian.'

'Yes, we know about that, you'll have to see the local police. Now Listen and listen good, we intend to wrap this job up today and get back to London. Now, we reckon that you got the bandages from the museum fire at Mairloch.'

'No way!'

'Just a village prank, and certainly not something we should be wasting time on.'

'Nay guilty.'

'As I said, it's a nice little earner you've got going here, be a shame to loose it. So, you stuffed the bandages with straw and stuck the imitation mummy on the bench.'

'Oh, did I?'

'Yes, but you were so drunk, you don't remember a thing about it. A small fine for being drunk and disorderly and causing a public nuisance.'

'I was sober that night.'

'You've forgotten, you were too drunk to know; a witness saw you staggering from the beach path.'

'Oh, aye, Ian and company I guess, and ye believe them?'

'You might as well own up, and of course, keep your little business running.'

'I suppose it could've been me.'

'Sign this Alex, then we can get back to some real crime.'

Unexpectedly, Alex's dad strolled in. 'What's going on?'

'We're just leaving, everything's sorted. See you Alex.' They left in a hurry.

'What did they want?'

'I took blame for the corpse.'

'Why?'

'They'd have done me for something else; they were going t' search the house.'

'They can piss off; why did you let them in? Where's the dogs?'

'In the yard.'

'Why do you think we keep 'em, nobody comes in here,' he fumed. 'Everything that happens in this crap village gets blamed on our house, well they can get stuffed.'

'It might have been me for all I know; the detectives said somebody saw me drunk. Drunk and disorderly, that's the charge.'

'Only the fourth time in two years, why don't they do Zoe and her gang, they stagger about the place and nobody says a dickey-bird.'

'How many times ye been done dad? I bet ye don't know!'

His dad opened a bottle of strong home-brew. 'Shut up, I'll be done again before the day's out.'

∾

Friday morning, Zoe and Jodie met on the college bus.

'Alex will be sore for a while; his dad was in the Tav last night,' Zoe said.

'I thought he was barred from the place,' Jodie queried.

Zoe burst out laughing.

'Come on what's the joke? Is he barred or not?'

'He is, but he stormed into the Tav half-drunk, and emptied the place. He was having a go at everybody, how he, Alex and the dogs got blamed for everything that happened in the village.'

'Well, he's done himself no favours at the Tav.'

'He grabbed hold of my dad, and was about to hit him, but then he fell and knocked all the drinks off the tables.'

'Which means the detectives believed Ian's story.'

'I guess so,' Zoe continued, 'and later, when dad left the Tav, he heard shouting, as if Alex and his dad where fighting. Then this morning at seven-o-clock, my mum went for the paper. Alex was sat on the doorstep with two black eyes.'

'Yes, well, he's used to it.' Jodie sucked her hair. 'Think he'll turn up at the cavern tonight?'

'Why would he do that?'

'He took the envelope off you, he's seen the plan; he knows the time of the meeting.'

'Tell me about it, but he won't get in without a key.'

'He could ask for one at the Tav.'

'What, Alex paying two quid for a key, I doubt it. Anyway, Pete wouldn't let him have one… You still okay for going then?'

Jodie played with her hair again. 'Just about I reckon.'

Later that day, Zoe arrived at the caravan and found the others already there. Ian was cleaning up. 'Sam's had a mad do, I've locked him in his cage.'

'Can I see him?' she asked.

'No, he's in a funny mood, like he was when he opened the guinea-pig's cage and pulled their heads off.'

'Jaws will quieten him down, I'll put them together tomorrow; see what happens.'

'Ian do you have to?'

Carl laughed. 'Yeah, no monkey, no parrot, no rabbits and no goats, just, a fat thirty-six-foot long python.'

'Next time, if Sam does something wrong, he sleeps with Jaws. When he sees what Jaws does with the rats at feed time, he'll mend his ways.'

'Made a mess hasn't he?' Emma said, coming through the door, 'I'm off to the Tavern with Stewart and Big John.'

'Roll on seven o'clock,' Carl licked the ends of his fingers.

'You've finally reached the end of the nails then,' Zoe commented, as she inspected her own.

'The doc said use clippers next time.'

'Try sucking your thumb,' Zoe grinned. 'Brings back memories.'

'What sort of memories?'

'Thumb sucking is a substitute for sucking on the breast. That sort of memory.'

'Funny, I only need go back to the last college party for that.'

'Really; who was that with then?'

'Nobody,' Ian butted in, 'he sucked his thumb.'

Carl grinned. 'I guess I can make do with my thumb, unless you're offering Zoe?'

'No, thanks, I've seen how you treat your nails.'

'Don't look at me!' Jodie snapped.

Carl went to the door and kept an eye on the Tavern

'We'll take the Land Rover, reach the dunes before the tide,' Ian said.

'They're going in the dance hall now.' Carl rubbed his hands together.

Ian picked up the keys. 'Let's go then.'

Ten minutes later, they parked in the dunes.

Zoe took the lead up the track to the cavern door, which was in the rock face near the top of the cliff. She unlocked the heavy metal door and passed the key to Carl. 'Lock it and leave the key in, that way, Alex or anybody else can't disturb us.'

At the top of the dark steps, Zoe pulled out her torch. 'Stay close Ian, hold my hand until it gets lighter at the bottom.'

'Not necessary, I can see what I'm doing.'

'Don't blame me if you fall.'

At the bottom of the steps, Ian's eyes lit up. 'Now I know why you call it the Cathedral, it's fantastic.' His voice echoed around the vast cavern.

'You should hear it when we bring radios,' Zoe said.

'What time is it?' Carl asked.

'Seven thirty.' Ian stared at the waters edge. 'There's air-bubbles coming from something.'

'Must be a whale in,' Zoe said.

Suddenly, a mini submarine surfaced next to the ledge.

Jodie looked at the others, her mouth opened, but nothing came out.

The sub was a navy blue metallic colour with lime green mayfly logos on the side.

'Who's this belong to then?' Ian asked.

'Good question, never seen it before,' Zoe answered.

Carl scratched his head. 'Yeah, but he must know what he's up to; finding a way in here.'

Jodie made for the steps. 'See you later.'

Carl followed her. 'I'm away. You two staying?'

Ian said nothing and stood firm.

'We're staying here,' Zoe shouted, 'we have a date, remember?'

Just then, the hatch opened on the sub. Ian held Zoe's hand as they stood there, expecting Waldo to appear, but no one came out.

'Hello again Zoe and Ian, it's Waldo Sultan.' The voice echoed round the cavern as if there were a dozen speakers in the place.

Zoe jumped on the sub and peered through the hatch. 'It's well lit, come on Ian.'

At that moment, the hatch closed. 'Sorry, the meeting is off,' the voice echoed out, 'you need to somehow persuade your friends back, but not tonight; the tide is turning. I'll arrange another time, meanwhile, you must say nothing to anybody and make sure Jodie and Carl do the same.'

'Yes, come on Ian, I'll kill them.'

They jumped off the sub and made for the steps. Zoe locked the door behind them. 'Bet they've gone to the Tav.'

Outside, Ian weighed up the tide. 'It's okay, I can get through, but I don't fancy the Tav; Dad, Emma and John are in there.'

'What do you fancy then?'

Ian said nothing until he pulled up behind the farm and stopped the engine. 'Bed.'

Zoe gave him a curious stare; her eyes wide open. 'Really, and I can stay overnight? Mum and dad have gone to Inverness.'

'You want to stay in the caravan all night?'

'Yes, we could do things; maybe check out the caravan for stability. You know, see if it rocks.'

'No point; I've had a spirit level on it and jumped up and down, no movement whatsoever.'

'Yes, but if two of us were at it?'

He blushed slightly. 'Zoe, you're a sod pot, you scare me. I think we'll go to the Tav instead.'

'Sounds okay, and then back here?'

'If you say so.'

'Super duper.'

When they entered the Tav, Stewart was carrying a couple of drinks from the bar. 'Come sit with us, but first get Carl and Jodie, they're in the games room.'

Zoe went to the games room, sighed, and shook her head. 'What a waste of space you two are, you spoiled everything.'

'Yeah well, I'm allergic to strange submarines.'

Jodie played about with her hair. 'So am I.'

Carl shot the white ball off the pool table. 'How did it go then?'

'It didn't, full stop. He'll arrange another time, and don't fluff it.'

'Yeah well you can count me out.'

Jodie shook her head. 'No way.'

'You get on my tits at times — nothing to do in this village, nothing ever happens and it's boring. Some adventure comes along and you blow it, how boring is that? Anyway, we've company in the other room; they want you to join them.'

Stewart announced that he was going back to London and introduced Big John as the farm manager and Ian and Emma as the new owners.

Zoe listened to him as if he was telling a secret, but half the village knew. 'What about my pets?' she asked.

Stewart laughed. 'Just don't buy any more, or the shed will need extending. By the way, I've booked a dinner for us all at the Stags Head in Mairloch next Friday. You probably won't see me for a while after that. I'm leaving on Saturday morning.' He looked around the empty room. 'It's a free bar here tonight. The drinks are on me, so make the best of it.'

Carl's eyes lit up. 'Everybody's in the village hall, do we get their share?'

'If you can drink it.'

Ian stood up. 'Okay if we go in the games room now, dad?'

'Yes, enjoy yourselves.'

Carl jumped up and down. 'What you having guys? I'll get them.'

'A gin and tonic, I can only have one or two at the most,' Jodie said.

'Double Bacardi and coke for me,' Ian said.

Zoe laughed. 'You won't last out at that pace. A sweet Martini and lemonade for me, please.'

An hour later, Zoe and Jodie were on their third drink, Ian and Carl had downed six doubles.

'The submarine, did you find out where it came from?' Jodie asked.

Ian gave her a glazed look. 'Submarine… what submarine? Anyway, what colour knickers you got on tonight?'

Jodie gave him a disgusted look, put her drink down and ran out.

Zoe chased after her, but gave up at the end of the beer garden.

Ian and Carl came out carrying more doubles and sat at a picnic table.

Then Carl stood up and started dancing, Ian jumped on the table, swinging his hips and singing. She'd seen Carl acting daft before, but it was so out of character for Ian she just burst into fits of laughter.

Carl went for more drinks and came back empty-handed. 'Making too much noise, he wouldn't serve any more.'

'You got any home-brew, Carl?'

'A few bottles.'

'Nip home and get them,' Ian said, in a slurred voice.

Carl returned carrying four bottles of the strong stuff. Ian grabbed one and guzzled half of it while doing a jig. Then he guzzled the other half, took off his shirt and jumped on the table again, singing in a gibberish voice.

Carl mimicked him on the next table. 'Fancy a taxi to the nightclub at Mairloch, anybody?'

Ian stumbled off the table and grabbed another bottle. 'No, we'll go in Zoe's speedboat, be quicker.'

'And more fun.' Carl nearly staggered over. 'What are we waiting for? Let's go.'

'I'm not taking the speedboat out,' Zoe followed them out of the beer garden, 'better if we call it a day. Let's go to the caravan Ian.'

They took no notice and headed for the harbour, with Zoe in pursuit. Every few steps they swigged their beer and zigzagged down the harbour road, laughing.

'Strong stuff this home-brew.' Ian promptly fell flat out on the grass verge. Carl tried to help him up, overbalanced and fell in a stupor next to him.

'Jesus, come on you two.' Zoe sat next to Ian and shook him, but it made no difference, he was beyond rousing. She left them snoring away as if they were in bed together. *Be a different story in the morning*, she thought.

The next day she went to feed the animals and met Emma in the garden. 'Don't disturb Ian, he's been sick all over the place, he's really ill. Carl's just as bad if not worse; his mother rang to ask what they'd been drinking. Apparently, he's pulled a muscle in his stomach through retching up.'

'I could go in and maybe cheer Ian up.'

'I'm not joking, he's beyond it, better if you remember him as he was before he had a drink. I reckon he'll be ill for a few days.'

'Hope he's okay for the dinner on Friday.'

'Tell me Zoe, how do they dress for dinner in this part of the world?'

'In boring clothes, compared to the ones you model. Katie used to scour the magazines at Mairloch; if you were in any, she bought them. I have them all at home.'

'Oh right, I'm surprised.'

'Well, I think you should dress like you would in London.'

'You don't think Stewart will mind.'

'No, you'll make his night… Emma, I really want to do modelling, how do I get started?'

'I know some good contacts, other than that, you don't need to do much; you're a natural. Practice flirting with the mirror.'

'I practice every day, but I've no proper clothes.'

'I'll give you some clothes; you're a touch shorter than me with a similar figure, I reckon they'll fit. Then we'll take some photos and send them off.'

'Oooh, thanks, Emma I can't wait.'

11 At the Stags Head, and unknown to Emma, there was an extra guest. Stewart introduced her as a 'good friend' and, as the night wore on, it became apparent that they were very good friends.

After the dinner, Big John, Ian and Carl entertained themselves at the bar, Zoe stayed with Emma at the dinner table. Stewart and his lady friend sat on a sofa just out of ear's reach.

Emma opened her eyes wide and shook her head. 'I guess he's deserted us.'

'Well, I didn't like his gawping, every time you looked away he undressed you with his eyes.'

'I know, I could feel it, you get a sense for that sort of thing and, to be honest, it makes me cringe.'

Ian made his way over from the bar. 'You two fancy a move?' Then, making sure his dad could hear. 'This place is a load of crap!'

Emma smiled at him. 'Just thinking the same.'

'Tell me about it.' Zoe said.

Big John went to Stewart. 'We're making a move; do you want picking up later?'

'No, I'm meeting some friends I'll make my own way back in the morning. I'm staying overnight.'

Emma watched Ian's face change. *Maybe it's a good thing he is staying here,* she thought.

Outside the hotel, two men acting very suspiciously, asked for the time.

John glared at them. 'There's a clock in the hotel.'

One man glared back. 'We aren't goin' in, just waiting for somebody.'

'In that case, they'll tell you the time when they get here.' He turned away and pulled out the keys.

At that point, Emma saw both of them spit on the ground and stick two fingers up at him. She pretended not to see it and climbed in the front passenger seat next to John.

'Anybody know them?' John asked, when they were all in the Range Rover.

'Trouble,' Carl answered, 'soon as you turned your back, they spat at you and gave you two—'

Emma cut him off. 'Let's just get on our way.'

John looked at her, raised his one eyebrow and grinned. 'I think they need a lesson.'

By now, the two men were leaning against a car, smirking.

John opened his door and sauntered over to them as if he were about to make friends. As he neared them, the smirks left their faces and they ran off. *Thank goodness for that,* Emma thought.

He climbed back in and started the engine. 'A couple of cowards. Right where we heading?'

'The Tav, then you can have a proper drink with us,' Ian said.

Four miles from Strathdale after a long straight stretch of road, Zoe gave a warning to John. 'A bad bend coming up, if you ever meet a car on this road, it'll be here... Jesus!'

'The brakes have gone!' John shouted.

They were the last words Emma heard. The Rover overshot the bend, hit the barrier, flipped over and somersaulted through the air.

Emma found herself floating above the burning wreckage at the foot of the cliff. She knew her body was in there, but she could see nothing for the flames. She looked to see if anyone was around the wreckage, but there was no sign, all incinerated, she guessed.

Thankfully, the pain and the screams were short lived. If anything, death by fire reminded her of drowning, except you can't scream under water, but the outcome is the same.

Still floating above the blazing wreckage, Emma knew there wouldn't be a body shell to climb back into. *This is no out-of-body experience; no returning to Earth this time,* she thought.

At that moment, it all disappeared in a euphoric state. She zoomed skywards as if she'd been fired from a gun; planets came at her at a fantastic speed until everything became a blur.

Within seconds, she came to a halt. When her eyes had focused, she found herself in familiar surroundings, the same space station she'd seen once before.

'You don't have a choice this time Emma. Your friends had no choice either. They arrived just ahead of you.'

She recognised the voice of Waldo. 'Where are they?'

'Four are in the shuttle. You outlived them in the fire on Earth by one minute. I held them back until you arrived, otherwise it could take ages before you met up again.'

'How did you know about the fire?'

'I was monitoring Ian and his friends for transition. I saw the crash.'

At that moment, she floated into the cubicle and went through the same mind-scan procedure as before. Then she drifted into the Duplico compartment. There were three rows of double seats. It reminded her of a fairground ride about to set off. A glass dome enclosed the carriage, and there were four shapes sitting on the seats in front of her.

'Can you hear me?' she asked.

'Emma, you made me jump! Can't see you properly. So, this ghost train is for real.'

'Nice one, Zoe,' a voice from a speaker at the front said, 'and close to the truth. You're in a spirit beam.'

An eerie silence came over the carriage.

'What's going on?' Carl shouted.

'Calm down.' Emma took charge of the situation. 'Who else have we here?'

'Me,' Ian said.

'And me,' Jodie said.

'So, Big John is missing.'

'Yes, where's Big John?' Zoe asked.

'Yes, where's Big John?' Ian echoed her.

Emma scratched her head in deep thought.

'Welcome aboard, I'm Captain Waldo Sultan. Big John has gone to planet Ungad, meaning he failed the Duplico test or he was sent there for some special reason.'

'This chamber, what is it?' Ian asked.

'It's a converter, normally the starting point of a journey from Earth to planet Duplico.'

'A converter, what does that mean?' Ian continued.

'It means it converts people from Earth into a paranormal frequency, an out-of-body time zone. Once converted distance becomes irrelevant, allowing teleportation instantly to our galaxy, via the spirit beam.'

'People converted… what's that for?' Zoe queried.

'Six-weeks ago, I was on my way to Earth when I came across Emma, in the space station. Out of curiosity and using her DNA, I found Katie and Ian at Strathdale. Then, two-weeks later, Emma arrived there. By then, I'd started my transition plan; Strathdale seemed a good place to take samples.'

Ian gave him a strange look. 'Samples? Did that include us?'

'Yes, but I had to abort my plan when your lives on Earth expired at the foot of the cliff. I saw it happen and came to the space station to escort you to your planet.'

'What happened on the bench?' Ian asked.

'My body was in limbo, neither in your world or mine. I could be visible or invisible, ensuring nobody else saw me. I left the straw-filled mummified disguise there to make it more interesting.'

'You looked so old, it was frightening,' Carl said.

'Sometimes, depending on the job in hand, I play with the age amplification. I've perfected it to such a degree, that I can walk about on your planet as a young or old man, or stay invisible and mingle wherever I am.'

'Seems a lot of trouble, sitting on the bench for days on end, then turning up in a submarine.' Ian said.

'We don't just whisk people away; it's a complicated method of transition.'

'And your intention?' Zoe asked.

'You were to be on Duplico for half a day of tests, but return home three days later due to the difference in our time zones. Dupliconians have a long life span, an average of five to six hundred years.'

'You're winding us up,' Carl laughed, 'Over five hundred years old?!'

'No more questions now.'

'My head's gone,' Carl said.

'I feel like I'm floating.' Jodie burst out laughing.

Zoe laughed with her.

Emma tried to keep her head. 'Waldo, what's happening?'

'The chip implants, attached in the cubicle, can't leave the station until the defragmenter's logged off.

'Oh, yes, the defragmenter, I'd forgotten.'

'The youngsters have lost consciousness; they'll hardly be bothered that Earth played a part in their previous lives. Any links with Earth will be almost dreamlike within a few months and they'll feel as if they've always lived on Duplico.'

'What about me?'

'Adults don't fall unconscious during transition. With adults, the computer deletes any stress accumulated in the mind. Apart from that, you keep your original memory. Of course, all your original memories were transferred to special storage disks before the defragmenter started.'

'The special storage disks, are they available to us?'

'No point; they'd be meaningless to you.'

'What are the copies for then?'

'Security, all mind-disks are scrutinized for criminal activity on Earth. The computer picks which planet a soul goes to.'

'Supposing I were a nun, would they still take a copy?'

'Emma, if you'd been a saint on Earth you couldn't enter our galaxy without a copy of your mind being deposited at security headquarters. You might be crime-free, but, as happens quite frequently, you could be innocently linked to a crime.'

'I think that happened to me.'

'There you are then. That's why every event in your life, including any deaths, accidents, murders or whatever, on Earth, is now recorded on a disk.'

'I remember a few deaths: one was my dog, one was my sister, and one was somebody I fell deeply in love with; the others, I'd rather not talk about.'

'Well, Earth will soon be a thing of the past.'

'The most wonderful feeling I've ever experienced seems to have taken over my brain, it's as if everything is new.'

'Correct, I just wish I could see you when you materialize, but I'm supposed to be bringing four more people back from Earth, so I'll have to return to Earth and start again.'

'Don't I get to see you?'

'The DNA profile tells me that you are all going to the same village. I just happen to work from your village. I'll make a point of seeing you if and when I get time.'

'Does the DNA mean we have relatives in the village?'

'Not necessarily, sometimes it can be a dog, a cat or some other pet, but they give out a weak signal. All your signals are fairly strong.'

'Meaning relatives?'

'Yes, but you have a stronger signal coming from planet Ungad, which means you have a parent or parents there. The computer ignored that signal though.'

'Why?'

'I don't know, but the computer is a high-tech machine with a God-like power to get inside your head then copy your mind to a disc. You can't dispute the computer.'

'Oh, sort of disputing my own mind. Well, I'm not about to argue with that.'

'And rightly so.'

'This village, is it like the villages on Earth?'

'You'll hardly notice a difference from your own village. We have three living worlds in our solar system. Ungadlings can be a problem. Extungadlings are a big problem. There are police and armed services on both, but you don't need to know about them; you're going to the premier planet.'

'Excellent.'

'No police, no armed services, agency captains and officers keep the place in order. Our agency controls all space travel. Nobody can enter Duplico without first going through our space station, which serves our three planets and Earth.'

Suddenly, Emma felt the euphoria go. She found herself struggling to recall events, some were like bad nightmares; others were illogical. On top of this, her mind was trying to deal with her present state; there didn't seem to be any reality. 'I feel ill, my head's burning and I can't see properly, I need a doctor or something.'

'Don't worry, it's the defragmenter; the old world's gone and the new world is kicking in. Things will settle down shortly.'

'How far are we from the old world?'

'Distance has no meaning in spirit travel, everywhere is the same distance, but we've certainly gone past the furthest point that Earthlings know about. Soon you'll be joining the people of our galaxy; all are rebirths or reincarnations from Earth.'

'I still don't understand; if you're from a distant planet how come you talk exactly like us?'

He laughed. 'I lived in Burnley, Lancashire, until my death under a bus. If you're expecting to see aliens you'll be disappointed; you're more likely to bump into a dead relative. We were all Earthlings we've just moved planets that's all.'

'So where is heaven supposed to be then?'

'Good question, but you'll have to live your life out here to find the answer to that one. Who knows what the next phase will bring us.'

Emma inspected the capsule; there was nothing to indicate that they were moving. 'What type of space craft is this?'

'It's not a spacecraft as such; it converts humans into subatomic particles for teleportation in the spirit beam or, as we call it, the dream beam. I use it for transporting Earthlings for testing. You wouldn't normally arrive on Duplico in one of these. Professor Davidoff, the most respected quantum physics expert in our solar system, discovered how to tap into the spirit beams and invented the teleportation converter.'

'When we died in the accident, I found myself floating above the scene and then zoomed off. How does that happen?'

'According to Davidoff, when a soul leaves the body, it hovers for while until a spirit beam draws you in. I don't know the energy source, but within minutes you arrive at the space station. The computer mind-scan processes the information it needs then selects your destination on one of the planets.'

At that point, Emma noticed the four shapes were moving. 'They're coming round.'

'My head hurts, what's going on?' Zoe asked.

'You're nearly home. Nobody worry about having a sore head, it'll be gone shortly after splashdown.'

'My brain's gone funny, I don't know what you're on about. Any chance of an explanation?' Ian asked.

'We're about to hit water and re-enter my launch pad, a submarine. This capsule is like a high-tech torpedo that travels between my base submarines on four different planets.'

'Yeah, pull the other one,' Carl said.

'Let's wait and see,' Emma butted in. 'Carry on Waldo.'

'After splashdown, Captain Homer will show you to your respective addresses, you'll soon feel at home.'

'You mean we already have accommodation awaiting us?'

'Yes. Right, prepare for disembarking. It's midday, the weather is sunny and a pleasant twenty degrees. You'll be leaving the capsule shortly, but first you'll enter the quantum entanglement receiver. After a series of bleeps, the red light will change to green, you'll materialize and then Homer will meet you outside.'

Zoe adjusted her clothes and re-arranged her hair. 'How do I look Jodie?'

Ian butted in. 'You'll pass.'

She gave him a suggestive smile. 'So will you gorgeous.'

Emma followed the others through the hatch.

'Welcome to Duplico,' said a tall, exceptionally handsome man, dressed in a pale-grey, tropical uniform. He had captivating blue eyes that flashed, a lightly tanned skin, and short-cropped blond hair. He held out his hand.

Wow, he's gorgeous, Emma thought, as she shook his hand and smiled.

'Captain Homer; pleased to meet you Emma.' He had lovely smile; his voice was clear and strong.

'Pleased to meet you Captain.' She held his smile.

They climbed a couple of dozen steps and went through a steel door that overlooked a harbour.

'Thanks for the trip,' Ian said. Then he turned to Zoe. 'Funny thing is, I can't remember the trip…'

'Nor me,' she said.

'You all fell asleep.' Emma said, looking around the harbour. 'This isn't Duplico, we haven't moved. That's the quarry track to Ian's farm over there, and the beach path to the Tavern… But it's too warm, and there are palm trees on the beach.'

'And silver sand and turquoise coloured sea.' Zoe eyed the deep blue sky and the landscape. 'It's as if everything's turned tropical. Otherwise, it's identical to Strathdale.'

Ian turned to Emma. 'Am I awake or dreaming; that was the cavern we just came out of?'

'Yes, are we all in the same dream, Emma?' Jodie asked.

'Yeah,' Carl said, 'one minute driving off a hundred foot cliff, the next, in paradise.'

'I remember that,' Zoe said, 'you remember, Emma?'

'I guess so, and it's no dream.'

Ian gave her a strange look and scratched his head. 'Well, that was the cavern, that's our beach and harbour and this is Strathdale.'

Just then, Homer turned and clapped his hands, they all jumped. 'Come on you lot! Wake up! Let's get you home.'

Emma walked directly behind Homer, in silence up the beach path. The scent of something sweet-smelling wafted over them in a warm gentle breeze. Exotic butterflies hovered over equally exotic wild flowers.

At the top of the path, Emma noticed the incredible range of vegetation growing at the edge of the village. They made their way up a cobbled road leading to the heart of the village. Here beautiful flowers surrounded the lush village green where friendly birds welcomed them. She stood surveying the scene. People in slow motion, some tending breathtaking gardens, others chatted on the street, unhurried.

An aura of timeless magical splendour hung over the whole village. She breathed in deeply. 'What's in the air?'

'Just ordinary air, pure of course.'

'My cottage, it's got an orange tree,' Zoe said, with open mouth.

Emma smiled. 'It's very pretty.'

'Come on Zoe, we're going in the Tav,' Ian said.

Zoe pointed to the sign. 'You mean the Swan.'

'We're all going in the Swan, it's my home,' Homer said.

The building had the same frontage as the Tavern, Emma noted, but it was the Swan Inn and had a huge extension at the side and rear. Homer took them round the side to an office in the extension.

He gave each of them an envelope. 'Here are your addresses; all the households were notified as you docked—'

'We know our addresses,' Zoe interrupted.

'Also,' he continued, 'in the envelope is a brief overview of the person or persons you'll be living with—'

'Person or persons we'll be living with!' Zoe cut him off again.

'Sorry, Zoe, no questions now, I've got to rush off. There'll be a welcome meeting in the Swan beer garden at seven o'clock; I'll be here to answer your questions then. Enjoy the rest of the afternoon.'

12 They all went outside, sat around a picnic table in the beer garden and read their letters. Emma looked towards the farm and felt a shiver go down her spine. The buildings seemed the same, except the animal hut was missing. She stared at the address again.

At that moment, Ian jumped up and ran to the farm.

'Seen my address, it's the same as back home on Earth,' Carl said.

Emma took no notice; her eyes were on Ian at the garden gate of the farm. Just then, Katie came out of the farmhouse, stared for a moment, then ran down the garden path and threw her arms around Ian and hugged him.

Emma ran over to the farm and they all hugged each other, not wanting to let go.

'What happened? Not that it matters. Did Ian find you in London?'

'No, I found him at the farm. I lived in the cottage for a while until six of us went over the cliff.'

Ian's eyes began to fill. 'I never felt a thing mum, honest.'

'I know, you spend half your life worrying about death and when it comes you couldn't care less, especially when you arrive here.'

He dried his eyes with his handkerchief. 'Is there a fishing rod here?' he asked, making his way towards the caravan.

'Not yet, should be here tomorrow along with your clothes.'

'I could do with a drink of something,' Emma said.

Katie smiled. 'You're not joking. Let's go inside.'

The layout was identical to the Earth farmhouse. 'This feels strange, you live alone.'

Katie opened a bottle of wine. 'Yes, it was vacant when I arrived.'

'Homer gave my address as the Farm Cottage, funny thing is I had just bought the same cottage off Stewart in Strathdale.'

Katie sighed and took a sip of wine, then went to the sink and cleared some dishes. 'He sold the farm I suppose?'

'I bought the farm off him and gave it to Ian.'

She turned away from the sink, tears in her eyes. 'Thanks, Emma.'

'Ian was over the moon, although he wasn't too pleased with his dad.'

Katie dried her eyes, took a long sip of wine and smiled. 'Doesn't matter anymore, we're on another planet, thank goodness.'

'So who owns this farm?'

'Not me. The farm, the Swan, every building in the village, and all the land for miles around is owned by Reno Salvos; but the villagers are quite happy.'

'You all pay rent to this Reno Salvos then?'

Katie laughed. 'I've paid nothing since I arrived here. He never bills anyone for rent. A manager runs his estate and he just uses it for holidays; he has another mansion in Inverbess. Homer says he is the nicest person you could ever meet.'

'And very rich by the sounds of it.'

'Apparently, he visits the Swan, but I rarely go in there, I've never met him.'

They sat and talked, only pausing to have a sip of wine. They talked about Gavin and Stewart and when they didn't talk, they sobbed.

'What made you stick with Gavin so long?'

'Because I was so busy modelling, I tolerated him.'

'Same with Stewart, I buried myself in the farm.'

Emma gave her a sly smile. 'Yes, literally; I attended the funeral.'

'Do you know, I was the tractor driver on the farm; I could drive it on a knife-edge,' said Ian. 'My last thought, as I went over the edge of the quarry was he had me well insured, and he'd done something to the tractor.'

Katie opened another bottle of wine and took them into the lounge where they talked and talked, until Emma fell asleep on the settee.

Later, in the Swan, everyone seemed quite happy with the new arrangements. Carl was with his great grandfather, Zoe was with her grandmother and Jodie was living at the Swan with her aunt Brenda.

'Were do the clothes come from?' Zoe asked Homer.

'From your mind disk, you should get two cases of clothes identical to the ones you wore on Earth, all ordered from various shops and factories by the computer.'

'What's a mind-disc?'

'It's a copy of your original mind. Clothes and anything you used for hobbies and pastimes will be duplicated and sent to you within a couple of days, all brand new, of course.'

Zoe smiled and looked at him warmly. 'My hobby was water skiing and scuba-diving; my dad gave me a speedboat.'

'In that case, keep your eyes on the harbour.' He gave them more envelopes. 'Your ID cards and your debit cards. The value of any Earth assets are already credited; the balance is on the printout. The cards are for all purchases. We don't use money; prices are in chips and blocks, ten chips to a block. Three chips will buy a newspaper, a block will buy a glass of wine or get you ten miles of travel. Menial work pays five blocks an hour.'

'Why is this village like ours?' she added.

'Suffice to say, wherever you go on Duplico you'll find similarities with Earth. Duplico, Ungad, Extungad and Earth are mirror images of each other.'

'This twin village shows ours up,' Carl said.

'We have an almost perfect climate on this coast.'

'What about the people?' Ian asked.

'The three planets have completely different lifestyles. Duplico, with an absence of crime, is the top-end planet. The people here are pleasant and friendly. Ungad is like Earth, they have similar traits and similar problems. Extungad is not a nice place: terrorists, dangerous criminals, rapists and murderers end up there; it's the next step to hell.'

Carl opened his envelope and fiddled with his card. 'It says here—'

'Right,' Homer cut him off, 'that's enough for today.'

'Okay if I have a word with you?' Emma asked.

'Yes, follow me.'

A passage connected the bar to the huge extension at the back. As they passed through a large room, that resembled a second-hand shop, Emma noticed some Egyptian and other Earth artefacts in a corner.

'Make-up department, it's always untidy.' Homer opened a door on one side, monitors, and radio equipment filled the room. 'Come through to the lounge.'

The massive lounge had ornate furniture befitting a stately home. A patio window led to a tropical garden where a fountain and a waterfall cascaded into a pond. Emma could see an outdoor swimming pool and the open sea beyond.

'This is beautiful, not your normal village pub type of place.'

'The pub is run mainly by my wife, Fiona. I work for the space agency; Waldo Sultan is my boss. I'm presently on paranormal duties with the transition squad, collecting and escorting, we borrow Earthlings for testing.'

Emma gave him an odd look. 'Testing?'

'Yes, for pollution. You'll be going for job assessments tomorrow, I'll tell you more then… oh, you wanted a word?'

'The mind-discs, supposing I knew of a murder victim on Earth, and knew the murderer, who also died. Would they be here?'

'Everyone that dies on Earth comes to our galaxy via the space station; the computer takes a copy of the original mind, then, according to what it finds, directs them to one of our planets. The security department keeps the disks under lock and key; they know the exact location of every individual and, of course, what they got up to on Earth.'

'So they'd know the whereabouts of a particular person that I want to find.'

'Yes, but the disks are top security, otherwise everyone would be running around looking for the person that murdered them or raped them or they fell in love with. We have three planets here, each as big as Earth, can you imagine that scenario?'

Emma sighed, 'When you put it that way, I guess so.'

'Look, that computer is something special, it directed you here through your mind scan and took you to your sister; the computer is never wrong. It wouldn't send you to your father or mother if something wasn't right. I've known it send people to a dog, a cat, a parrot and even hamsters, rather than a relative.'

'If the person I'm interested in finding was a good person on Earth then he should be on Duplico, am I right?'

'Well, you might have thought he was a good person, but you wouldn't know for sure what was on his mind.'

Emma laughed. 'Everybody knew what was on his mind.'

'Hate to correct you, everybody *thought* they knew.'

'Yes, and the computer will know exactly what he was thinking, but I'll never get to know.'

'Fiona was my girlfriend on Earth; we're married now. We found each other, but it took ten years.'

'I can't wait ten years; I'll be too old to start a family.'

'Worry about that in a few hundred years.'

'Oh, right… What's the point in taking copies of the mind?'

'Mainly to help the security service. The computer can put blocks on parts, or all of your memory, removing information from the subconscious.'

'That's a liberty, to say the least.'

'They can reprogram a person if they so wish. However, that only applies to those bound for Ungad and Extungad, on Duplico, at least half your original memory is retained.'

'Did the disc help find your girlfriend?'

'Eventually, yes. Everybody in our galaxy has their memory on discs at Fort Locks on Ungad. In your previous life, were you married?'

'Yes.'

'Fairly simple then; you give his name and the date when he died, they check his mind-disc; if all's okay, they'll give you his location.'

'But we were about to be divorced, it's another person I'm interested in.'

'In that case, he might well be in another galaxy or back on Earth. They won't open files on lovers; I tried for five years, it's painful. But if you live on Ungad they don't mind opening the files for partners, lovers or even a bit on the side.'

'How do you get to live on Ungad?'

'Break the law here a few times, or just once if it's deemed to be a three point category, but it's a long road. I got myself demoted to get to my file and found that Fiona was living on Ungad. But you can't return to Duplico, until you've earned enough star points to re-establish yourself.'

'That's a bit harsh.'

'I soon earned the points, but it took Fiona a while. You wouldn't want to live on Ungad permanently; it can change people. When I found Fiona, she'd taken to drugs. She managed to kick the habit, but now she's become a problem again.'

∽

In the bar, Zoe gave Carl an inquisitive smile. 'What were you going to ask H about your card?'

'I just seem to have lost some interest, can't grumble though, everything I had in the bank has been transferred here. And guess what, I'm living with my great grandfather.'

'I'm with my grandmother, and they've put a hundred blocks on my card to get me started.'

'They gave me a hundred blocks,' Jodie said, 'and you'll never guess where I'm living.'

'By the excitement on your face it must be somewhere good, and anywhere's better than where you were living before.'

'I'm happy, and living with the most gorgeous guy; well, not exactly with him, but in the next bedroom but one.' Her eyes twinkled.

Carl laughed and winked at Zoe. 'She's been drinking.'

'Tell me about it, what's come over you Jodie? Never seen you so blissed out.'

'I'm living with Homer and my Aunt Brenda, here at the Swan.'

Carl gave her a sarcastic look. 'Yeah, living in t' staff quarters wi' your aunt Brenda, that's not living wi' Homer.'

'Well, so what.'

'Yes, so what Carl; if she's happy here that's good enough for me, she doesn't need you to pull her down.' Zoe remembered all the depression that Jodie had suffered on Earth, how her perverted stepfather had changed her outgoing bubbly personality and made her into a slave. *Jodie deserves some happiness,* she thought.

Fiona, now dressed in clothes more suited to a nightclub, came over to their table and gave them a broad smile. 'Get you a drink, friends?' Diamonds sparkled on her fingers, on her wrists, in her earrings, and round her neck.

'Two pints and two halves of lager, please,' Ian said.

She gave him a strange look. 'Are you from Ungad? You won't find lager on this planet.'

Ian rubbed his chin and turned to Carl. 'Where we from?'

Carl suddenly fell off his stool and just missed banging his head on a table. 'That reminds me, wonder if there's a doc around here?'

Fiona bent over him, put her arms around him and lifted him up, as she did so, her cleavage brushed against his face. 'You all right love?'

He stood back, his eyes wandering over her body. 'Yeah I'm ok. Turned out nice hasn't it?'

She gave him a broad smile. 'We do a large or small Ambry ale, cider, wine and a variety of hot shots.'

'Two large Ambry ales,' Ian said.

'And two small,' Zoe added.

Fiona headed to the bar.

'I wonder why she's dressed like that, the place is empty,' Carl grinned at Zoe.

'For you, I guess. Did the fall make you dizzy?'

'She had the same effect on me.' Ian had a wry grin on his face.

Carl followed her legs to the bar. 'Young lookin' for him, not much over twenty.'

'Plus maybe two or three hundred years, for all we know.' Jodie reminded him, her eyes fixed on Homer, who was coming over to their table with Emma.

'How's everything going then?' Homer asked.

'Funny thing, living with grandparents and a neighbour, who died on Earth,' Carl answered.

'Yes, but as you can see, they didn't die, they reincarnated like the rest of us.'

'How safe are we here?' Zoe asked.

'Because of the low crime rate, there are no prisons on Duplico. Anyone incurring three crime points go to Ungad, where they do have prisons. However, on Ungad for the hardened criminals there is the ultimate deterrent of a transfer to Extungad. If you watch the news, you'll get some idea of the other planets. Channel one is the national and regional news, two is global news and three is the galaxy news.'

'Okay if I take them up to the guest lounge?' Jodie asked.

'I'm going back to the farm; enjoy yourselves,' Emma said.

'I'll end up drunk, I feel a bit woozy now,' Jodie said as they entered the guest lounge.

Carl grabbed the TV magazine. 'Put channel 18 on, it's the cartoon channel.'

'No, the galaxy news, put that on first.' Ian said.

'Just put anything on,' Jodie said.

'Right, it's number three then.' Zoe switched on in the middle of a gun battle.

'That's not news, I've seen it; it's an old film,' Carl said.

'You're right, it's The Untouchables; that's Al Capone and his mobsters. But H said number three was galaxy news.'

'Switch over,' Jodie said, 'I'm not watching that rubbish.'

'In Extungad this afternoon,' the newsreader said, *'Galaxy news took these pictures of a bank robbery. Al Capone and his team shot dead four of the bank robbers and arrested three more. The robbers were part of the Pall Mall hoods.'*

'I haven't seen that bit before.' Carl scratched his head. 'That's Al Capone in person, not an actor. I used to have a scrapbook with cuttings of the real gangsters.'

'It isn't a film,' Ian said.

'Last night,' the newsreader went on, *'a man shot dead one of the staff in a coffee bar, apparently they had served him cold coffee.'*

'That's terrible,' Jodie said.

'It's not real,' Zoe said.

Fiona came in carrying a tray, still dressed in the short low-cut black outfit. 'Supper's up, a selection of treats; I hope you like them.'

'They look very nice,' Carl answered.

'I see you're watching the Extungad news. Bad things happen when all the horrible people are lumped together on one planet.'

'At first we thought it was a film,' Carl said, 'Al Capone was a gangster in Chicago on our planet.'

'He died long ago, what's he doing here?' Ian asked.

'Spirited to Extungad along with other mobsters; he has been a good boy over the years.'

Ian laughed. 'If that's being a good boy, what do the bad guys get up to?'

'You don't understand, he shoots the bad guys; he works for the security force. They can easily recognise the top mobsters from Earth. Then they fiddle with their mind disk, implanting whatever. Al Capone is in charge of the Special Branch, in the largest country on Extungad.'

13

When Emma arrived at the farm, Katie was cutting up a salmon on the worktop.

'What are star points?' Emma asked her.

'You needn't worry about them here. Star points are the opposite of crime points, for good behaviour on the other planets. However, you would practically have to turn into a saint, to get from Extungad to Ungad and then to here.'

'I'm only interested in Ungad to here. How do you gain the star points?'

'Charity work, hospital volunteer and things of that nature, but it's a minimum of four years to gain two points and an extra year for the third.'

'And the crime points?'

'Dropping any sort of litter on two separate occasions will see you with one point, as will threatening behaviour, anything above that is two or three points at one go.'

'But there are no police, how do they enforce the law?'

'We are the police, we report an offence to one of the captains, they give you a lie-detector test, then issue the points to the accused, that's all there is to it.'

'So if I drop two separate pieces of litter, that's a point gone?'

'Yes, if someone reports you. Why are you asking?'

'I'm going to Ungad.'

'Why?'

'I need to find Alistair, but because he wasn't my husband, I can't access the mind-discs unless I live on Ungad.'

'Well, don't go rushing into things. According to Homer, there are so many unmarried people arriving, they'll have to make some changes to the computer so they can link up lovers here. Trouble is, it doesn't work on Ungad and the governors here aren't too keen on a change.'

'Yes, well, I guess I'll just have to add myself to the crime list here.'

'You've only been here for half a day. He might be living in the next village for all you know.'

'If Alistair brought his wealth with him, he wouldn't be living in a village; he'd be living on the outskirts of a city in a mansion.'

'I think you're right, because everyone here from Earth seems to keep their original standing, and from what you told me about him earlier he'll be on Duplico and in this country.'

'Is there a London here?'

'Yes, but with a different name, the map here is like nothing we know.' Katie pulled out a Duplico World Atlas and one of Earth that had come with her luggage. 'See that's the world map, but if you compare them, everything is muddled up, the countries are the same shape, but with different names.' She put her finger on the map. 'Look, we are in what's called Genland.'

Emma studied the map. 'I see what you mean.'

'Yes, a bit confusing.'

'Does Homer know you have an Earth World Atlas?'

'Yes, he has one; he can tell you things about Earth as if he'd been round it a hundred times.'

'Right, and I suppose he has; he could probably do it in a day. I just wish he would help me find Alistair.'

'He won't bend the rules you know, and anyway there's no rush; the life expectancy here is five to six hundred years.'

'I know, but I'm not waiting that long. Alistair was called away by a supposedly urgent call, just as we were about to make love for the first time. We were planning to marry. I never saw him again because he was murdered. How do you think I feel now that I know he didn't really die, but is here on this planet?'

'Well, if he left at such a crucial moment, I wouldn't be too hasty to take up with him again. I mean, what sort of a man is that?!'

'The best guy I ever met on Earth, and he had waited eight years for that moment, that's how long I'd put him off. I've already told you that he was set up.'

'Yes, but you also told me that Gavin and his two friends met their deaths accidentally, an eye-for-an-eye sort of accident.'

'I know, but they were out to kill me. Self-defence in an accidental way, Big John said.'

'I'm worried about that.'

'Why?'

'Because it's murder.'

'Yes, but it cleared the air and it's gone now.'

'That's why I'm worried. I thought my death was dubious: Stewart had threatened to kill me, more than once. I told Homer, he said, "forget it, when he arrives here, the mind-scan will pickup on that."

Then I told him that I was thinking of killing Stewart. "In that case," Homer said, "one thought cancels out the other. When Stewart dies on Earth, providing he's otherwise okay, he'll probably arrive on Duplico. Unless he carried out his threat."'

'I bet you're worried about that.'

'Well, he won't arrive here at the farm; he'd already sold it to you and Ian. Anyway, he'll go straight to Ungad. I think he did carry out his threat.'

'So what you getting at?'

'If Gavin murdered somebody and then he was murdered in retribution, the computer will cancel out both murders.'

'They murdered five people: Alistair, his mother and father, Trish and Amy.'

'Yes, but you told me that you didn't know for definite who killed who. And supposing just one person killed all five, John C, the hit-man for instance?'

'Gavin had planned Alistair's death for years; everything he did was part of an elaborate plot.'

'Okay then, that's one murder. But supposing James the butler did one, and John C the other three?'

'That's feasible, but you're not trying to say that they could be here on Duplico?'

'Depends on what else they got up to.'

'Well, they were into drugs in a big way, and what about the armed robbery against your Stewart then taking over your jewellery business?'

'Oh, yes, is that what he told you? Well, he had a girlfriend in London, and when we moved to the farm in Scotland, she was only living in the next village.'

'Why would they want to get at Stewart then?'

'The truth is we never owned the jewellery shop; it belonged to James the butler, a front for laundering drug money. One day Stewart sold all the jewellery to a dealer and did a runner. Of course, I knew nothing of this; as far as I was aware, the house and business had been sold to buy a new life in northern Scotland.'

'There you are, murderers and drug barons, and if they are on this planet I want off.'

'They won't be on Duplico, but if the murders were cancelled out then that leaves the drug issue; the computer would send them to Ungad.'

'So why be concerned?'

'There's only three star points between them and us, in five years they could be here.'

'Why would they want to come here?'

'Normally, I don't think they would, but if Gavin asks Fort Locks to check his mind-disc, because you're his wife, they'll give out your location.'

'Hell.'

'Yes, it will be for me when Stewart arrives on Ungad.'

'Do you know Katie, your story is almost as bad as mine; so trusting and naïve, the pair of us.'

'Yes, and you can imagine how I felt when Stewart told me he'd done a runner, then said we had to cut all contact with anybody south of the border or we'd be dead. Then, as if to rub salt in, I found clues that his girlfriend had arrived, almost next door, the week before us. I just hope she milks him of his ill gotten gains.'

'Well, I met her briefly and she looked the type.'

'I'd like to get my hands on him when he does arrive here.'

'Do you think you ever will?'

'Put it this way, we are here for five to six hundred years; he's got at the most forty on Earth, and my disc will find him when he arrives.'

'Yes, but he will probably go to Ungad.'

'For the moment it doesn't matter, and I think I can help you find Alistair; I have a plan.'

⁓

At the Swan, Fiona left the four eating their supper. Jodie and Zoe sat at the table while Ian and Carl stayed glued to the telly on the sofa.

'Zoe, pass us a treat.' Carl said, without taking his eyes off the telly.

'White filling, orange, or yellow?'

'Orange.'

Ian glanced at the pile of triangular shapes on the tray and frowned. 'What are they?'

Zoe cleared her mouth. 'Hmm, tasty, I would say the orange one is smoked salmon, the bread tastes like crusty doughnut.'

'I'll try one of each colour.'

'Sorry, either get them yourselves—they look very nice treats—or I could ask Fiona back. My, oh my, she'll be a handful! Loads of experience and dripping with diamonds.'

Jodie, her voice slightly slurred, laughed. 'A few hundred years experience, that's all!'

'Yeah, just think, Jodie, I could then pass the experience on to you.'

Ian interrupted, 'You're all talking stupid; I'm trying to watch the telly.'

'Let's go down to the bar,' Zoe suggested.

Homer was sitting on a barstool with a slight grin on his face.

'Fiona told me that you've been watching Extungad news; it's not a place you'd want to live.'

'No way, they even have one of our legendary gangsters in charge of the police,' Ian answered.

'You mean Al Capone? He's ace and he's got the toughest job in the galaxy.'

'What happens when you die here?' Zoe asked.

'That's an interesting question. We live a long time, but we're not immortal. We hope to go to the abode of angels when we die, in the same way that earthlings do.'

'Who decides which planet we are sent to?' Ian asked.

'The mind-scanner decides. Earthlings arrive here via four paranormal beams transmitted from Earth to our galaxy. The space station intercepts the beams, a computer scans every soul and takes a copy of the mind.'

Ian scratched his head. 'You're joking.'

'The computer is a very high-tech machine with a God-like power. He enters the mind and knows all the thoughts you've ever had, even the ones you've forgotten.'

Ian laughed, 'I'm into computers, but they can't do anything without our input.'

'Yes, quite, but it's the other way around here.'

'Why four beams?' Zoe asked.

'According to Professor Davidoff the spirits are tuned into predetermined beams; when the signals hit our atmosphere, one goes to Ungad, one to Extungad and one arrives here.'

'Seems a bit strange,' she replied.

'We think our planets are stepping-stones — a stopping off place between Earth and the abode of angels or the abode of the damned.

'Duplico gets the good guys, all types go to Ungad, and the really bad guys go to Extungad.'

'If the planets are a stopping-off place, where do the beams go when they leave here?' Carl asked.

'Our physics experts have tapped into the paranormal, the spirit beams coming from Earth. Curiously, they've failed to find any moving from here to the abode of angels or to the abode of the damned.'

'You talked of four spirit beams, but you only mentioned three. Where does the other go?' Ian asked.

'I'll tell you on the way to Gosglaw, I'm closing the bar.

You'd better get some sleep, we've an early start tomorrow.'

'Bed sounds a good idea,' Zoe yawned, 'any chance of sleeping here with Jodie?'

'They're her quarters, it's okay by me.'

Jodie gave him a big smile. 'Thanks, H.'

'In that case, I'll go sleep with Ian in the caravan,' Carl said, 'ok if we take a bottle with us?'

'Sorry, I just told you the bar is closed.'

'You can leave the tops on, the police won't know,' Carl persisted.

Homer gave him a stern look. 'I am the police! Everyone meet here at seven in the morning for breakfast. Emma won't be with you; she's going to the assessment centre on Monday instead. Jodie, if you need anything just let me know.'

Zoe watched Homer's facial expression then turned to Jodie and saw her face melt as they locked eyes on each other. *What's happening here,* she wondered. Throughout the conversation with Homer, Jodie had sat watching him starry-eyed, as if he was her idol. This was a huge change in Jodie's personality: normally she looked elsewhere, embarrassed if a man looked her way.

'What did you make of all that then?' Zoe asked as they entered Jodie's bedroom.

'I like it here, what do you think?'

'I'm not too sure about Fiona, she was flirting with Carl, and H had roving eyes.'

'Yes, gorgeous roving eyes, he's nice.'

The next day, Fiona met them in the dining room. 'Morning, hope you all slept well.'

'All snores in the caravan,' Ian answered.

'We were both unconscious until six-o-clock,' Zoe said.

'Good, the Captain shouldn't be long, he's gone to get the chopper ready, meanwhile enjoy your breakfasts.'

'Meaning, we're going to Gosglaw in a chopper?' Carl queried.

'Yes you are.' Homer walked into the dining room. 'When you've had breakfast, go up the steps on the side of the building; the helipad is on the roof, I'll meet you there.'

An hour later, Homer welcomed them aboard. 'Jodie, you can be co-pilot.'

'Oh, I wanted to sit in the front,' Zoe said.

'Sorry, you can swap places coming back. Fasten your seatbelts please.'

Homer gave the chopper full throttle, smiled at Jodie, and they headed skywards. 'When we return you should all know what your employment options are and you'll be given a week in which to make a start.'

'I haven't a clue what sort of work I want to do yet,' Carl said.

'Neither have I. Do they have universities?' Zoe asked.

'You'll each be given two choices by the assessment centre, otherwise you have no say in the matter.'

'Thought you said this was a nice planet. Only two choices of jobs?' Zoe said, in a raised voice.

'The centre is the only place that has access to your mind-discs at Fort Locks. After scrutinizing your original minds, the computer picks out what your capabilities are, and makes your mind up for you. It matches you to the most appropriate employment.'

Ten minutes into the flight, Carl pointed below. 'Heck, that must be the longest and fastest train ever.'

'It's not a train, it's the Sedan Express Line. It runs at three hundred miles per hour non-stop, the length and breadth of the country. Next question please?'

'Non-stop. So how do you get on?' Ian asked.

'You'll soon find out. Everybody uses it for commuting.'

'I have a question,' Zoe said. 'You work with a transition squad, plucking people from Earth; it sounds a bit sinister. What's that all about?'

'It's about testing Earthlings for the affects of pollutants. We have special laboratories to analyse every pollutant that enters a person's body on Earth.'

Zoe scratched her head. 'Must be important, going to all that trouble.'

'We need to monitor what's going on, it's in our interest to know exactly when Earth will be used up.'

'What do you mean, *used up*?' Ian asked.

'The tests tell us many things about your planet.'

'Like what?' Zoe asked.

'Air pollution and pesticides are altering your planet.'

'Why choose the north of Scotland, miles away from any pollution?'

'We take samples from every corner of the Earth; pollution is everywhere, it's out of control and the damage is irreversible. The land is contaminated, the streams, rivers and seas are dying; animals, birds and fish are disappearing.'

'The fish aren't vanishing, my dad's catching more salmon than he's ever caught.'

'Good point Zoe. Amongst other things, we monitor your fish stocks. Our findings have turned up some alarming facts.'

'In what way?'

'Fish farms have sprung up throughout your planet, especially salmon farms. So you see Zoe, your father is either farming the fish or catching escapees, not the real salmon. Thousands of farm fish have been escaping and pushing out the native salmon to the point of extinction.'

Jodie put her hand on his knee and looked into his eyes. 'Yes, but you know darling they are still salmon, and now that we've managed to farm them, everyone can eat salmon.'

He put his hand on her hand and gently stroked it.

'Precisely, and everyone can become slowly poisoned. These farmed fish, along with other fish in the rivers and oceans, are changing sex, caused by a hormone getting into your water — entire fish stocks irreversibly affected. That's how bad it is love.'

Zoe looked at Ian and Carl; they both raised their eyebrows and shrugged their shoulders, as if nothing was going on. *Well, they'll be kissing next,* she thought, never in her life had she seen Jodie like this, the change was scary and embarrassing. *At least, it is a massive change for the better - apart from the problem that H is already married,* she thought

She peeked over the front seat again. Homer's hand was on Jodie's leg and, a fair bit past her knee, stroking it. Jodie was smiling, looking out of the side window, oblivious to the others.

At that point, Zoe coughed loudly. 'But not everybody eats salmon.'

He quickly took his hand off her leg. 'We've checked your food chain, it's contaminated. Pesticides containing chemicals that disrupt the hormone system have been widely found in your food and drink, also your food is mass produced and genetically modified. On top of this, the air pollution is causing acid rain, which is wiping out forests and creating holes in the ozone layer, causing global warming. Nature will not accept these changes and nothing can be reversed.'

Zoe tickled the back of his neck. 'Sounds as if everybody should be half-dead already?'

'Close to the truth. Earthlings have created and adopted many life-altering substances; fish are already changing sex, and before long earthlings will have to be produced by artificial means.'

'What's the fishing's like here?' Ian asked.

There was no reply, Homer looked at Jodie, and for a moment, they locked eyes on one another.

Zoe touched him on the shoulder. 'He asked about the fishing here.'

'Oh, yes, the fishing, it's good, and definitely not farmed fish.'

'Let's not go there; it's all Ian ever does.'

'How well up are you on the bird life around your village?'

'Jodie's the bird expert.'

'How are the birds doing in your garden Jodie?'

'Some birds have disappeared completely.'

'Correct, birds disappearing from under your noses. Nature's alarm bells have been ringing for some time, but they've gone unheeded.'

'Is it really that bad?'

'I'm afraid so. The self-destruct button has already been pressed. Earth, is surrounded in a toxic atmosphere, which will eventually kill the planet. The tests help us to keep track of the decline.'

'Last night, you mentioned a fourth spirit beam,' Ian said.'

'Yes, this was the first beam that Professor Davidoff worked on and the start of our space shuttle program, our shuttle line between here and Earth. It's also the odd one out of the four beams.'

'What's odd about it?'

'It's odd because unlike the others it didn't enter our atmosphere. The fourth beam hit our atmosphere and bounced straight back to Earth. 'We set up a space station to receive and intercept the beams. The professor 'unlocked' the beam and discovered earthling spirits arriving here, then doing an about turn and going back to Earth.'

'How did he know they were going to Earth?' Carl asked.

'He stumbled across a way of releasing his own soul – or energy body. After two years of trial and error, he came up with the energy body converter.'

'That's incredible.'

'Yes, then I went with one of the rebounds to your planet. That was our first Earth landing, thirty years ago. Later he developed a subatomic quantum capsule for transitions. We've used the capsules for space travel ever since.'

'What happened to the rebounds?'

'The spirits re-materialized in their own bodies. We discovered that these rebounds had what you call 'out of body experiences,' we call them the 'half-dead'. These individuals started the after death process and when almost here, at the last minute, managed to abort the process and returned to their own bodies on Earth.

But now, depending on the mind scan, we give them a choice.'

Jodie rested her hand on his leg again and smiled. 'I've heard of that, people seeing their bodies when they are dead, then climbing back in and coming back to life.'

'Right, that's the end of question time, the job assessment centre is below us.'

He landed the chopper on the helipad in the grounds.

A pleasant, extremely good-looking, blonde-haired nurse greeted them at the reception desk and took them through to a waiting room. Smiling, she looked at Carl's hair. 'What do you call that hair style?'

'Elvis-style.'

'I've met your double, exactly the same hair and denim clothes, he's a singer.'

'What do they call him?'

'Reno Salvos, he's a top artist.'

'Huh, not the one I was thinking of.'

She gave Carl a warm smile. 'Who would like to go in first?'

'I'll go,' Jodie answered.

'The mind-disc report takes about five minutes. Follow me Jodie, the rest can find something to read.'

Zoe picked up a magazine turning the pages.

'That's the agency journal, on page six you'll find an article by Professor David-off,' Homer said. 'I'm off to the office, catch you up later.'

Zoe found the article and began reading it aloud.

'Too little too late, Earth continues to slide into the abyss. Work continues in helping us to pinpoint the actual time when Earth becomes a dead planet. Preparations are underway for an increasing exodus of earthlings to our galaxy, which will occur over the next two hundred years.'

Zoe frowned and looked at Ian. 'Well, at least we won't be there.'

Carl sniggered. 'What you on about?'

'Earth is definitely on its last legs.'

'Yeah, and Duplico is made of green cheese.'

Zoe carried on reading.

'Over the last twenty years we've noticed a rapid increase in the level of harmful chemicals, and the hole in Earth's ozone layer just keeps on growing. Climactic changes have already started; icebergs and glaciers will melt, followed by widespread flooding, droughts and crop failures.'

'Yeah, so what's new, it's always been that way in Africa.'

She turned to Ian. 'This is serious stuff, you should read it.'

'To be honest, I can't be bothered, just read it out.'

'The last bit goes like… 'This man-made hole in the ozone layer will ultimately lead to the death of planet Earth, and will kill off any Earthlings that haven't already died from chemical poisoning. Birds, the first casualties, have been arriving here in ever increasing numbers.' She looked back at Ian. 'So, what do you think?'

'I don't believe Earth's dying.'

At that moment, Jodie returned to the waiting room. 'She wants you next Carl.'

He immediately sprang up, almost went flying over a chair leg.

Ian shook his head, looked at Zoe and laughed. 'Bet he's at the doc's before the week's out.'

She smiled back. 'Yes, and maybe before the day's out.'

What's going on, she thought, *Ian laughing was something rare without a bottle of booze, and Carl chasing nurses — totally out of character. Jodie acting as if she were a seductress, making a move on H, that was something major. Everybody seems to have gone funny in the head,* she concluded.

'How was it in there?' Ian asked.

'She just put my ID card in a pad and emailed a copy to Fort Locks; a few minutes later she got a printout and sent me back here.'

Carl arrived back with a smug look on his face. 'She's gorgeous.'

After Zoe and Ian had their turn, Homer came in and handed them an envelope each. 'Your job choices, you have until Tuesday to pick one of the two. Then on Friday you go to meet your employers and start work on the following Monday.'

'Supposing the interview goes wrong?' Zoe said.

'There is no interview; the jobs are automatically assigned to you.'

'Even if we don't want the work?' Carl asked.

'Well, the computer used your own minds to come up with the most suitable work. Wait until we're in the chopper then open your envelopes, see what you think.'

On the forecourt, the charming blond nurse waved goodbye and blew a kiss to Carl.

'So that's why you took longer than everyone else,' Zoe quipped.

'Yep, I've arranged to meet her.' Carl threw a triumphant fist in the air.

Homer turned to him. 'Erica taken a liking to you?'

'She's coming to the village next Friday.'

'Yes, I know, she's booked into the Swan with her partner.'

'Her partner?' Carl screwed his face up.

'Yes, her regular partner, they've been coming to the Swan once a month for a couple of years now.'

'What's the attraction then?' Jodie asked, in an upbeat voice.

Homer turned to her and smiled. 'The attraction is the monthly show. Reno Salvos sings at the Swan, Friday and Saturday night once a month.'

'Do we need tickets?'

Homer smiled at her again as the chopper took off. 'Yes, love, and you're invited… better open your envelopes now.'

14

Meanwhile, at the farm, Emma sat outside with Katie, eager to hear her plan.

'Supposing I told you that I work in Forensic Science? Monday will be the start of my fourth week.'

Emma raised her eyebrows. 'Never?!'

'True, that's what the assessment centre threw up, crime or counselling. I couldn't believe my eyes when I saw the printout; I'd always fancied myself as an undercover detective.'

'No mention of farming or the jewellery trade then?'

'Thank goodness no. I once did a twelve month course in counselling and then two years on forensic, they must have picked up on it.'

'You're not trying to tell me that they use forensics to track down litter louts?'

'I wouldn't put it past them; no, it's a bit more gruesome. Where do you think I work?'

Emma shook her head, grinned and looked her in the eye. 'A forensic scientist, I just can't believe it.'

'I work on Ungad, normally three days on site, two days at the lab.'

'How do you get there?'

'The shuttle, it takes me five minutes to walk to the cavern, where the converter is, less than a minute to arrive on Ungad, then fifteen minutes to head-quarters.'

'Who looks after the farm?'

'A man from the village, Bill, but there's not much work on the farm, a couple of cows, a few sheep, my pet goats and a few hens.'

'I've not seen him yet; is he hiding or what?'

'I hardly see him myself; he keeps the place tidy though.'

'Okay, brains, how can we find Alistair? How many halls and mansions do you reckon there are here?'

'Too many, but there is an easier way to find Alistair.'

'Go on.'

'This is my plan; if you give me your ID card I'll take it to Ungad on Monday and email a copy to Fort Locks. That will give us his location when he arrived on Duplico.'

'So simple?'

'I'll have to answer five questions. I know four of the answers, your date of birth, date of death, and your husband's name—'

'Forget that,' Emma cut in, 'I'm not looking for Gavin.'

'It's one of the questions, if you had a husband give his name, whether you're looking for him or not. The next question says, if you're looking for a partner-lover give his name, then they ask if you had a favourite pet, and to give a name.'

Emma gave her an odd look. 'How do you know all this?'

'A couple of friends at work, they did it when they arrived here.'

'And did they find their loved ones?'

'Yes, but they were living on Extungad, so my friends let the matter drop, even though they both had access permits for Extungad... I've forgotten your dog's name.'

'That's because I didn't tell you, but he was called Pal, a strapping Alsatian, I loved him to bits and he loved me.'

'Emma, you're crying.'

'I'm okay, honest.'

'Do you know, Emma, I think I'm almost as interested as you are in finding Alistair.'

On board the chopper, the only sound apart from the noise of the rotors, was the tearing of envelopes.

'Yippee!' Zoe made everyone jump. 'Modelling or acting, and I wanted to do both.'

'That's good, because you're the most stunning girl I've ever seen,' Homer said.

'Thanks, H... What you got Jodie?'

'Classical music or sport, namely golf. How do they know?'

'The computer analyses your mind-disc from birth to present day and misses nothing. It never gives anyone the wrong job choice; we don't have any unhappy workers on Duplico.'

'I'm a domestic electrician or a computer programmer,' Carl said, 'and I've never changed a plug or touched a computer.'

'No matter; after twelve months in college, you'll be an expert in one or the other.'

Zoe looked at Ian. 'Well?'

'Agriculture or the River Board... Well what do you know...'

'That we'll probably never see you—'

'On Friday,' Homer cut in, 'you need to make your way to your places of employment for the introductions. Before then, I'll show you how to operate the Sedan cars.'

'Some of us can't drive,' Zoe said.

'They're self-drive; you can sit and watch TV, play a computer game or take in the countryside.'

Homer hovered the chopper above the Swan then landed gently on the roof.

Fiona met them in the bar lounge. 'Your cases have arrived. Yours are in your room, Jodie; the rest have been delivered to your homes.'

Jodie ran upstairs, the others made for the door.

Zoe ran across the village, her gran was watering the garden. 'Slow down, slow down, you'll meet yourself coming back if you're not careful.'

'Has my stuff come, gran?'

'Yes, but get something to eat first; you must be starving. There's some broth and dumplings on the stove; it'll fill your tummy, make your hair shine and make your skin glow.'

'Thanks gran, you're too kind.' (Though it was a perfect salad day and Zoe was sweating.)

It seemed crazy to start eating hot food, but not wanting to upset her gran, she ladled a bowl of broth into a deep bowl and took it to her room, sampling it on the way. She sat on the edge of her bed, 'Jesus, this is good.' For a moment, she was torn between the broth and opening her cases. She put the bowl on the bedside table and proceeded to open the cases while spooning in the broth, but the cases won in the end and she left some broth to go cold.

I can't wait to try on the new outfits. There were clothes that she'd not seen before. *I'm a model now, I've got to act like one,* she said to her image in the mirror. *You look gorgeous baby, give us one more twirl; we want to see those long legs. Yes, well you can talk to my agent about that.* Not only did the clothes transform her body, they transformed her way of thinking.

She went downstairs and crept past her grandmother who was now asleep in the rocking chair. Once outside, she walked confidently across the village to the farm and knocked on the caravan door. 'Ian, can I come in?'

The caravan door swung open. 'Come in, what do you want?' He spoke with his back to her.

'What do you think?' He turned round as she did a twirl, 'You like the outfit then?'

He took one glance and quickly looked away, went to his desk and began messing with some papers, but she could see he'd changed colour. 'You don't approve.'

'First time I've seen your bare shoulders… and wearing a skirt.'

'What's that supposed to mean?'

'Nothing; It suits you, you look sexy.' He put one lot of papers in a pile then moved them to another pile and then seemed to get them all mixed up and started again.

'From a week come Monday I'm a model, these are the type of clothes I'll be wearing.'

'Good for you,' he turned and eyed her over, 'but I prefer you in your lumber-jack shirt, combat trousers and boots.'

'Oh, Jesus, what do you like? You never notice me whatever I wear.'

'Yes, I do Zoe. You're a real outdoor girl, and you were about to take up fishing.'

'And you were to be my tutor. I still want to go fishing, nothing's changed.'

'It will change though once you're a big-time model.'

'Don't be silly, I haven't even started yet, and what makes you think I'll be a hit?'

'Everything about you, and the mind-disc is never wrong; H told us.'

'Oh, so we're using the mind-disk now. I'm only interested in your real thoughts.'

'Zoe, my mind's gone blank; I can't look at you and talk at the same time.'

'Okay, I'll do the talking. Do I look lovely, glamorous, gorgeous or stunning?'

'All four.'

'You said I looked sexy so that makes five, I'll give you my five. You look hand-some, attractive, electrifying, kissable and arousing.'

'Do you know, Zoe…?'

'Yes, go on.'

'I can't wait for my fishing rod to arrive.'

'My, oh my, I wish I could get a copy of your mind-disc. Come on I'll take you for a drink.'

As they neared the Swan, they saw Carl sitting outside on his own. 'Hi, Carl, where's Jodie?'

He eyed her from head to foot. 'What an incredible makeover… She's in her room.'

'I think I'll join her, see you in the bar shortly.'

Opening the bedroom door, she found Jodie sat on her bed.

'God, you look beautiful. Where did the clothes come from?'

'Found them in an extra case. You all right Jodie?'

'So, so. I was watching the telly with Carl and he tried it on with me, it was embarrassing.'

Zoe laughed. 'He wouldn't know what to do.'

'He's changing fast, and he's arranged to see that nurse Erica here next week.'

'I know, but I can't imagine it. Mind you, when he saw Fiona in that dress he went all googly-eyed.'

'I know, he's become randy all of a sudden, that's why I made him leave the room.'

'So, if you'd thought he just wanted a kiss, you'd have let him stay?'

'Maybe, mind you, if H had been here instead of Carl, I'd definitely have let him stay; he's gorgeous.'

'Yes, but he's married.'

Jodie's face glowed. 'Not happily though.'

'Really, what makes you think that?'

'He told me.'

'Well, in that case you need to keep clear of him.'

'I know, but I'm not bothered. Guess what? Your new speedboat's coming tomorrow morning.'

'Who says?'

'H. He had a phone call, all the diving and snorkelling gear should come with it.'

'Brilliant. Fancy a splash then?'

'I do, and the water's much warmer here.'

'Good, I'll see if I can tempt Ian into some diving gear; you and Carl can snorkel.'

'Okay by me.'

An hour later, as they sat by a window in the bar lounge, Zoe noticed a scruffy-looking man approach Fiona and ask for a coffee.

Homer, setting eyes on him, seemed livid and rose from his stool at the other end of the bar. 'What are you doing here? Why have you left your room?'

'Just wanted a coffee.'

'Get yourself back to your room, and press the buzzer next time.'

'Sorry Captain.' He picked up his coffee and made a quick exit.

'When are they going to Ungad?' Fiona asked, in an abrupt manner.

'Soon as possible, Wednesday at the latest.'

She put a glass under the 'Indiana' nozzle and poured a double. 'They're a bloody nuisance; I'm fed up with them.'

'Tuesday then.'

She took a sip of the Indiana. 'Why the bloody hell can't you take them now?'

'Okay, I'll take them after dinner.'

Homer joined Jodie and Zoe. 'Sorry about that, we have two salmon poachers awaiting deportation to Ungad. I'm afraid my wife is heading in the same direction and I'm helpless to stop her.'

Jodie gave him a sympathetic look. 'She did something wrong?'

'Outbursts in public normally get you a crime point, becoming an alcoholic gets you three. People are beginning to wonder why she's still here. I just can't send my own wife back to Ungad, not when I spent years getting her out of there. Hope you're not getting a bad impression of our planet.'

In full view of Fiona, Jodie put her hand on his. 'That's okay, don't worry about it.' Zoe kept her eyes on Fiona, it was as if she approved, or her mind was elsewhere.

As Homer left the room, Ian and Carl came in from the beer garden.

Zoe smiled at Ian. 'We're going diving for salmon tomorrow, but you don't need to come if you don't want to.'

He burst out laughing. 'Diving for salmon, there's little hope of that; you won't get near them.'

'So is that a no then?'

'Not unless you happen to have a boat, some diving gear and a spear-gun.'

Jodie tapped him on the shoulder. 'She has.'

'Oh, in that case, I might give it a go.'

'I fancy a bit of snorkelling,' Carl said.

Zoe gave him an inquiring look. 'Sure that's all you fancy?'

'Yeah, well, Jodie keeps giving me the eye, and Fiona—'

Jodie slapped his arm. 'You've changed so much Carl.'

'Well, you've changed from what you were on Earth, but my chances have dwindled since H came along.'

Zoe interrupted, 'Everybody she meets is in with a chance now.'

Jodie frowned at her. 'I don't think so.'

Carl and Ian went to prop up the bar.

'Keep quiet Jodie, let's listen.'

'Hello, Carl, what can I do for you?' Fiona gave him a solicitous look.

'Two large Ambries please.'

'I need your card first.'

He passed his card over. 'First time I've used it.'

'You've got the best type of card in Thrastdale'

'How come?'

She pulled her shoulders back, flaunting her cleavage. 'You have unlimited access.'

'What about me?' Ian asked.

'Same as Carl, unlimited access.'

Zoe nudged Jodie and laughed. 'Well she won't be accessing Ian's body; he views girls as if he's a detective on a case, and they won't get any favours throwing themselves at him.'

'Well, you should know.'

'Tell me about it, but in future I'm going to play hard to get...' She turned her ear to the bar.

'Forget the Ambries, could we have two double whiskies instead?' Carl asked.

'Yes, no problem.'

'Cards with unlimited access…?' Ian queried.

'Just for alcohol, for one week; it applies to all newcomers, after that, if the limit is exceeded the card rejects payment. Only a captain can endorse your card to exceed the limit.'

'Well, we'll worry about that in a week's time,' Carl said.

Zoe went over and touched Ian. 'Right, I'm going. I'll sort out the boat in the morning and meet you all at the harbour at twelve o'clock.'

15

Mid-afternoon on Monday, Emma arrived back at the farm with her job assessment. She found Zoe playing with a rabbit next to the caravan. 'I heard the good news; you're doing a photo-shoot for Verona? I'm happy for you.'

'I'm absolutely over the Mono.'

'Oh, right, so that's what they call it.'

'Officially, but H says everyone calls it the moon and they no longer call the stars sarts.'

'Thank goodness for that, I mean, who'd want to sit under the mono and sarts? Sounds more like a hangover than a romance.'

'Did you read the magazine that Katie bought?'

'Yes. Verona, the most prestigious cosmetic company on the planet are taking on a new generation of models. They opened a new glitzy studio at Inverbess four weeks ago.'

'That's where I'm going, it only takes half an hour on the Sedan Expressway.'

'Hey, I might be travelling with you.'

'I wish!'

Emma pulled out her printout. 'What's that say?'

Zoe put down the rabbit and read the printout. 'Modelling or photography for Verona.' She threw the paper in the air and with tears in her eyes, hugged Emma. 'I've never been so happy, and my new speedboat arrived in the harbour yesterday morning. I took Ian diving.'

'Did he enjoy it?'

'A guy in the harbour confiscated our spear-gun. Ian wasn't happy about that, but he enjoyed seeing all the varieties of fish in their fancy colours.'

Emma looked at the caravan and saw a fishing rod on the hooks.

'Yes, his gear must have arrived while I was at Arimlock and that's his trout rod so I presume he's out salmon fishing. I've never seen anybody so besotted with their hobby.'

'And there's worse to come Zoe, he's taking the River Board job.'

'Well, we won't notice any difference.'

'I'm not too sure about that. Did he tell you which river he would be looking after?'

'This one here I presume!'

'No, similar though, only it's on Ungad, that's where he starts work on Sunday.'

'Great, that's all I need, worlds apart.'

'Absence makes the heart grow fonder you know Zoe.'

'My heart can't get any fonder than it already is.'

'I'm talking about his heart.'

'You think so?'

'Absolutely, you can be in each other's face too much. Let's see what happens when you're doing a gig in another country and he doesn't see you for a while. I bet he doesn't go fishing when you arrive back home.'

'I wish… So when you used to travel abroad, it made your husband really, really, glad to see you?'

'I married a man I didn't love. I could be away for a few weeks and it was as if I'd just been out shopping. I fell in love with someone else, Alistair, and planned to marry him, but he was murdered.'

'That must be awful.'

'It's the worst pain you could suffer, but imagine my delight when I discovered that he wasn't really dead and probably still alive on this planet.'

'He wasn't murdered, then?'

'Yes he was murdered, and we were killed in a car crash, but we're still alive. I won't rest now until I set eyes on him.'

'Alistair, what a lovely name. Think you'll find him?'

'Just waiting for Katie; I'm expecting some news about him.'

'According to Bill, the farmhand, she'll be home at six.'

'Where is Bill?'

'He might have gone fishing with Ian. I must go; I'm taking Jodie and Carl snorkelling. I'll be back to feed the rabbits at six thirty and you can tell me the news.'

Emma went to her cottage, poured a glass of wine and sat outside watching the sea. Nothing came into, or left the harbour. Out at sea she counted three vessels that appeared to be fishing boats, but she'd need binoculars to see what they were actually doing.

She looked over at the sandy cove; the beach was empty apart from Zoe, Jodie and Carl, who were snorkelling.

In the village, she could see every house; the village was deserted apart from a couple chatting at a garden fence and the woman sitting outside the store.

Well I've the best vantage point for people watching, but there's nobody to watch, how disappointing is that? She looked at the sky, but it hadn't changed; there were no clouds of any description.

She looked at her watch, it was ten minutes to six. She decided to meet Katie at the shuttle port and went by way of the harbour.

'You looking for someone?' a man mending some fishing nets asked her.

'Are people allowed in the shuttle port?'

'You see the steps above the cove,' he pointed, 'and the door at the top? That's where they come and go. But it belongs to the Space Agency. You can't go in; you need to see Captain Homer, at the Swan first; that's if he's not commuting.'

'Commuting?'

'Yes, let's see, Waldo does Thursday, Dan does Tuesday, and I think Homer does today, anyway we'll know shortly because the shuttle's due in.'

As he spoke the door at the top of the steps opened. Emma counted eighteen people come through the door, but Katie wasn't among them. She watched the people disperse, and began to wonder if something was wrong, but the door was still open. *Maybe she's chatting to someone inside*, she thought.

The fisherman looked up at the sky and shook his head. 'Could be bad news for somebody, nineteen departed to work on Ungad this morning.'

She rested her chin on her hand and closed her eyes. 'And what does that frigging mean?' she opened her eyes and looked at him.

He raised his eyebrows and gave her a dirty look. 'Pardon?!'

At that moment, she saw Homer come through the door and it closed behind him. 'Sorry, it doesn't matter.' She set off at a fast pace up the hill to the Swan, and sat breathless at a picnic table until he arrived.

'Hello Emma, lovely evening.'

'Is it? Where's Katie?'

'Good question, she wasn't at the pick-up port, could be anywhere on Ungad.'

'Oh, frigging hell.'

'Pardon.'

'I said, frigging hell, and please, don't you start on me.'

'Careful you don't say it in public or you could be in trouble.'

'How many crime points would I get for that?'

'Depends on the situation; better if you forget the word and just keep calm.'

'Oh, great, but a fisherman said it was bad news if all the workers didn't return?'

'Well, on Ungad they have knives, guns, drugs and unlimited access to alcohol, not to mention drugs and the traffic accidents. Sometimes a worker goes missing for various reasons.'

'Please don't say that.'

'It's a fact, but I wouldn't worry too much about Katie, a message from Forensics said she was at a crime scene; she should be home tomorrow.'

'Thank goodness for that.' She dabbed her brow with her handkerchief. 'I'm sure it's gone warmer.'

He glanced at his watch. 'You're right, by one degree, not normally enough to make you sweat though.'

'It is if you rush up the hill from the harbour.'

'You fancy a ride out tonight? You need to familiarize yourself with the Sedans and I'm taking your friends out at seven thirty.'

'Good idea, I'll be there.'

She then returned to the farm, and met Zoe in the garden.

'Katie's not here, nobody's here.'

'I know, she's staying overnight, something's cropped up.'

'No news then?'

'Not a thing, I'm disappointed to say the least.'

'You ever been on a speedboat Emma?'

'Yes.'

'Ever been snorkelling or scuba diving?

'Yes, it's my favourite pastime when on holiday. Why?'

'Super, I've enough diving gear for four, but Carl and Jodie are too scared, they draw the line at snorkelling. You fancy a dive tomorrow?'

'What time we going?'

'Oh thanks Emma, the water is crystal clear, so warm and the sea life is amazing. But while diving yesterday, just off the cove, I saw something that startled me.'

'Not a shark, I hope!'

'Yes, but don't worry they have a brilliant shark-barrier system around the cove and harbour. H told me it's an invisible beam that stuns them if sharks touch it, but first they get a shock that normally sends them away.'

'And what about us?'

'It's the same at this side of the beam, you get a warning shock and soon back off; it made me shudder.'

'Really? I'd like to know more. I'll ask him later.'

At seven-thirty Homer took them to some steps at the far end of the green, which led to an underground car park. There were about fifty identical metallic-blue Sedans, which were more like stream-lined campervans than cars.

Homer opened one of the doors. There was a settee at the back and fixed seating on each side, a coffee table in the middle and a computer on a desk at the front, no steering or driver's seat. 'Who wants to drive?'

'Only Ian can drive,' Carl said.

'Can you all use a computer?'

'I can,' Zoe answered.

'Just.' Emma said.

'No,' Carl said.

'No matter, it's simple. Sit at the computer Zoe, put your ID card in the pad and type in Reno Salvos Club, Arimloch, then click on Express and then click Start. You can come and sit down now.'

Emma went to the computer and watched the onscreen map, the others gathered round.

Homer put his finger on the screen. 'That's the branch road that we're moving along and that's the main express line two miles outside the village.'

'What's the other road?' Emma asked.

'Coast road.'

'Why didn't we go that route?' Zoe asked.

'We'll return that way, and normally we'd go that route. For short journeys, you just type in the address and click Start, but if you want to go via the express, then you click Express first. Right you'd better sit down and hold onto the handles or you'll be thrown backwards.'

The Sedan slowed to a crawl and drove onto a single rail, wheels straggling off the ground.

'This shoots us onto the main express line; we'll be in Arimloch in five minutes.'

Emma kept her eyes on the red light at the side of the track, it changed to green and they hurtled along like a dragster. The main line zoomed into view, where Sedans were spaced at intervals. They hit a gap in the Sedans on the main line with the computer showing two hundred and twenty miles an hour. The scenery sped past as if they were taking off in a jet.

'Hells bells!' Carl began…

'And dynamite!' Ian cut in. 'How did that work?'

Four minutes and twenty miles later, they were on the Arimloch branch road, and pulled into an underground Sedan park just a few minuets later.

'So, it's as simple as that, just remember to plug into the meter before you leave the Sedan. When you return, check the mileage meter and jump in a Sedan with enough mileage showing to get you back. Don't take one with two hundred miles on the clock if you're only going forty.'

'Are there any pubs here?' Carl asked.

'Three or four in the square.'

'We can drive ourselves back, is that okay? Zoe asked.'

'You're free souls, when you're ready to go just type in your address or the Swan and you'll arrive safely in the village Sedan park.'

'We'll see you later then,' Carl said, as he ran up the steps, closely followed by the others.

At the top of the steps, Emma gazed round the town centre. A solitary carved stone belfry tower, with a clock, dominated the centre of the square. Men sat on stone steps surrounding the column. Women sat chatting on benches in central areas with lawns and flowers. More flowers grew in hanging baskets and window boxes on the buildings. Quaint narrow cobbled alleyways led to shops with fruit and fish stalls outside. The square was a mixture of sounds and smells.

At one end of the square, taking up the full width, was a town hall-like building where neon signs, looking distinctly out of place, advertised The Reno Salvos Club. Emma looked at Homer and pointed to a poster. 'That's Elvis Presley.'

'No, it's Reno Salvos, the owner of the club, he's a brilliant singer.'

'Absolutely, so Elvis is alive after all, and living on this planet.'

'You knew him on Earth?'

'Everybody on Earth knew of him; he was a megastar.'

'He's mega rich, I can tell you that much, and most of the famous people from Earth normally change their names after arriving here.'

'Katie said he owned the village, where does he live?'

'Two miles away, in a mansion that could accommodate everybody in the village.'

'Oh, right.'

'You staying Emma, or coming back with me?' he said, with a glint in his eye. She'd seen it before and didn't fancy the idea of just the two of them on a settee in the Sedan.

'Think I'll have a walk around town, see what the kids are up to.'

'We could take the coast road, some nice stopping-off places.'

'I'm sure there are and I'll see them on my way back later.'

16

Tuesday afternoon after the scuba diving session with Zoe, Emma showered, then glanced at her watch, just in time for the six o' clock shuttle. She went outside and kept her eye on the cavern door. This time Katie came out with the others. Emma went to the garden gate to meet her. As Katie drew closer, she smiled and waved a sheet of paper. 'Got the address!'

Emma gave her a big hug. 'Thanks, you don't know what it means to me… I daren't look.'

Katie passed her the email printout. 'It's not far from where you're going on Friday.'

'Oh, great, well, I won't be waiting until Friday.' She read the printout, *Last known address, the Hilltop Inn, Loch Bess.* 'Is that it?'

'Yes, they don't give much away.'

'Not even a name!'

'Nope, they expect you already know it, and of course, you should recognise the person when you knock on the door.'

Emma cupped her face in her hands, looked at the sky and said nothing, thinking of that knock on the door. However, if it were an inn she could just walk in and surprise him. *Wouldn't that be the best day of my life? — she smiled to herself — or my death?* 'I'm going in the morning.'

'Let's go inside and open a bottle of wine, I'm pleased for you.'

At that moment, they heard Zoe, singing and humming behind them. 'Hi everybody, any news?'

'Yes, one of your rabbits had babies, you've now got six,' Emma said.

'Honest?'

'Go and have a look, and if you want a glass of wine come inside after.'

Katie poured three glasses of wine, then went through a pile of maps, pulled one out, and spread it on the kitchen table. 'This is the one we want.' She traced her finger over the map.

'Can't see it though, but it must be on here somewhere.'

Just then, Zoe came in. 'They're lovely, and so cute. Sorry, what you looking for?'

'Hilltop Inn,' Katie said.

'Well, it won't be down there next to the water.'

'You find it for us Zoe; I can't think straight,' Emma said.

'The brown bits are the mountains, so it won't be up there, must be lower down… There it is, just above Loch Bess.'

'Ski lifts nearby?' Emma queried.

Katie topped up her wine. 'Yes, there's snow on the mountains even in summer I'm told, and the place has the highest rainfall in the country. It's only a hundred miles away; yet we are in the driest and warmest area.'

'Is that where your man lives then?' Zoe asked.

'Yes, and I'm going tomorrow, fancy a run out?'

'Please.'

'Wish I could come with you,' Katie said, 'Ian and the others might want to go though.'

Wednesday morning Zoe and Carl met her at the Sedan park. Emma typed in the address, via the expressway.

Half an hour later, the Sedan turned up a private road; a sign said: *Hilltop Inn - 20 miles.* Emma was quiet, playing with strands of her hair, the other two were chatting away, but she wasn't listening her mind was elsewhere. A picture of Alistair kept flashing at her; she began to wonder if this was the right way to go about it.

Maybe I should have written him a letter or phoned; maybe he has a girlfriend or married even… She tried to brush the thought away.

'We'll be there in a few minutes… You look worried, Emma.'

'Absolutely, to say the least.'

At that moment, the Sedan pulled up, making a bleeping sound. Zoe jumped up and went to the computer. 'It says rock fall, road closed. Make detour, yes or no.'

'Shit, click yes.'

The Sedan turned round, and took them to a boatyard on a canal side and pulled in. A man knocked on the window. 'Yes, I know,' he said, 'you're going to the Hilltop, but the road's closed and you want a boat.'

Emma gave him a strange look. 'Do we?'

'Well, if you're desperate, there's no other way to get there.'

Zoe gave him a furtive look. 'She's desperate.'

'In that case, stretch your legs and choose a boat.'

They opted for a grand six-berth cruiser and climbed aboard.

'You been on a boat before, you know how everything works?'

'Yes, I'm okay with this,' Zoe said.

'Good, here's a map and the waterway code; waterproofs and life jackets are under the seats. The Hilltop mooring is on the left, about two hours away.'

They set off cruising along the canal.

'Wonder if they have a Loch Bess monster here,' Zoe said.

'Yeah, well if we've got one on Earth I suppose his granddad could be here.'

'We're nearing the canal end, the weather's changing though.' Emma lifted the seats in the cabin and found the waterproofs and life jackets. 'If you're staying on deck you'd better grab a waterproof.'

'Much cooler here.' Zoe shivered.

'I'm not surprised, look at the snow on the mountains,' Carl said through chattering teeth.

Emma eyed the dark clouds coming their way. 'Can't understand it, half an hour ago it was quite warm and cloudless.'

At the canal end, the weather deteriorated, bringing with it a strengthening wind. Two warning buoys marked the entrance of the loch.

'Don't go through there.' Carl was reading the waterway code. 'It's too narrow; the water will be too shallow. Go through the wide gap.'

'I'm supposed to go through the buoys.'

'It's twenty times wider at the other side of the buoys, that must be the right way!' Carl shouted.

'Who's the skipper?!' Zoe yelled back at him.

Emma looked at the codebook, but by then, Carl had persuaded Zoe to go through the wide gap.

They promptly ran aground. At the same time a large wave hit the boat, turned it on its side and threw all three into the loch.

'Hell, I've never felt water so damn cold.'

'Jesus, tell me about it.'

Carl stood speechless, taking in breaths in rapid succession.

Fortunately, the water was only three feet deep.

They managed to push the boat upright, but try as they may, they couldn't budge it off the rocks.

After they'd scrambled aboard again, Emma rang the emergency number on the cabin wall, then grabbed some blankets from the sleeping quarters. 'That was a shock.'

Zoe wrapped herself in a blanket. 'Exactly, must be the melting snow from the mountains.'

Carl, wrapped in two blankets, picked up two broken plates. 'Well, don't just sit there laughing. I can't move without stepping on plates!'

Zoe had a fit of the giggles. 'How come we managed?'

'Yeah, only by walkin' like cats. Come on, help me.'

Within a short time, six sea cadets arrived in two dinghies and towed the cruiser to deeper water, and they continued their journey.

However, the further they went the stronger the wind became. With the wind came the rain and a thick mist, bringing the visibility down to twenty yards, with ever increasing waves.

'Turn back!' Carl pleaded.

'It's all right, this is nothing compared to the North Sea in Scotland; you just keep heading into the waves and you won't capsize.'

Emma could tell that Zoe was surprised at the height of the waves, which by now were higher than the boat, and still growing. The wind had changed to a gale, lashing the waves over the boat. They had to shout over the wind, and the rain was hitting their faces like needles. On top of this the boat seemed to be making little progress. She moved close to Zoe. 'This is frightening.'

'I'm having to fight with the steering; something's not right, there's no power.'

'I've just spotted a harbour, you'll see it when we're on top of the next wave!' Carl shouted.

'You're right; I'll try to edge over.'

The sheltered harbour, in stark contrast, seemed too calm to be part of the same loch. The sun broke through and within minutes, everything around them was steaming.

They discarded the blankets and soaked up the warmth.

Emma glanced at her watch and spread out the map. 'That took us five hours and we still don't know where we are.'

Carl didn't hear; he had his head over the side of the boat throwing up.

Zoe patted his back. 'And nobody to ask… It's as if we're the only boat on the loch… You okay Carl?'

'No, just leave me alone.'

Zoe looked at Emma. 'What do you reckon we should do?'

'Stay put. It's still rough out there.'

Zoe nodded in agreement, jumped off the boat and tied it to a ring on the harbour wall.

Emma followed and stretched her legs on the deserted harbour walkway. After walking fifty yards, she spotted a wooden board fixed to a tree and went over to have a look. The weather-beaten board turned out to be the remains of a sign, but she could hardly make sense of the few faded letters. She called Zoe over. 'What do you make of this?'

'F-o———h -o —e ———t— —n. I've no idea, but there's a Word Master in the boat.'

Zoe returned to the boat. Emma went to the end of the harbour and sat on the pebble beach, wondering if she was doomed never to find Alistair. At that point, she noticed that the wind had changed direction, blowing straight at the harbour. Dark clouds blotted out the sun and the mist rolled in off the loch.

In the time it took her to reach the boat, the waves were a couple of feet high.

Zoe had secured the boat at both ends and she was sitting on a log with Carl, her face beaming. 'Come on get your coats, we're going for a walk. The sign says Footpath to the Hilltop Inn.'

Emma felt her heart thump against her chest. She sat on the log and breathed in deeply.

'You okay Emma.'

'Yes, fine, just give me a minute.'

Zoe stood up. 'Great, can't wait to see your faces.'

Rolling on the waves for five hours had taken its toll on Carl; he walked just behind them, as though he were a worn-out drunk. 'I don't feel sick anymore, but one leg feels shorter than the other.'

They negotiated the footpath that zigzagged up from the harbour and into a thick pine forest.

After the pine forest, they made their way along a cliff top path.

Zoe, by now twenty-yards ahead, turned back to Emma with a startled look. 'Where's Carl?!' she shouted.

'He was here a minute ago. Carl!' she screamed.

Zoe was back at the cliff before Emma's scream had stopped echoing. 'Quick, grab my legs,' she blurted, lying down and shuffling herself over the edge. 'Hold me until I get his hands to the top then grab him, he's unconscious.'

'Shit, I've got his hand!'

'Pull, pull, keep pulling don't let go!' Zoe scrambled to her knees and they dragged Carl clear of the edge and laid him out on the grass.

Zoe felt his pulse. 'Carl, wake up.'

Emma put him in the recovery position. 'I think he's fainted.'

'What's wrong with you lot? Huh… My side's killing me.'

Zoe stroked his hair. 'Nothing's wrong, try standing.'

'Wow, my side's really sore. What happened?'

Emma ran her hands over Carl's ribs. 'Maybe a couple of cracked ribs, but when you see where you've been the pain will ease off.' They held his hands until they were well clear of the cliff.

At the end of the cliff-edge path Zoe took Carl onto an outcrop above the cliff face.

'See that Carl, a five hundred yard long cliff face, with a two hundred-foot drop.'

'Yes.'

'On that cliff face, do you notice anything?'

'Nothing, except for a single tree growing near the top; what's special about that?'

'Tell him, Emma.'

'I'm shattered, you tell him.'

'Well, if I do, he'll faint again. Better if he faints over a beer later.'

'What's all the fainting gibberish?' he mumbled.

'It's so funny,' Zoe said, as they came towards a clearing.

'Yeah, what's bloody funny?'

'Nothing, I was thinking about a cartoon sketch I'd seen somewhere.'

They went through the clearing and, unexpectedly, were in the grounds of the hotel, perched above the loch.

Emma's face dropped, the look of the hotel definitely wasn't worth the effort they'd put in. The ancient doors and windows had bits of paint clinging to bare wood. The surrounding garden would have looked better if left wild.

As they made for the door she felt apprehensive. A hand-painted, lopsided sign over the door read *Sheep Dip Bar.* In the hallway, cobwebs hung on the walls, as if some special decor. Emma stepped back and let Zoe and Carl go in first; as they did, two hens ran out, chased by a piglet. Carl stood there wiping his boots on a wafer-thin mat on the flag floor.

Zoe gave her an odd look; Carl raised his eyebrows.

'This must be the place.' Emma pulled out the e-mail print-out to check, but it didn't make her feel any better.

She inspected the room while Zoe and Carl went to the bar.

A single light bulb in the centre of the ceiling glowed like a small candle. The only other light came from moth-eaten holes in the closed curtains, which were moving in the draught coming from cracks in the Victorian-type windows. She sat down on a stool next to a table with dominoes scattered on it.

Carl gave a huge bell an almighty clang that must have made the mice cover their ears and run for the door.

When the ringing in her ears had stopped, Emma wondered why nobody else had heard the bell. Carl clouted it again. This time, she heard the distinctive sound of clogs clattering on the flag floor and a man appeared. Zoe left the bar, covered her face with her hands and sat with her head hidden behind Emma, giggling. Carl stayed put.

The man took off his cap, scratched his head, replaced the cap and scratched his hillbilly grey beard. He then pushed his thumbs behind two bicycle inner tubes that he used for braces.

'Look what the storm's blown in,' he said.

Carl turned to Emma and screwed up his face, then turned back to the man. 'Can we have a drink?'

The man came to their side of the bar, twanged his rubber braces, whistled "Three Blind Mice" and tap-danced with his clogs as though he was a professional clog dancer. 'What do you think, not bad for an old codger, eh?'

'Yeah, it was great, made me thirsty watching you.'

'Tha needs a drink, young'un, but tha won't get one here.'

'Why?'

'This is back a pub, farmers' side; tha needs ta be next door, it's at front.'

When Emma opened the door to leave, the two hens and the piglet ran back in.

'Thank goodness for that,' she said, as they entered what looked like a different hotel. 'Quite posh really.'

'Yeah, but anything would look posh after a—'

Zoe stopped him from falling. 'When you going to learn how to walk on a carpet?'

He bent down and checked the pile. 'They should have warning signs for carpets this thick.'

A smartly dressed barman with a charming smile greeted them.

Zoe gave him a cheeky grin. 'I brought my friends for a pleasant cruise. You know, sunbathing on the deck, a bit of fishing and some sky diving.'

'Oh dear, you picked a bad day for it; we had a weather warning this morning. They stopped all boating on the loch, just to be on the safe side.'

Emma gave him a surprised look. 'Oh, pity they didn't tell us… But it's made us all hungry; three dinners would be very welcome.'

'No problem.' He gave them a menu. 'Take a seat and I'll send in the chef.'

They sat in a bay window overlooking a blanket of mist below.

'Aren't you going to ask the big question?'

'Not yet. I need a drink more than I've ever needed one.'

'Same here,' Carl said.

She beckoned the barman and ordered a bottle of wine.

Zoe weighed him up as he came towards them. 'I'll ask him if you like.'

'I was going to have a drink first… but go on then.'

A waitress interrupted the barman. 'I'll take their drinks in. Come through to the dining room please. I've put you at a table overlooking the loch, but you can't see anything at the moment.'

'What happened at the cliff? I remember nothing,' Carl asked through a mouthful of roast beef.

'Have more wine first, then you can laugh about it.'

Carl drank half his glass of wine in one go. 'Right, go on then.'

'Well, somehow you either fell, or fainted, off the edge of the cliff.'

'Never!' He turned pale and took another good drink of wine.

'A single tree saved your life; how lucky can you get?'

'Hell!' Wine spluttered out of his nose. 'Don't get me a sweet, please.'

Zoe carried on. 'We're taking a photo of the cliff face, on our way back.'

'I think he's had enough of that.' Emma sipped her wine and looked down at the blanket of mist. 'This is not where you'd ever expect to find Alistair; you'd have to be a complete dropout to live out here.'

Zoe patted her shoulder. 'Loads of people used to drop out of London.'

'Yes, but you don't understand; Alistair was London's top party guy, no way would he be here unless there were a vibrant party going on with two hundred guests.'

Zoe looked around the room. 'You'd probably get sixty in here and maybe hundred in the bar; you could have a good party.'

'Oh, right, and the guests, where would they come from? More to the point, how would they get here?'

'Yeah, easy, call in all the farmers and round up the mountaineers.'

'Quite.'

Zoe finished off her chocolate gateau. 'Jesus, we haven't even asked for Alistair yet, let's go in the bar.'

The waitress began clearing their table. 'I'll bring your drinks through.'

'Thanks.' Emma played with her lips, glanced at Zoe, then the waitress. 'Do you have many parties here?'

'One or two a month. Tomorrow is a big event; it's a five-hundredth birthday party, a surprise do for a farmer.'

Emma played with her glass on the table. 'Could you tell me who owns this place?'

'Jake, that's his great-great grandson, Robert, working the bar lounge.'

Zoe shook Carl. 'Wake up, we're moving.'

Emma went over to Robert. 'Is Alistair around?'

He looked puzzled. 'Sorry?

'Alistair, he's supposed to live here.'

'We don't have an Alistair.'

'Oh... I was led to believe that he lived here.'

'I'll go to the other bar and ask my great-great grandfather if he knows anybody by that name.'

He returned a few minutes later. 'Can't help you I'm afraid.'

Zoe came alongside her. 'Something wrong?'

'No, I feel awful, he doesn't live here.'

Just then, Emma felt something licking the back of her leg, she spun round, an Alsatian licked both of her legs, her arms, then sprang up and put its paws on her shoulders and licked her face.

'You're privileged,' Robert said, 'he normally won't go near anybody.'

'PAL!' she squeezed him, tears of joy filling her eyes.

'He's called Laddie, had him about six weeks. I must say, we can't handle him like that.'

Emma wiped her eyes. 'It's my dog. I lost him six weeks ago.'

Zoe stroked his head. 'What a gorgeous dog.'

'You sure it's yours, lady? We brought him from the kennels at Inverbess; they never said it was a lost dog, can you prove he's yours?'

'I think so. Lay down Pal.' He curled up at her feet. 'Now, you try to get him away from me.'

'Here, Laddie... I said, here LADDIE!'

He whined and began licking Emma's legs.

'Come from behind the bar and try to take him.'

'Thought I had him trained.' He lifted the hatch and made towards them. Pal stood up and bared his teeth, ready to pounce.

'I wouldn't come any closer.'

'That'll do for me lady, I guess he's yours. Do you want to take him now?'

'We hired a boat, but it's broken down.'

'They won't repair it until tomorrow, and by then the road will be open. Would you like a couple of rooms?'

'Thank you. Is Pal allowed in my room?'

'Of course!'

Thursday morning, Emma was up before dawn and took Pal down to the loch. The day broke with a flat calm over the loch. Two eagles soared in the early morning sun; deer drank at the water's edge. It was as though they were in a different place. After breakfast, they headed home in a Sedan.

'Bet you're glad to see Pal.'

'Absolutely ecstatic, but I don't know how it came about. We just have to find Alistair now.'

17

On the journey back to Thrastdale, Pal lay next to Emma's feet and growled every time Carl tried to move.

Zoe tickled Pal's belly. 'Just play with him Carl, he won't bite your hand off.'

'Yeah, I'm full of tricks like that. I'm not stupid.'

'He's growling 'cos he knows you're scared. I used to have an Alsatian, if you let them think you're a wimp, they'll go for you; they use their size to frighten you, but it's all bluff; the smallest dogs are the worst.'

'Yeah, but they've only little teeth.'

The Sedan drove into the underground park and pulled into a parking space.

'That was great, I do like these things, and you don't even need to pass a test.'

'Absolutely, and no bad drivers, no good drivers, and no road-rage.'

'Yeah, and they all go at seventy miles an hour and it's impossible to crash.'

Emma nodded. 'I know. Right, I must go. See you later in the Swan maybe.'

At the farm, Katie was sitting in the garden. 'Hey, he's a beauty, where did you find him?'

'This is Pal, my dog, that Gavin killed on Earth. He was at the address you gave me.'

'What about Alistair?'

'They got it half right, Pal was living there; I'm quite pleased. You'll have to send them another e-mail.'

'Can't, you're only allowed one.'

'Tell them they sent me to the wrong place.'

Katie shook her head. 'Really, they won't buy that.'

'Love for a dog is not the same as love for a person; maybe it was a computer error.'

'They won't buy that either. We might end up being sent to Ungad; they'll treat it as a serious malfunction of the computer and check it out.'

'What do you mean, we?'

'They'll find out that I used your ID card. In fact, that's a six crime pointer; we'd both go to Extungad. It could take twenty years to work your ticket back here, that's providing you weren't murdered in the meantime.'

'Right, better forget that then.'

Katie went to the wine rack. 'Fancy a nightcap? I've some white in the fridge.'

'Yes, fine.'

'While I'm at lunch tomorrow, I'll make some enquiries. If necessary, we can go through every hall in the country, eliminating them one by one. I can only do it in my spare time at work though, but a couple of workmates will help me.'

'Thanks, Katie.'

'We'll start at the southern tip and work our way through the country from there. It could take quite a while; we're not looking for a serial killer. We've no backup team, it's a single-handed job.'

'What else can we do though?'

'There is another way, and it's the one that I think will save us from prating about here, there and everywhere.'

'Carry on.'

'You'll probably hit it off at Verona. I'm sure they'll use you big time; your face will soon be in the media. Why not let him find you. Why chase him?'

'Sounds okay, trouble is I don't want to go back to modelling, I'm thinking of photography.'

'Well, he won't find you at that side of the camera. If you want my honest opinion I think you're going a bit over the top on Alistair, you want to see some of the captains around here that are single.'

'I know, but why haven't you got one?'

Katie shrugged her shoulders. 'Look at Pal, he's fast asleep, must wonder what's going on.'

'I tired him out on the beach, he enjoyed himself; it's as though we've never been apart.'

'You need to get a form off Homer; you might have second thoughts when you see all the regulations for keeping a dog. I reckon you've broken a few already.'

'You're joking.'

'I'm not, they have dog schools and you have to take them from when they're puppies until they are properly trained.'

Emma took a sip of wine and nearly chocked on it. 'Oh, and they all sit in the classroom and be good dogs and bitches, raise their paw to go to the loo?'

'Yes, you have it right; two paws if they're hungry and so on.'

'Right…' Emma topped up her glass and held it up to the evening sunlight, 'Tell me, what percentage is this stuff?'

'Listen, the classes are for the dog owners; they have to know exactly how their dog's brain works, what the signs are.'

'I wondered what Pal was playing at. Why don't they just give the dog a mind-scan, then stick it on the computer for everyone to see?'

'They do, and so I'm told, there are islands on the other planets where dogs and gorillas are completely in charge of the humans.'

'Really? I wonder how that works.'

'I don't know; I haven't been there yet. Okay, I'm off to bed. I won't see you in the morning, so good luck at Verona studios.'

'What should I do with Pal? I can't leave him in the cottage all day.'

'He can have the goat pen; the goats can go in the field.'

'Great, he will like that, thanks Katie.'

Friday, Emma was home at five thirty and sat in the kitchen waiting for the shuttle to arrive, hoping for some good news.

Just after six, Katie arrived. 'It took three of us in our lunch break using the Forensics computer, to eliminate fifty addresses.'

'That was good going.'

'Think so? There are twenty-three thousand, six-hundred and forty cities, towns and villages, most of them with one or more halls, mansions, or a stately home.'

'Wow; where did you find that info?'

'A forensics guide to stately homes and mansions covering the country.'

'Eliminating fifty in your lunch break is not so good then.'

'Well, at that rate, we could be giving up our lunch break for ten years, and we do spend half our time away from the labs. So we can't do it that way. My friends would help for a couple of weeks, that's all I dare ask for.'

'It's okay, thank your friends for me.'

'I will… So, how did you get on at the studio?'

'I was chosen to launch their new perfume but I turned it down, it's too big. I'm doing their new beachwear range instead. As it happens, I did Zoe a big favour; out of the other fifty girls that turned up, she qualified, one of five short-listed. They'll pick the winner of the contract next week. The winner will become the new Verona perfume icon.'

'I'm glad for you both, beachwear is a good choice for you Emma; it got you noticed before.'

'I know, that's why I decided to forget about the photography… And guess what? Zoe and I will be partying next week. Meetings with modelling agents and advertising executives; they said it was going to be a huge launch. We're off to Donlon on Wednesday.'

'That's London in our vocabulary.'

'Right.'

'Whereabouts in Donlon?'

'Sordwin. We log on to Charlene o-three-six-four on the Sedan computer, and when we leave the expressway we'll pull up alongside her in the Sedan park, she'll take over from there. As our chaperone, she'll fill us in before arriving at the place. So we don't feel lost; she'll see to everything, make all the introductions and so on.'

'Great.'

'It's mega; you should've seen Zoe hugging everyone and jumping for joy. You'd think she'd won the contract. If she does I just hope she can cope; from nobody to a hell-raising social life is one hell of a leap.'

'Well, it was her dream on Earth; let's see how she copes with the reality... I did the Verona family at lunchtime and, after a dozen phone calls eliminated them. They have two stately homes and three mansions in this country, and various residences abroad.'

'Are there any in London?'

'Yes, two stately homes on the outskirts; Sark Hall at Sordwin, owned by Lord and Lady Verona... Sordwin... did you get it...? That's Windsor. All this playing around with words is so that we won't confuse Earth with Duplico, but it's so stupid.'

'And the other?'

'Yes, the other, I think you'll get this one, Stock Lock Hall near Rombley.'

'Absolutely, Lockstock Hall near Bromley, oh right.'

'Well, don't get too excited, the present owner is Earl Verona, he's been there since sixteen-eleven.'

'And?'

'I didn't speak to the Earl, he's a recluse, and according to his butler, they've had no visitors at the hall in over ten years, let alone anyone staying there.'

'What a rotten shame, Alistair would go mad if he knew.'

'He probably doesn't want to know, that's why he's not there.'

'So this place where I'm going, any info on that?'

'Lord and Lady Verona live alone, apart from an army of staff. I spoke to their secretary. In the last six weeks they'd had a party virtually every night she told me, and there were some overnighters, but no long stays.'

'Sounds a nice place.'

'Yes. Now you're going into the fashion industry I think Alistair will find you. Presuming he wants to of course.'

'Well, he spent eight years of his life on Earth wanting to. I'd like to see his face when he sees me in the media here on Duplico.'

'If he does find you, I'd still play hard to get, pretend you're not interested; don't just give yourself over to him.'

'Okay, supposing I wasn't here and he walked in, I bet you'd give yourself over to him.'

'I bloody well wouldn't!'

'Yes you would.'

As Emma slowly described him in detail, Katie went to the wine rack, opened a bottle and filled two glasses.

'I never saw a female shun him, including lesbians.'

Katie studied the ceiling, the walls and the floor. Then, with an excited look on her face, she took a long sip of wine and said, 'Emma, you've just got my juices going, I'll definitely start going out more. I've noticed a captain that goes in the Swan every other night at nine o'clock.'

'Good. So I got you going just by describing Alistair?'

'I don't know how you kept off him for so long… This captain, he always stops for a moment and looks out at the farm.' She took another long sip of wine. 'Sometimes, he sits in the beer garden for a while. He's called Richard; I asked Homer about him.'

'Great, all you have to do is start going in the Swan then.'

❧

At seven o' clock, Zoe entered the Swan with a big smile on her face. She went to the bar and prodded Jodie who was sitting on a barstool. 'Guess what?'

'You might be a model for a new perfume.'

'How did you know?!'

'We knew at lunchtime, somebody rang Homer, all the village knows.'

'Yes, well, I'm glad to be in the top five, can't think beyond that. Verona is the very best in cosmetics; they have all the top models, but they want a new face to launch the new perfume.'

'What's it called?'

'Nobody seemed to know, but the girls I talked to said it would be like Christmas when it hit the stores, but very expensive.'

Jodie screwed up her face. 'I'll just rub up against you then.'

'Don't worry, I'll get you some; you'll have Homer slobbering all over you.'

Jodie's eyes lit up. 'Oooh, thanks.'

'Don't get me wrong Jodie, thing is he's married, and twice your age if not more.'

'I know, but I don't care… Guess what, you're going fishing with Ian tomorrow, and I'm playing golf with Fiona and Carl.'

'I'll say one thing, you get some good inside info.'

'I told him you liked fishing, he's sorted some gear out for you.'

'Good thinking.'

Ian and Carl came from the games room. Zoe told them about Saturday's agenda.

'Fishing, that'll do me.'

'I can stand a round of golf,' Carl said.

Carl and Ian went to the bar.

'Hello Carl, your friend's here with her partner; they've gone to change for dinner, then they're watching the show.'

'Is Homer staying?'

'No, he'll be away all night.' She gave him a wry smile. 'I hate sleeping on my own.'

Carl locked his eyes on her. 'Yeah, so do I, how about—'

'Two large Ambries please,' Ian cut in.

'Okay, but take them through to the dining room.'

'I'm disappointed,' Carl said, as they made their way to the dining room.

Zoe glared at him. 'Why?'

'Well, Erica said she'd meet me here, but she's brought her partner with her. She gave me the impression she was single.'

'Oh, really, well you'll be busy with Fiona I guess.'

'Evening folks,' the waiter greeted them in the dining room, 'you're by the window.'

The waiter passed Carl a note. Carl scratched his head then read it out. 'See you both in the function room at nine o'clock, Erica.' Bewildered, he looked at the waiter. 'Where's the function room?'

'Downstairs, the couple finished dining just before you arrived sir. They've gone to Arimloch.'

'With her partner then?'

'Yes,' then looking back over his shoulder, 'if it's any help, sir, they slept in separate beds.'

Ian, taking a sip of his drink, coughed, and it spluttered out of his nose.

At that point, Fiona came to their table. 'I've finished, Brenda's taken over the top bar. Enjoy your meal; I'll see you guys later downstairs.'

Zoe gave Ian a puzzled look. 'The note says see you both later, what's all that about?'

He shrugged his shoulders. 'Don't ask me.'

'You better not freak me out with some other girl.'

Carl cut in. 'Come on let's go to the function room.'

A rendition of "Jailhouse Rock" came from the stage as they made their way downstairs.

'Look who's on stage,' Zoe said as they entered. 'White suit: black shirt, suede shoes, same face, same hairstyle and the same voice. It's incredible; just like your Elvis posters, Jodie.'

'And the same gyrating body.'

'It's too noisy for me, I'm going to the top bar,' Ian said.

'I think I'll join you.'

'And me,' Carl said.

In the bar, they immediately spotted Erica talking with another girl.

'Hi guys, you haven't met my friend Sarah, she's a model.'

'Hello… Sarah.' Carl glanced at Ian with a puzzled look and then turned to Erica. 'Is your partner in the gents then?'

'No, no, I'm single.'

'Pleased to meet you Sarah,' Ian said.

She shook his hand. 'It's my pleasure,' she said in a low soft voice.

Zoe noticed a twinkle in his eye. Sarah was dressed in the most elegant of clothes, with the softest shiny brunette hair, striking hazel eyes and a smile that seemed to captivate Ian.

'Hello Sarah, I'm Zoe, a good friend of Ian's. I'm also a model.'

'Hmm, I thought so, but I haven't seen you around, which agency you with?'

'I'm a beginner, I'm doing a photo-shoot next week for the new Verona perfume.'

'You lucky thing, I applied but was eliminated, Verona don't normally take on beginners. It's the hottest company to work for; perhaps you can give me some tips?'

Zoe shrugged her shoulders. 'I'm here totally by accident.'

'I'll get the drinks in,' Carl interrupted.

'A Guitar and a can of B P,' Sarah said.

'Can a BP...I'm not sure, but a goldfish can fart, I've seen the air-bubbles.'

She gave him a cynical look. 'Oh, you like watching goldfish then?'

He scratched his head and made for the bar.

Jodie bumped into Carl carrying his tray of drinks. 'Hi, we've just been talking to Reno, and it is Elvis, he's gorgeous... Fancy a drink. What's that?' she asked, pointing at a can.

'Can a B P?' he replied.

'Can a B P?'

'Yes it can, and wait until you see some of the other fancy-named drinks. They even have one that's named after Charles Dickens.'

'That sounds fancy.'

'Yeah, but it's just a sweet cider.'

'Oh, I'll try a half when it's Ian's round.'

Fifteen minutes later, Ian picked the tray up.

'Okay, what can I get you then, cans of B P or Guitars?'

'Jodie wants a Dickens cider,' Carl said.

Zoe gave Ian a furtive smile. 'So do I.'

As Ian left for the bar, Fiona arrived and caught them all laughing. 'What's the joke?'

'Oh, it's the drinks, they have queer names,' Zoe said.

Ian returned. 'They didn't have any Dickens cider, I got you Guitars instead.'

'Thanks Ian, I'll just have to manage without,' Zoe said.

'We'll have some on tomorrow,' Fiona said. 'Ian might oblige then.'

'Yes, no problem.' Ian replied.

'Is that a promise?'

'I said no problem; it's a promise. Don't keep going on about it.'

'Thank you, Ian,' Zoe chuckled to herself.

Carl turned to Erica. 'How long you staying at the Swan?'

'We're here until Tuesday, but we'll leave you guys for now, see you all later at the party.'

'Yes, and I've some work to do, I'll meet up with you later,' Fiona said.

Zoe nudged Ian. 'What did you think of the supermodel?'

'Yes…' he hesitated, 'she's very…'

'Go on!'

'She fancies him,' Carl cut in.

'Oh, terrific!'

'He has a mind of his own you know. Calm down, he's spreading his wings.'

'Not with some alien bloody supermodel, he's not.'

Ian butted in. 'You're all talking like I'm not here. Is it okay if I join in the conversation?'

'Depends on what you're going to say,' Zoe retorted.

'Well, I don't belong to anyone, I'm a free spirit.'

There was a long pause. 'I'm going to the powder room.'

Jodie patted her shoulder. 'I'll come with you,'

Zoe stormed off. 'I might go home.'

Jodie caught her up in the loo. 'You'll miss all the fun.'

'If I hang around here, I'll probably spoil it.'

'Just forget about it, let's have a good drink.'

'Okay, you win.'

They bought two bottles of wine at the top bar, each taking a long swig from the bottle before they went downstairs.

Ian suddenly went to the dance floor and started acting daft and making everybody laugh. Carl joined him and they took over the dance floor.

'That's not dancing,' Jodie said.'

Zoe took another long swig of wine. 'No, but it's hilarious. It's called the drunken stupor, a new type of dance.'

Fiona came over to their table and picked up some empty glasses. 'Aren't they a laugh, they won't be fit to walk by the end of the party. I can fix them up with a room now the poachers have gone. You can stay in Jodie's room if you like, Zoe.'

'Fine by me, thanks.'

Fiona took the glasses to the bar.

Jodie kept eyes on her all the way, shaking her head. 'Do you think H will kick her out?'

'Maybe he won't have a choice, whatever she was up to on Ungad. I don't know, but I reckon she's addicted to everything that's going here.'

'I feel tipsy, I'm off upstairs, see you later Zoe.'

Carl and Ian staggered back to the table. Carl fell flat on his face.

'Come on Carl, stand up!' Zoe and Ian helped him to his feet. On standing, he fell again, taking Ian with him; they both lay motionless.

Sarah and Erica helped to lift them into two chairs.

At that point, Fiona came over to help. 'Come on Carl, I'll find something to bring you round.'

'Sure you can manage? Want us to help?' Erica asked.

'I'm fine, I'll help him to his room.' Fiona put her arm around Carl and helped him across the room and out of the disco.

Sarah held Ian's arm. 'What about you? We're going to bed, do you want a lift?'

'I'm... okay... No...'

Sarah kissed him on the cheek, Ian fell back in the armchair and promptly fell asleep.

Zoe shook him. 'Ian, wake up, or I'll get mad.'

'Where am I?'

'You're on another planet, come on, wake up, I'll take you to your room.'

She got him to his feet and helped him upstairs. 'Got the key? The door's locked.'

'What key?'

'Somebody's locked the door. Okay, you'll just have to sleep on the floor in Jodie's room.'

'Don't keep waking me up then,' he said, in a slurred voice as she opened door.

Jodie's bed was empty. *Must be still out*, she thought.

Ian fell onto Jodie's bed and closed his eyes. Zoe sat on the spare bed, watching him.

Just then, she heard the toilet flush in the bathroom. Jodie opened the bathroom door, took one look at Ian and burst out laughing.

She looked at Zoe and covered her face with her hands. 'What's he doing here, and how did you manage to get him up here?'

'Easy, he got drunk, and he's locked out of his room.'

Jodie raised her eyebrows. 'When I passed by I heard voices; it sounded like Fiona with Carl.'

'Yes, Carl was blind drunk so Fiona took him to his room. Watch this Jodie...' She went to Ian and gave him a lingering kiss.

Jodie laughed aloud. 'What're we going do? I need my bed.'

'This is my plan. We undress him and put him in the spare bed with me.'

'You wouldn't dare... Well...yes, I suppose you would; I'm not sure I want to see him in the nude though.'

'Just help me undress and move him. We'll leave his underpants on. I'll take them off when I get in bed with him.'

'All right, but it's your funeral.'

'Or my wedding!'

18

Saturday morning, Homer knocked on the bedroom door at six o'clock. 'Fifteen minutes Zoe; I'll meet you in the studio.'

Ian, slowly stirring, put his warm hand on her bottom, and quickly withdrew it. 'What's your bum doing in my bed Carl?'

'Jesus, do that again Ian. By the way, it's Zoe,' she whispered in his ear.

'You're jesting! What am I doing in your room?'

'More to the point, what have you been up to in my bed?'

Ian retrieved his briefs from the floor and put them on under the duvet. Then he collected his other belongings strewn around the room. 'Okay, I can't remember a thing about last night, what happened?'

'Thanks Ian, it was fantastic.'

He made for the door, speechless, checked the corridor and ran over to the spare room.

Zoe went to the bathroom and shut the door on Jodie's loud snoring. 'Fishing, okay, but why six o'clock in the bloody morning? she said to herself. She hardly dared look in the mirror; she knew her eyes had lost yesterday's sparkle.

She turned on the hot and cold taps and dabbed her eyes, first in hot, then cold water. She did this for a few minutes then looked in the mirror; the redness had faded somewhat. *Thanks Emma,* she said to her reflection, *it really works.*

She suspected Ian had gone to the farm for his gear. She was eagerly slipping into a pair of wellies, in a side room off Homer's studio, when Ian strolled in.

'Morning Ian, I see you're geared-up. Zoe tells me she's a learner at river fishing.'

'She'll struggle, but I've found her a small trout fly rod.'

'Well, you've all day in which to turn her into a fly-fisher lady, but there's not all day for her to try on all the various fishing outfits. However, I've just been called out, so I can't come with you today. But I'm sure you don't need me around…'

Zoe, listening to every word in the side room, stopped what she was doing and smiled to herself. *I'm positive that we don't need you around; thank you very much,* she mouthed to a mirror.

'Come on Zoe, there's enough gear in there to fill a fishing tackle shop,' Ian retorted.

Finally, she plumped for an olive sleeveless waistcoat, which complemented her lumberjack shirt and combat trousers. She topped it off with a Robin Hood-style hat with a fancy array of coloured feathers in the side. She bounced out of the room and twirled her new look. 'What do you think guys?'

Ian eyed her over. 'One thing's for sure, if clothes could catch fish, then you're in for a good day.'

'You should catch plenty then too.'

'Come on you two, it's not a fashion show.' Homer led them outside. 'One thing, Ian, you'll notice that your lures are different to the ones that you used on Earth.'

'Yes, they briefed me on it yesterday. I'm a River Board bailiff on Ungad come tomorrow you know.'

'Straight in at the deep end eh, and that's where you might end up.'

'It's okay; I can swim with my clothes on.'

'You won't need to; the poachers take your clothes first then throw you in the river, or shoot you. But good luck in your new venture!'

'Thanks.'

'By the way, if you both come back here at nine, they'll make you breakfast.'

'Thanks again.'

'How far is it to the river?' Zoe asked as they walked through the farmyard.

'Two fields away, why do you ask?'

'Because these wellies are rubbing my feet like mad, I won't make it that far.'

'Nip home for your boots then, I'll wait in the caravan.'

Ten minutes later, she arrived back. 'Can't we fish later? I'm really tired.'

'The salmon won't wait, it's got to be early morning or late evening; they won't bite once the sun's up.'

'We could sleep, then after breakfast go trout fishing on the loch.'

'Okay, you have a sleep, I'll wake you in time for breakfast.'

She stripped off, jumped in his bed and hugged the pillow. She caught a whiff of the mint-scented shampoo that he used; it made her feel close to him. *Wonder if he'll climb in bed when he returns…* She let her imagination explore the prospect as she fell asleep.

She woke to the sound of the door-latch, quickly moved the duvet part way down her back, and pretended to be asleep.

'Zoe… Zoe, come on.'

She lay motionless, breathing deeply, feigning sleep as best she could.

'Zoe.' He put his hand on her back and gently shook her. 'Zoe, are you going to come?'

Jesus, I hope so, she thought.

At that point, he removed his hand. 'I'm going for breakfast.'

She turned over and sat up, exposing her breasts.

For a long moment, he froze; his gorgeous deep blue eyes wide open with shock.

She gave him an alluring smile. 'Are we going to do things?'

His face took on a different colour and he turned away. 'You frighten me Zoe. I'll wait outside while you dress.'

She covered her face with her hands and shook her head. *What am I supposed to do? Am I doing something wrong? You love someone and you've a good idea that they love you, but they run away all the time. How the hell do you turn it round? Go fishing with them I suppose. Yes… why didn't I think of that first thing this morning? Open countryside, fresh air, just the two of us on the riverbank, birdsong for the mood…* She threw on her clothes and rushed out to catch him.

'Sorry if I snubbed you, I had the jitters, ' he said.

She gave him an odd look. 'Why?'

'Two girls once overpowered me when I was ten: they were strong and much older; they held me down on the grass; one sat on my legs, the other knelt on my arms. They were horrible and just did whatever took their fancy.'

'That must have been awful.'

'They terrified me. Eventually I passed out when they forced me to eat live worms and shoved soil in my mouth.'

'They were a right couple of perverts, most women aren't like that.'

'I know, but sometimes I think back to it.'

'Well, you're safe with me. We going on the loch after?'

'If you're up for it.'

She tickled his ribs and giggled. 'You come out with some good ones. Of course, I'm up for it. Why else would I want you to take me fishing? I might catch a big one on my first day.'

'Maybe, but more likely an average size one and probably more luck than management.'

She gave him a cheeky look. 'Really? Hope it's my lucky day then. What type of gear will I need?'

He stopped walking and eyed the cloudless sky. 'Well, I'll probably use a Hairy Mary fly, on a deep sinker fly line then maybe a shooting head fly line, but you'll just use a simple floater.'

'What a clever combination: first, a deep sinker then a shooting head with a Hairy Mary on the end. That should send them crazy.'

He didn't reply, he just marched on in a matter-of-fact way. She watched his face, it was blank and, as usual, oblivious to her comments. *In a way, I like that part of his personality; he's so innocent that you can't help playing on it, but then you feel guilty. He's brainier than the rest, but hardly smiles at a joke, even while others fall about laughing. Yet, on occasions, he comes out with the most hilarious pun, and you laugh tears.*

He stooped down, picked up a small clump of hair and inspected it. 'Badger, I'll catch a sea-trout with that.' He shoved it in his pocket. 'I wouldn't say crazy, but a very successful salmon fly, the Hairy Mary.'

'Well, whoever thought up that stupid name for a fly, must have been married to a gorilla called Mary. The mind boggles.'

'Is that how you see it?'

'Yes, unless she had a beard.'

'No way, she probably had a good head of hair though.'

'I was only joking. His wife was probably quite attractive with hair under her arms, hair on her legs and an untrimmed bush between her legs. These days we don't go in for the hairy look.'

'I don't know about that, but I've trimmed the Hairy Mary down, and it catches the big trout.'

'Good, can't beat a good trim. Let's hope it catches something today then.'

When they arrived at the Swan, Jodie and Carl were in the dining room.

'I just caught the biggest salmon of my life,' Ian declared.

'Okay, where is it then?' Carl asked.

'I put it back.'

'Yeah, some hope.'

'They don't kill the fish here, except the odd one for the table. They don't use hooks either, just Velcro with feathers on, and it works, sticks to their teeth.'

'I bet the fish still won't like it though.'

'Homer's caught the same fish three times in one day. He says they enjoy the struggle, a bit like a dog playing pull and tug with a rope.'

Fiona interrupted. 'You two ready for golf?'

'I can't wait,' Jodie said.

'I've always fancied golf,' Carl added.

'Right, come on we'd better make a move.'

Zoe glanced at Jodie and gave her a cheeky grin. 'Good luck with the golf you two.'

Jodie smiled back. 'And good luck with the fishing.'

After breakfast, Zoe and Ian headed along the bridleway towards the loch.

'I wish I'd left this fishing coat where it was, I've never known it so warm at ten o'clock.'

She took off the coat and hung it on her bag.

Ian stopped and peeled off his coat. 'I reckon there could be a good rise today.'

'Wow, do you really think so?'

'Yep, it's that kind of morning, but by noon it'll go dead.'

'We'll have had a good two hours by then, though.'

He raised his eyebrows and smiled. 'Yes, and with a bit of luck, a nice bag full.'

She looked him in the eye and promptly went into a fit of giggles.

'What you laughing at?'

'Nothing.'

He paused at the end of the bridle-way and gave her a strange look. 'Come on, why were you laughing?'

'I was thinking about us two in bed last night.'

'Okay, here's your rod, let's make a start.'

'It was my first time.'

'Well, we all have to start somewhere. Now, hold the rod straight up.'

'I know what you mean, it's not right when it's bent over.'

'Correct, it must be straight up, that's how the power is unleashed.'

'You mean, like last night.'

'I wasn't fishing last night. Was I?'

'No, you were having sex with me.'

'As your rod comes forwards… What?' He fumbled about in his fly box. 'Here put one of these on. Let's see if you can catch anything.'

'You were good, did you enjoy it?'

'Um…it was all right.'

'Is that it? All right?'

'I mean, it was excellent. Try casting over there.'

'Problem is, you didn't wear a condom.'

'To be honest Zoe, I haven't a clue what you're talking about.'

She was about to complete the con by saying she could become pregnant, but guilt crept in. 'Just fantasizing aloud, that's all, sorry.'

'I know you were; you can't fool me Zoe.'

'Come off it Ian, you didn't know which planet you were on, anything could've happened.'

'Nothing did though.'

'You were unconscious, you can't remember a thing.'

'I know, but I can tell a full bag from an empty one, and nothing had changed.'

'Oh, really?'

'One other thing, while I was unconscious, you spent some time kissing me.'

'Go on, Sherlock Holmes.'

He gave her a wry smile. 'I can still taste your lipstick.'

'Great, what do you think of the flavour?'

'Yes, well…' he surveyed the water, 'let's get started.'

'I'm not bothered about fishing;' I'd rather do some sunbathing.'

'That's a boathouse over there. Sunbathe if you like, but do some rowing in between while I fish.'

As they approached the boathouse, Zoe noted that it was no tin hut affair, but a fancy stone building with lots of ornate features, as if some wealthy person had over-indulged. Inside, a fridge stood in one corner, fishing gear in the other. Ian opened the fridge and took out two bottles of wine, two glasses and a corkscrew. *Compliments of Homer,* a note read.

The rowing boat also turned out to be a bit special, with two padded bench seats across the middle and sunbathing mats at each end. Ian put the wine in a cool-box that was under a seat.

Once out on the loch, he dropped anchor in a likely looking spot.

While his back was turned, Zoe dropped her combat trousers, took off her shirt and, just as he turned, sat down in her underwear. 'You don't mind do you?'

'I'm fishing, you please yourself, but the sun's hot, you'll need sun cream.'

'It's okay; I spotted some oil in the fishing bag.'

'Fish rising all over the place… drat I just missed one.'

A few minutes later, she lay in the back of the boat. 'Ian, just rub some oil on my back, please?'

'Hang on I can only do one job at a time… Got one, it's a good fish too.'

'Well, super-duper!'

The fish snagged his line under the boat and escaped. 'That was some fish, more like a salmon than a trout.'

'Give it a rest Ian and put some oil on me before I burn. Unhook my bra first, I'm going topless.'

To her surprise, he unhooked her without a word of complaint.

Then he smoothed oil on her back with one hand while holding the rod with the other.

'Got one!' He grabbed the rod with both hands. 'Another good fish.'

'Mind if I tell you something? It's about how I'm feeling.'

'Blast, it got away… Pardon?'

'Supposing I said I really love you?'

'Don't talk stupid.'

'It's true.'

'He pointed over the loch. 'Look at that, an osprey just grabbed a trout.'

'I reckon you love me, but you're too shy to tell me… Do you love me or not?'

'Maybe.'

'Is that a yes or a no?'

'I don't know what love is, that's why it's a maybe.'

'Okay, do you have strong feelings for me?'

'Yes, in a brotherly sort of way.'

'But I'm not your sister, so obviously the strong feelings mean something else.'

Just then, she turned over. 'Anyway, what do you think of the body, Ian?'

'Marvellous, and such streamlined plumage.'

'No, I mean this body, my body, not the stupid osprey's. The body that I'll be modelling.'

For a long moment, his eyes examined her figure; a wry smile spread across his face. 'Oh, *your* body, I thought you meant the osprey.'

She slapped his leg then lay on her back. 'You're freaking me out. Right, you can carry on with the oil please. That's if you dare.'

Sweating, he took off his shirt. 'Do you fancy a glass of wine?'

'If it helps things.'

They sat opposite each other on the bench seats.

The first glass went down with Ian talking about fishing, his eyes mainly on the loch. The second glass went the same way. Zoe took it all in with a happy smile; she would change the subject before long.

Not until he was on his third glass did he take a good look at her. Ian flicked his eyes up and down her body then locked eyes on hers and smiled. 'Zoe, you are the most beautiful thing, and I've never taken much notice of you.'

'Tell me about it.'

He ran his hands over his shoulders. 'I can feel my skin prickling, I could do with some oil on.'

'I know, and I'm still waiting.'

They went to the back of the boat; she was about to lie down on the mat when he stopped her. 'You do me first; I'm burning.'

'Drop your pants then and lie on your back.' She chuckled inside; it was an off-the-cuff remark with next to no chance of him responding, but to her surprise, he did. *Wow, where are we going from here?* she wondered.

She straggled his near-naked body and began massaging oil on his chest. He closed his eyes, smiled and ran his fingers over her body. She guessed they were having much the same thoughts.

An hour later, she woke with a start as a ladybird tickled her nose. The boat rocked gently in the warm breeze; their oil-clad bodies lay glistening in the sun. She sat up, feeling ecstatic. *No wonder people make such a big thing of sex,* she thought. *Jesus that was something else, never have I felt like this, never have I felt such pleasure, what a wonderful day.*

She watched Ian wake up, his eyes sparkling. She smiled at him, proudly. 'Aren't you just gorgeous.' There was a long silence as he dressed.

'Thanks… I reckon you're going to make a good fishing partner.' His voice had a modest tone, but his face had the triumphant look that you see on a gold medallist.

'I'm definitely interested in this sort of fishing, I'm well and truly hooked,' she said, pulling on the oars and rowing towards the boathouse.

'Well, you certainly know how to handle the rod.' He gave her a droll smile. 'Wait until you see the evening rise.'

'You mean it gets better?!'

'The fish normally have a mad hour just before darkness falls, they come to the surface to feed; it's called the evening rise.'

'Oh, I thought you meant something else!'

At the golf course, Jodie, after playing two holes on her own, went to drag Carl out of the clubhouse. Fiona suggested she should have a couple of drinks before setting out again. However, before she got chance to answer, Fiona ordered three double brandies, then continued a flirty conversation with the steward, whom she seemed to know well.

Jodie wet her lips and poured the rest in Carl's glass.

'Thanks Jodie,' he said, in a slurred voice.

'Carl what's come over you?'

'If it's on offer you can't turn it down.'

'Yes, but we're here to play golf, not prance about.'

'You make a start, Carl, I'm just having another drink with the steward,' Fiona said.

Jodie spent some time showing Carl how to stand, hold the iron and put the ball on the tee, without him falling over. After a few divots, he managed to get the ball in the air.

A couple of holes later, 'Jodie!' he shouted from the bushes. 'Help me find this.'

'No chance, I'll get Fiona, she's good at finding balls. Anyway I've had enough, she can try playing with you.'

In the clubhouse, Jodie interrupted Fiona's conversation with the steward. 'See if you can do anything with Carl, he's bringing my game down; you'll find him in the bushes at the second hole.'

'Sure, no problem,' she said, in a cheerful voice. 'That's where I usually end up.'

Jodie glanced through the window and watched Fiona swaying up the fairway. 'Glass of fresh orange, please,' she asked the steward. He moved as though she'd asked him to do a day's work, and looking at his appearance, she wondered if he'd seen a mirror lately.

'Fiona's very nice, known her long then?' she asked.

'Yes, we worked the same club on Ungad. She was very popular.' For a moment, he speeded up while he poured himself a whisky.

'You a three star man then?'

'Certainly am, I've been here four months now. Where are you from? How did you meet Fiona?' he asked in a tired voice, looking over her body as if she were a commodity.

'I'm on holiday; I met Fiona at the Swan. She seems to be a celebrity there.'

'That's due to her husband; he's a big shot around here.'

'A top golfer then?'

'No, he doesn't even play. I've never seen them together, he does his fishing and whatever, and she does her own thing.'

'She's very attractive.'

'You're not bad looking yourself.' He topped up his drink from the optic.

'Thanks, but she's much better looking.'

'Well, she was a top paid escort on Ungad, and wealthy until she overdid the drink and drugs. We were going to get married when she went off the rails. He got her back on her feet and she married him instead.'

'Looks as if you're still friends.'

'Only by good fortune and hard work, you see…' He topped his drink up yet again. 'I bumped into a deportee who happened to have seen her. I was already on two stars and put all my effort into getting the other one, and here I am.'

'You've done very well.'

'Yes. Did she say your name was Jodie? I'm Ricky. It's my night off tonight if you fancy a drink somewhere?' he said without a hint of a smile. His bloodshot eyes avoided contact with hers, but he searched the rest of her as if he was looking for something.

'Thanks, but I've an important appointment tonight.' She suddenly felt uncomfortable. 'I'll go see how Fiona and Carl are doing.'

Fiona, looking quite smug, met her on the steps. 'You're right about Carl,' she brushed some leaves off her clothes, 'he seems to like being in the bushes more than on the fairway.'

Jodie looked the other way. 'Yes, part of the learning process I suppose.'

'Well, he's doing okay.'

'Is he? I must have missed something. Where is he now?'

'Still in the bushes by Fairway Two,' she grinned, 'but you won't get much out of him.'

Jodie left her and headed for the bushes, wondering what Homer would think if he knew. *You won't get much out of him, because it's all running down your legs Fiona,* she thought to herself.

She shook the bushes. 'Carl, wake up, what's she done? Drugged you or something?'

He came out, rubbing his eyes. 'Nice golf course.'

'Pity you didn't see much of it. Plied you with drugs eh?'

'You could be right.'

19 Ian and Zoe were first to arrive back at the Swan. Erica and Sarah were enjoying the sun and a cool drink on the picnic benches with Homer.

'Well, how did the fishing go?' Homer asked.

'I got my first ever on a rod,' Zoe replied, smiling.

'Yes, I also caught one.'

'It was a first for both of us, we really enjoyed ourselves.' Zoe tried to keep eye contact with Ian; he avoided hers by watching the birds flitting across the village.

'Good, I'm glad you both enjoyed it. Perhaps you'd like to take Erica and Sarah out on the boat and teach them. They might take to it.'

Ian had a blank look on his face and said nothing.

'Yes, I'm willing, sounds okay,' Sarah said.

'I fancy it, providing it's okay with you Ian?' Erica asked.

'There you are Ian, they're both up for it and you've nothing on tonight. Be a sport.'

Zoe made a quick exit for the loo to let her giggles out.

When she returned to her seat, she gave Ian a questioning look. 'You going then?'

'Looks like being a pleasant night, should be a good evening rise.' Homer commented.

'What's the evening rise?' Sarah asked. 'I'm not too well up on these things.'

'It starts a couple of hours before dark. Ian will show you.'

'What about tackle?' Erica asked.

Zoe looked at Ian and raised her eyebrows. 'I know that Ian's okay, I'm not sure about Carl.'

'Do you mind if I borrow yours then Ian?' Sarah asked.

'Zoe wants to use it I think.'

Zoe looked from one to the other. 'Sorry girls I had a practice with it this afternoon, it was just right for me. Jesus, it's a dream—'

'We're not lending it out, full stop,' Ian cut in.

'Look, Sarah, no need to fight over one rod, I'll sort you both out,' Homer said.

'I've changed my mind,' Ian said, 'I can't go fishing; I've to get ready for Ungad.'

162

'I don't think I can go either,' Zoe said. 'I've to feed the rabbits, sort something out with Ian, then do some packing.'

'No worries, I'm doing nothing, I'll take them,' Homer said.

As he spoke, Fiona arrived. Jodie and Carl joined them in the garden Fiona went in the pub.

'Will he make a golfer then?' Homer asked.

Jodie laughed. 'I don't think so, he's too easily distracted.'

'Fancy a bit of fishing tonight Carl?' he asked.

'Not really, I was thinking of staying around the Swan.'

'Oh, come on Carl it'll be fun.' Erica said.

'Well, if you're going I might tag along.'

Homer looked Jodie up and down. 'What you doing my little petal?'

'Staying here, watching telly, might have a drink.'

'I might join you later.'

'I'm off to my room. You coming Zoe?'

Ian winked at Zoe. 'I'm going, see you when you come to feed the rabbits.'

In Jodie's room, 'How did the fishing go then?'

'Extremely well, how did it go with Carl?'

'Need you ask?'

'I guess Fiona got him in a bunker?'

'She got him in the bushes.'

'Sounds about right.'

'Yes, and while they were in the bushes her boyfriend tried to chat me up.'

'What boyfriend?'

'The golf club steward. He's a right crank, like an advert for skid row; he drank six whiskies in no time. It seems they worked together in a club on Ungad; she was some sort of escort.'

'And?'

'Drugs. I think he's supplying her with drugs. I'm seeing Homer tonight. Think I should tell him?'

'What you seeing him for?'

'To discus my future at the Swan.'

'In that case, tell him, I'm sure he'll be interested. I think you'll be in her bed before the week's out.'

A big grin came over her face. 'What a thought!'

Just then, the phone rang. Jodie answered it.

She smiled. 'H wants to see us in his office, didn't say why.'

They went down to his office, knocked on the door and walked in.

'Sorry about this.' He put his hands on Jodie's shoulders and looked in her eyes. 'You'll do for me.'

'Oooh, thanks H.'

He went to Zoe; she opened her eyes wide. 'Okay, what's this about?'

'You'll pass.'

'Pass what?'

'Tell me Jodie, what happened at the golf club today?'

'Do you know Fiona's steward friend?'

'A smart, well-dressed chap, I saw him when he arrived with one of the other captains.'

'He's not looking too smart now, you'd be shocked.'

'In what way?'

'He looks awful, like an alcoholic or drug addict or something. Fiona seemed to know him very well.'

'Were they smoking?'

'Yes, some hand-rolled cigarettes.'

'What about Carl?'

'I didn't see him smoking.'

'Well, he's been on something, and it's not just alcohol, I reckon they've all had a dabble.'

'I don't think Carl would touch drugs,' Zoe said.

'No, that's not like Carl,' Jodie added.'

'Okay, let's see then. They think I've gone out, I left them chatting at the bar.'

He switched an intercom on that picked up the conversation at the bar.

'Roll-ups, what sort do you smoke?' Carl asked.

'The same as you,' Erika said.

'And when you're rolling, I suppose you add something?'

She laughed. 'Add something when I'm rolling?' She laughed again. 'Makes you feel in love, yes? Are you in love?'

'Yeah.'

'How long?' she asked.

'Since arriving here.'

Sarah laughed. 'This is a romantic place, you will like it. It makes you feel in love.'

'Yeah, but it's the stuff you put in your cigarettes...'

'Yes, makes you in love,' Erika repeated.

'Where do you get yours from?' Carl asked.

'The same place as you.'

'Yeah, that's when I fell in love with Fiona.'

'It's not the weed either,' Fiona said, 'we really are in love, aren't we Carl?'

'Yeah, and you're beautiful. But so are you Erika, you should hit it off with Ian.'

'Thanks, he doesn't smoke though, and Zoe seems to be in the way.'

'We'll have to convert him then, won't we?' Sarah said.

Bram Sol

'I'll soon sort that out,' Fiona said.

'Anybody fancy a smoke while he's out?'

'Carl, that's stupid, he has a nose like a bloodhound; he'd smell it even if he didn't come back for two days,' Fiona said.

Homer switched off the intercom. He had a pained expression on his face and stared at the blank wall.

There was a long pause.

He rubbed his chin. 'It's all gone wrong. I was on the verge of taking her back to the clinic for treatment.'

'She laces peoples' drinks to get her way with them, she's done it to Carl, he's besotted with her,' Jodie said.'

'Anything else?'

'I think the steward is supplying her with drugs. He worked at the same club as her on Ungad.'

'I'm afraid it's the end of the road for Fiona. I feel terrible.'

'Like you said Captain, "love is blind".'

'I'll organise a search of the golf club, and the foursome at the bar. Any drugs and it'll be Ungad for the lot of them. I'll be back in a minute.'

'Oh dear, poor Carl,' Zoe said.

'Well, he's acted stupid since we got here, something was bound to happen.'

'Tell me about it, but Fiona's well out of order, using drugs to charm him out of his pants.'

Homer returned. 'You won't see them again; in half an hour they'll be on Ungad.'

Zoe gave him an odd look. 'Just like that, no trial, no goodbyes?!'

'We don't have trials and there are no goodbyes for drug offences, just on-the-spot removal from the planet.'

'Yes, but it's your wife that that you're losing.'

'It was coming. I lost her a while back. I should have got her to the clinic earlier.'

'What did they say?' Jodie asked.

'The girls said nothing, Carl asked me to tell you all that he's sorry, but not to worry, he'd be okay with Fiona.'

The girls fell silent, tears in their eyes. Homer passed a box of tissues. 'They'll be okay, they'll be taken to a good treatment centre, but I think you'll see Carl again.'

Zoe gave him a nasty look and wiped her eyes. 'It's cruel, he's only taken drugs for a few days and that's your wife's fault, he hardly needs treatment.'

'He needs treatment for something or he wouldn't be having it off with a married woman, would he? That's an offence here.'

'Only if they go with a captain's wife, I suppose.'

'Zoe, stop it,' Jodie cut in.

'And what about married captains with roving eyes chatting up girls? I bet that's no offence.'

'Zoe, calm down, you're upset,' Homer said.

'Course I'm bloody upset, we all learnt to walk at the same time. Carl is our best friend.'

'Yes, and he's never done anything wrong since we've known him. Can't you do something?' Jodie started crying again.

'That may be, yet he's done nothing right while I've known him, but yes, I can make it easier on him. Trouble is, in doing so it would make it doubly hard on Fiona.'

Zoe gave him a questioning look. 'Why?'

'In my report I'd have to implicate her. She's the cause of Carl's undoing. Carl would be credited with two stars, meaning he'd only need one to get back here. But what they give, they then take away. Fiona would need more than the normal three. Worse, if she then lost a crime point she'd go to Extungad.'

Zoe looked daggers at him. 'Who the bloody hell cares about Fiona?'

Jodie locked her eyes on him and raised her eyebrows. 'Yes, who cares about Fiona?'

He looked her in the eye then slowly his eyes drifted down her body, stopped at her knees and drifted back to her eyes. They both stared at each other, oblivious to Zoe.

'H, wake up, you haven't answered the question.'

'Zoe, go and feed your rabbits, please. My report will be in Carl's favour.'

'You're a darling, and I'm sure that you'll soon find someone else.' Zoe made her exit and closed the door behind her, but she didn't leave, she put her ear to the door.

'You can't move in with me yet.'

'Why not?'

'Don't be silly Jodie, Fiona's only just gone.'

'Yes, so we don't need to keep creeping to a spare room; we can sleep together in your four-poster bed.'

At that moment, the phone rang. Homer answered it.

A few minutes later, he took up the conversation again. 'The steward has been arrested. A team are clearing the place. He was cultivating hemp and opium poppies in the disused function room; he had a drug processing plant in there.'

'Good... What do you think about what I said?'

'Well, we don't have a problem now that Fiona's gone, and because she's left the planet I'm entitled to an instant divorce.'

'Love you H.'

'You can't love someone just by sleeping with them a couple of times. Especially when you hardly know them.'

'I can. I said I love you. My heart pounds every time I hear your name, and when I'm close — just put your hand there — feel it?'

'Put your hand on mine then, it's beating faster than yours.'

She giggled. 'That's because your hand is on my tit.'

Zoe had never intended to listen beyond a few words and felt ashamed. She forced herself to leave. *Well, you could do worse than marry a captain I suppose. Good luck to you Jodie,* she said to herself.

She intended to feed the rabbits, but went over to Emma first, who was sitting outside the cottage.

'There's been a drug swoop. They've taken Carl to Ungad.' She then told Emma everything that had happened.

'I saw them going in the shuttle station and wondered what was going on. Carl will be devastated.'

'Well, according to Homer, he didn't seem devastated, more like he was looking forward to it. He's hit it off with Fiona, I think she's hypnotised him.'

Emma lowered her eyebrows and screwed up her nose. 'Carl will end up being her slave no doubt. But at least he only needs one point to get himself back here.'

'Somehow, I don't think he'll be keen to return here. Carl won't mind being a slave to her; she fits his idea of the perfect woman.'

'Oh, right, in that case good luck to them.'

'Yeah, good luck to them; might be a good match for all we know.'

'Absolutely, we shouldn't knock them.'

'You seen Ian?'

'On the river, says he will see you in the Swan tonight. I might call in myself, seeing that Fiona's gone. You might see Katie going in there now. Fiona was off-putting to say the least, not what you'd expect from a captain's wife.'

Zoe smirked. 'Well, I wouldn't say Homer was exactly the nicest guy around.'

'You mean he's tried it on with you?'

'So, so, but nothing I couldn't handle. He has Jodie entranced though. I reckon she'll marry him. They've been sleeping together, she's fallen in love with him.'

'So her head's gone too.'

'Yes; is it the sun, or something in the air? Even Ian has changed.'

'I know. I'd never heard him whistle before, now he's whistling all the time, I think he's picked it up off you.'

'Well, I've never heard him whistle, must have been practicing on his own.'

Emma gave her a wry look. 'By the look on his face, he's been practicing something other than whistling; he's completely spaced-out.'

Zoe inspected her fingernails, first one hand and then the other, smiling to herself.

'You mean he looked pleased over something?'

'To say the least, funny thing is, you have the same look about you. If you look like that on Wednesday, you'll have the edge over the rest; that's a look that you can't imitate, it'll win you the contract.'

'I wish.'

'I started modelling at fourteen, I've seen everything, but I've never seen anyone with such an aura around them. Just sitting next to you is giving me an energy boost. The camera will pick it up. You'll have people crying at your feet.'

Zoe laughed. 'I can't imagine Ian doing that.'

'Here's what you've to do at the audition, pretend Ian is the camera and you're trying to win him over. With each shot imagine he's coming closer.'

'Supposing I don't like the cameraman?'

'Ignore the guy taking the shots, just flirt with the camera; kiss it, fondle it, and do whatever crosses your mind to seduce it. Ultimately, the camera becomes your lover. Of course, Ian's in the back of your mind.'

'You mean just think my normal thoughts, but exaggerate them for the camera?'

Emma laughed. 'Yes, Zoe, just make sure you don't overdo it.'

Zoe giggled. 'I get it; stop before I reach a climax on set.'

'Come on Zoe, this is serious stuff; it's not about a stroll on the river, or meeting friends in the pub. Don't underestimate the camera, it can turn your life upside-down and probably will. This isn't twenty pound an hour catalogue-modelling, which is where I started. You've bypassed all that.'

'I don't care; Ian loves me. I might turn modelling down, even if I get top spot.'

'Ian loves you? Since when?'

'Since he first met me, but I didn't know until recently.'

'Oh, I wondered where the climax thing came from.'

'Trouble is Emma, I can't think straight for thinking about the next time. Was it like that for you?'

A tear rolled down Emma's cheek. 'I'm glad for you Zoe… No, it wasn't that way for me.'

'Not even when you were courting?'

'Nope, there was no courting, but I expect there will be, if and when I find Alistair.'

'You will, I'm sure.'

'According to Katie, there are fifty million people living in this country; he's not tied to be here, could be anywhere on the planet among five billion people. Faced with that, I think I'll have to forget about looking for Alistair, just hope that he finds me.'

Zoe gave her a sympathetic look. 'I wonder how many dogs there are on this planet, yet you found Pal, how did that come about?'

Emma told her about the Fort Locks help line and how they'd mixed up Pal with Alistair. 'Thing is, they know where Alistair is, just like they knew where Pal was, but they only allow one inquiry.'

'I'll do it on my card then, I'm not going to need it.'

'From Duplico they only accept inquiries for husband, wife, mother, father, brother or sister. On Ungad, they'll find your pet snake.'

'If I'm a success at modelling, I might have to travel to Ungad to promote products.'

'Zoe, even those at the bottom of the pile don't need to leave the planet to get work.'

Just then, they heard whistling coming from the field.

'Here he comes.' Emma watched Zoe's face melt as she straightened her hair.

Ian, still whistling, placed a fish on the patio table. He stroked it, turned it over and stroked it again. 'That is a perfect specimen of a sea trout, wait until you taste it; you'll not sleep for thinking about the next.'

He leant over and gave Zoe a quick kiss on her lips. 'You going in the Swan tonight?'

'Yes, and Emma, and maybe your mum.'

'Good, I'll see you later, some things to pack for tomorrow.' He picked up the fish and turned towards his caravan. 'I'll gut this first.'

Zoe looked down to the harbour, and appeared to be in deep thought. She then turned to Emma, eyes open wide. 'I've an idea!'

'Oh, really. What?'

'Ian's going to Ungad. He could use his card to find Alistair.'

20

Later, at the Swan, Emma and Zoe arrived together at eight o'clock. Jodie was behind the bar with her aunt Brenda and looking quietly pleased.

'Tell them the good news then,' Brenda said.

'I will, let's serve them first.'

'Two medium white wines, please,' Emma said, and pushed her card over.

Brenda smiled and pushed the card back. 'You won't need that tonight. Homer says it's a free bar for Jodie's friends.'

Zoe watched Jodie from the corner of her eye; her face was a mixture of bewilderment and excitement. Her hands were picking things up for no reason and putting them back down again.

Zoe took a sip of her wine and winked at Jodie. 'You just helping out then?'

Jodie grinned and raised her eyebrows, picked up a glass and held it against the light, then put it in the glass washer without saying a word.

At that moment, Ian came in whistling away, but it suddenly faded away when he saw Jodie behind the bar. 'Carl in the pool room?' he asked.

'Well, he could be, but not on this planet. Didn't get a chance to tell you before, there's been a few changes.'

'Oh yes, in what way? Large Ambry please, Brenda.'

'I'll tell you after.'

Brenda gave Ian his card back. 'It's on the house, compliments of Homer.'

Ian looked at Zoe. 'What's going on?'

Brenda butted in. 'Tell them, Jodie.'

'I'm marrying H next Saturday,' she blurted out.

Ian burst out laughing. 'How do you work that out? He's married to Fiona.'

'Not any more,' Brenda said, 'she's vacated the planet, and her marriage.'

Ian took a good drink of his Ambry ale. 'I suppose Carl's with Fiona then?'

'I guess so, they've become an item,' Zoe said.

'Let's find a seat,' Emma said. 'That's half of the gang sorted, and we haven't been here two weeks yet.'

Zoe gave Ian a quick kiss. 'Wrong, all the gang are sorted. We're getting engaged.'

'Oh, right, I wondered why all the whistling, that's lovely news — I just hope my man comes along as quickly,' said Emma.

Zoe then told Ian about Emma's search for Alistair; how she'd found Pal instead, and asked for his help.

'No problem, tell me what to do.'

Emma gave him a hug. 'Do you think you'll have access to a computer?'

'I'll be on one in the morning at the River Board, going through the histories of the known poachers and their methods.'

Emma wrote out the details for Fort Locks and the date of Alistair's death. 'After you've put your card in, just click Male Friend in the questions box.'

'Got it, I'll do it tomorrow, chance permitting.'

'Pity it's going to be a week before we know the result,' Zoe said.

'Well, I'm supposed to contact Homer at five o'clock every day to let him know I'm okay. They have a special line at the shuttle station. And, I'm allowed to pass on a personal message.'

Emma patted him on the back. 'That will work out great. I'll ring Homer after five.'

Just then, Ian stared out of the window and screwed up his face. 'That's odd, mum's sat talking to a guy at a picnic table.'

'He's Richard, a regular here, an agency captain,' Zoe said.

Emma smiled. 'So she's finally plucked up courage.'

Ian widened his eyes in alarm. 'Courage? What for?'

'Oh, just to talk to him.'

Zoe grinned. 'By the way they're talking I'd say they were smitten with each other.'

'Yes, well let's not be nosy. I'm heading for an early night. See you when you return from Ungad, Ian. See you in the morning Zoe.'

Sunday morning, Emma noticed a commotion outside the village store. She slid open the patio door and sat at the table wondering what the fuss was. She could see Zoe in the middle of a dozen villagers; some were patting her on the back, while others were reading the Sunday papers.

Zoe broke away and set off running towards the farm, waving her newspaper and pointing at it. 'We're on the front page!' She ran up the garden path and onto the patio. 'Look!' She spread the paper on the table.

Verona to celebrate five hundred years of perfume creation. The headline read. *Their new cosmetic range, 'Bram Sol' will be launched at a glitzy party next week.*

Emma smiled at Zoe then inspected the pictures. 'Oh, you do photograph well.

Your face is lit up: beautiful, fresh, wide-awake brown eyes; your whole body is illuminated. You were born to be a model; a photographer's dream.'

'What do you think Ian will say?'

'I think he'll be worried, might chain you up on the spot when he sees this.'

'Oooh, I wish.'

One of the models in our picture, the paper stated, *will be chosen on Wednesday, to represent the new Bram Sol perfume. She'll become Verona's new icon, effectively the planet's highest paid model. The other four models will promote the rest of the new range.*

'You'll beat them Zoe. The other four girls are stunning, but they don't have the same aura.'

'You're in here also, and on the front page of the supplement magazine.' She pulled out the magazine. Above Emma's photograph - *The ravishing figure of Emma Noble, Verona's new swimwear girl.* 'I think you look terrific.'

Just then, Pal came bounding out of the cottage, stared at Emma, jerked his head twice to one side and pointed his paw towards the beach. Zoe tickled his chin. 'What's wrong Pal?'

'He wants to go to the beach. If he points at the bridleway, then he wants to go to the loch.'

'How do you know?'

'I took him to the dog school at Arimloch; I know everything he wants to do. You get a read-out from their mind-disc; it interprets all your dog's sign language for you. I can ask him questions and he will give me a yes or no with his head.'

'That's brilliant.'

'The read-out also tells you what all his different expressions mean. I ask him to confirm my interpretation and he nods or shakes his head. Isn't that right Pal?'

He nodded and pointed his paw at the beach again.

'I'll have to take him Zoe.'

'It's okay. I need to clean the rabbit hutch out. I'll be in the Swan before five though.'

'Good, I'll be there at half four.'

Later, when Emma was on her way back from the beach, Homer phoned her mobile. 'Fort Locks rang me. A man from Security has interviewed Ian. He's coming to see you on the six o'clock shuttle.'

'What for?'

'He wants to clear up one or two things with you, nothing serious, he told me. When he arrives I'll send him over to the farm cottage.'

'Oh right, for a moment you had me worried.' *Security interviewing Ian,* she thought, *that doesn't sound too good at all.*

Emma met Zoe leaving the farm. 'I've had a message from Fort Locks. They're sending someone to see me at six, but according to Homer, it's nothing to worry about.'

'Must be something to do with Alistair.'

'Well, they've interviewed Ian and we know he was making inquiries, I guess we'll have to see.'

'Any point in meeting at the Swan at five then?'

'I don't think so, but you can come here for six if you like.'

'Honest?'

'Sure, but if he wants to see me alone, you'll have to leave.'

Zoe looked up at the sky and let out a whistle, then winked. 'You mean, if he's drop-dead gorgeous, you'll want him to yourself.'

Pal cocked his head to one side and gave her a menacing look, as if to say, I'll be here.

Zoe patted him. 'Sorry, Pal I forgot about you.' She stroked him, rubbed her nose against his and then set off home whistling away.

Emma asked Pal if he wanted an early dinner, he nodded. 'Rabbit, chicken, beef or pheasant?' He nodded at pheasant. 'Well, I'm having duck, sure you won't change your mind?' He nodded again.

After dinner, she heard her mobile ringing on the patio table outside; she glanced at the clock, it was ten past five. When she picked up the phone, it was Homer. 'Ian sent me a massage, says they've found your friend, and the security man that's coming at six is taking you to meet him.'

'Thanks Homer, thanks ever so much.' She threw the phone in the air and caught it as it came down. *Excellent, to say the least,* she thought. She picked up the watering can and began watering the flowers round the edge of the small lawn in front of the patio. Then she realized she was doing Bill out of a job and put the can down.

She went to the kitchen, opened the fridge and shut it again, wondering why she'd opened it in the first place, picked up a cloth and went in the lounge dusting anything and everything, even though there was no dust. She rearranged papers and magazines and then went back to the fridge, opened the door and scratched her head.

At that point, Zoe entered the kitchen. 'Sorry I'm late Emma.'

She shut the fridge door, and spun round. 'Late? Why what time is it?'

'Time for the shuttle.'

'Listen Zoe, Ian's found Alistair's address; the man that's coming at six is taking me to see him.'

'Jesus that's terrific!'

'I know, my head's spinning.'

They went out to the patio and sat watching the shuttle station entrance. Within minutes, the door opened and a lone man came out. He took in the surroundings then, with a walk of authority, struck out towards the Swan, paused for a moment outside, then entered.

'I guess that's your man Emma, I wouldn't say he had the wow factor.'

'He certainly seemed in a hurry.'

When he came out, Homer was by his side and pointed to the farm. They shook hands and he set off across the cobbles, each stride broke the silence in the village.

He opened the gate and made towards them. 'I'm Ken, you're expecting me.' He had a serious face with hard brown eyes and head of dark curly hair. He wore a grey suit with a startling yellow shirt and shiny brown brogues. He smiled but this soon faded.

'This is Zoe, is it okay if she stays?'

He shook hands. 'No problem, I'll only be a few minutes. Your friend is living on Alzimo, a small private island on planet Extungad.'

Emma screwed up her face. 'Extungad?'

'Don't worry it's a completely safe island. I'm the only security person there.'

'How come he's on Extungad?'

'Not my department; my instructions were to collect you in the morning for the eight o'clock shuttle and escort you back at six. So I'll meet you at the station before eight.'

'If you're staying at the Swan, we'll be in there tonight Zoe said.'

'I'm dashing off to see my parents in the Midlands. Where's the Sedan park?'

Emma pointed to the railings by the green.

'Nice to meet you Zoe. See you in the morning then Emma.'

He hastily strode off. Pal followed him to the garden gate, sniffing every inch behind him and then sniffing his way back to the patio.

Emma watched the man disappear down the Sedan park steps. 'Well, he wasn't for giving much away.'

'Tell me about it. Alzimo, it sounds like some new fizzy drink. At least he's taking you to meet Alistair.'

'I know, but I can't think why he's on Extungad, that place is for hardened criminals.'

Zoe smiled. 'Don't look so worried, there are people on this planet that own property and businesses on Extungad.'

Emma opened her eyes wide. 'How do you know?'

'Homer told Jodie. Fort locks franchises out thousands of security businesses that operate on Extungad and Ungad. Seventy five percent of the franchises are owned by Dupliconians, the others are from Ungad.'

'Interesting, did she tell you anything else?'

Zoe shook her head and giggled. 'Nothing that you'd believe.'

'Why?'

'Because, in some places on Extungad dogs and gorillas are in charge, how bizarre is that!'

'Katie mentioned it to me. It's very bizarre, hard to see how that could work.'

Pal pawed Emma's leg, looked at her then at Zoe and nodded his head as if to say it was true.

Emma ruffled his coat. 'You couldn't know Pal, you've never been there.'

Zoe hugged him and laughed. 'If you had, you'd have stayed.'

Pal blew a long blast of air down his nostrils and sloped off, head bowed, into the cottage.

'He didn't like that, Zoe.'

'Well, dogs knowing more than us, it's just not on.'

'To be honest I don't care if demons are running the place, as long as I meet Alistair.'

'You will, I'm sure.'

At that point, Katie came from the farmhouse and joined them. 'Who was that chap?'

Zoe grinned. 'He's just arranged a blind-date with a gorgeous guy for Emma.'

'You're kidding.'

'They've found Alistair on Extungad; she's meeting him tomorrow.'

Katie threw her arms around Emma. 'That's excellent... but Extungad!'

'I know, but according to my escort, Alistair is on a private island called Alzimo. Wouldn't surprise me if Alistair actually owns the island.'

Katie patted her on the back. 'Well, you're soon going to find out.'

Monday morning, Emma walked with Katie to the shuttle station.

'What's it like on the shuttle?'

'Well, they call it the Dream Beam and that's how it feels; the capsule doesn't move, but you do.'

'How do you travel then?'

'You stand in a glass-sided capsule that holds up to thirty people.'

Within a minute of the doors closing, everyone dematerializes and you go through the space station interchange. According to Homer, that's where you're directed to your chosen planet. You notice nothing until you materialize, in an identical tube, on the other planet.'

'Okay...that's my escort, Ken, waiting outside.'

He held out his hand as they approached him. 'Morning Emma.'

She shook his hand. 'Morning, this is my sister Katie, she's going to Ungad.'

'Nice to meet you Katie.' He shook her hand.

They entered the shuttle along with twenty others.

In the station, the capsule was the size of a single-decker bus; there were two computers, one on each side of the sliding, glass doors. A sign over one read Ungad, the other read Extungad.

'This is where we log in our destination,' Katie said.

Ken went to the Extungad computer, put his ID card in a pad and typed in, Alzimo. 'You do the same, Emma. You always type in your destination and you're dropped off at the nearest station.'

In the capsule, Katie looked at Emma's feet. 'Keep inside the circle.'

'Yes, we don't want to leave half of your body here,' Ken said.

'Take good care of her, won't you,' Katie said, as the doors closed.

Minutes later, Emma re-materialized with Ken and ten others in a station on Extungad.

'One thing they don't have here is Sedans,' he said, as they made for the exit.

Outside, there were five cabs, each with an open-backed jeep behind carrying two armed guards. Emma gave Ken a strange look. 'Is this what you call a safe island?'

'Don't you feel safe with two armed guards?'

'No, it's quite scary.'

He patted her back and smiled. 'We're on the mainland; they're just taking us to the harbour ten minutes down the road. Unless you fancy some sightseeing in the city it won't take long.'

She fixed her eyes over the road where a spectacular gold covered palace stood in breathtaking gardens. She thought of Alistair. *Has he one of these? More than likely, and I'm so close to him, why should I rush?*

'Okay then, why not.'

Ken used his mobile and within minutes another armed jeep arrived and took up position in front of their cab. They set off towards the city centre with armed guards front and rear of their cab.

Ken gave her a running commentary on the way.

'On the left is a five-mile graveyard, on the right is Al Capon's palace.'

'Really?'

'Look over the bridge on the left, you'll see hundreds of bin-liner homes on the dried up riverbed, and on the right a palace, owned by Bonnie and Clyde.'

Emma began to doubt him. 'How come they have a palace?'

'They're the top bank robbery investigators on Extungad.'

In the city centre, single-deck buses were carrying so many people they were hanging on the bumpers and windows. There were old bikes, old mules and queues of battered old cars going in any direction they wished. Troubled men with handcarts, pulling massive loads, struggled along; stretch limos, with blacked out windows, edged their way through the mayhem.

Ken pointed to a side street. Eight bedraggled, shifty-looking youths, stood chained to a wall. Uniformed police were whipping them while painfully thin dogs licked their blood. A slim young woman — six hens in a basket on her head, a carpet under each arm — stood by nonchalantly watching.

Emma turned away. 'That's awful.'

'Petty thieves; they can't scream; they've lost their tongues.' He pointed over the road. 'Execution square, they'll be losing their heads next.'

She screwed up her face. 'Can we go back now?'

'Sure. I don't like it myself and it's really no place for a woman.'

Half an hour later, they were at the harbour. The guards stayed with them until they climbed in a speedboat.

Ken took out his mobile phone. 'Meet you at the kennels in one hour,' he said, then put the phone away. 'Forty minutes on water, an hour on land and you'll meet your friend.'

'Did you just speak to *him*?'

'No, that was Bruno; he's taking us to the farm. I've no transport today, a couple of zomb mechanics are working on my jeep.'

'What's a zomb mechanic?'

'A motor mechanic.'

'Oh, right… And the farm, does Alistair own the farm then?'

He gave her a strange look. 'Bruno owns the farm.' As he spoke, they pulled into a small harbour.

'So what is Alistair doing?'

There was a long pause; he tied the boat to a ring on the jetty.

'Alistair?'

'Yes, my friend I've come to see.'

He scratched his head. 'How did you find out he was here?'

'The mind-disc at Fort Locks, they sent you to pick me up.'

'That's because you're not allowed to travel here alone, but we don't have an Alistair on the island… Our cab has arrived, we'd better jump in.'

Emma held back. She wanted to scream. 'You're jesting!'

'I'm not, and you'd better hop in the cab if you want to see your friend.'

'Alistair's the only person I want to see, I'm not looking for anybody else.'

'The mind-disk pinpointed the farm here. Have you any other friends that crossed over recently?'

'Just one and I don't know were he is.' She climbed in the cab.

'Describe him.'

She gave him a description of Big John including graphic details of his deformed face. 'If you ever meet him you'll know instantly.'

Eyes wide-open he held her arm. 'Extraordinary, I've already met Big John; he's my new boss at Fort Locks. He knows more about security than anyone I've met.'

'You're not telling me he knows you've brought me here?'

'No, different department, but that brings us back to your friend at the farm… This Alistair guy, what did he do on Earth?'

'Incredibly rich, ran a business empire, why do you ask?'

'You've done a search before with no success, and this search is through another card, yes? Ian's card?'

'Yes.'

'You'll never find Alistair that way; both your cards are C Grades.'

'Meaning?'

'This guy on the farm could be anybody from your previous life with family ties. I'll tell you in a minute about the grades.' He tapped the driver. 'SPCZ kennels, please.'

'What's that mean?'

'The society for the prevention of cruelty to zombs, that's where we're meeting Bruno and his wife. They're picking up a zomb for their stud farm.'

'Zombs?'

'Zombies, you not been told?'

'No.'

'You're in for a shock, dogs run this island, gorillas run the other. But I won't spoil it for you.'

'Ken, frig off, you've just done that.'

'You don't need to hold back, you can swear as much as you like on this planet.'

'In that case—'

'Going back to the mind-discs,' he cut in. 'There's three levels of access: A' cards are for royalty, B' cards for aristocracy and C' cards for commoners. You can only access info on people in, or below, your category. When you search, and the person is in another grade, it comes up with the best match in your grade. I guess you're about to meet someone that was close to you.'

Emma shivered. 'I don't want to go any further. I want to go back to Duplico.'

'Don't worry, he's a bottom of the line zomb; he won't recognise you.'

Emma gave him a puzzled look. 'Does the zomb have a name?'

'Yes, Gavin, poor soul.'

She glared at him. 'Oh no, not Gavin! The last person I want to see; he's my worst enemy.'

'In that case, you might be glad to see how he's ended up.'

21

Twenty minutes later, they entered a room lined with huge cages on each side.

'Back in couple of minutes; it's okay they're harmless.' Ken went through a side door as though he knew the place well.

The cages had zombie-like people inside. Emma felt a hundred eyes staring at her, she shivered, inspected the floor and then the ceiling.

While she was pondering what was going on, a door at the far end of the room opened and two Alsatians walked in, accompanied by a zombie-like nurse dressed in white.

The Alsatians weren't your ordinary Alsatians, they were bizarre and scary. They had human-like bodies with Alsatian heads, but the teeth were human-like and they were talking to the nurse.

They walked round the room inspecting each cage and having a discussion with the nurse.

'This is Robert,' the nurse said, as they came to the cage close to Emma. 'He has quite a good pedigree with nine offspring on Earth. Two major and three minor crimes, almost an Ungad entrant.'

'What do you think, Meg?' one of the Alsatians said.

'Looks intelligent and a good pedigree, I like him, but you're the expert, Bruno.'

'Yes, we'll take him,' he said to the nurse.

She unfastened the cage. 'Well, you won't need shackles with this one, he's quite placid; we've not heard a grunt from him.'

'The pups will be really pleased,' Meg said, smiling and patting him on the back. 'I just hope he gets on with Sue.' She patted him again and stroked his hair.

Just then, Ken came through the side door. 'Bruno, this is Emma; she's here to see Gavin.'

'Yes, well, we knew she wasn't a zomb. Nice to see you again Ken, and pleased to meet you Emma.'

They shook hands. Bruno had human hands, with dog fur on the arms. *How weird*, Emma thought.

Once outside, Bruno opened the back doors of an old transit van. Emma looked at Ken, raised one hand to her mouth and opened her eyes wide. He just grinned at her.

There were two wooden benches on each side, and cardboard had replaced the back windows, and a side window. The driver's seat was well torn and an ordinary chair had replaced the passenger seat.

They climbed in the back; she sat next to the only window that hadn't been replaced with cardboard. Ken sat opposite with the zomb.

He grinned at her again. 'I did warn you about everything; just enjoy the experience, you're never likely to see the place again.' He closed his eyes. 'Wake me if you need me.'

She sat in worried silence as Bruno drove on.

Meg prodded Bruno's shoulder. 'What shall we call him?'

'Robert will do for now.'

Meg tapped his shoulder again. 'Stop at the town store, we need some more zomb food.'

Emma wiped the dust off the side window and peered through. Three gorillas were standing outside the store, dressed in dark suits with white shirts, black ties, black hats and dark sunglasses.

They're window-shopping, she thought, *as if it were the normal thing to do.* They were proper gorillas, but on such a hot sunny day, with all that fur, and wearing clothes... *A bit odd, to say the least.*

Rickety van or not, she was thankful she wasn't out shopping. She looked at Ken; he was snoring away. She looked at the zomb; his eyes were wide open and vacant yet he seemed to be asleep.

Bruno eyed the gorillas. 'Tourists from Conking, we are overrun with them at the moment.'

Emma tapped him on the shoulder. 'Excuse me, where is Conking?'

'Two hours away by boat, a small island like this, nice beaches, but you can't move for towels and most of them talk in a different language. If you go in town, young gorillas are tearing about all over the place on motorbikes. You need eyes in the back of your head; I wouldn't recommend it.'

'You have holidays then?'

He sucked on an empty pipe. 'Yes, but we rarely leave the island; armed guards are expensive and you need two on the mainland... Get me some pipe tobacco while you're in the store Meg. Oh, and some zomb biscuits, we're running out.'

When she'd entered the store, one of the gorillas came sauntering over to the van. 'Where's the nearest tourist information centre, friend?' he asked, in a Russian accent.

'One mile down the High Street, turn left at the Afghan take-away,' Bruno said.

Then he turned to Emma and laughed. 'It's the other way really, but I always send them in the wrong direction. I can't stand the Conking lot.'

A bit risky, you wouldn't want to upset a gorilla, Emma thought, *especially a mafia-type gorilla.*

Meg climbed back in the van carrying tins of zomb food and passed Bruno his tobacco. 'Come on, let's get going, the pups will wonder where we are.'

'Thanks, Meg.' He began to fill his pipe while steering with his knees.

Meg knocked his knees off the steering wheel and snatched the pipe from him. 'Watch it. There's an Afghan taxi overtaking us on the bend, you'll cause an accident yet!'

Bruno blasted his horn at the taxi. 'He'll be the one that causes a crash. He won't have passed his test; they can't drive in a straight line unless they're on a bend. Afghans have taken over every taxi firm in town and they can't drive for nuts. When I was a pup, it used to be just Bulldogs and Labradors.'

'What about the paper shops?' Meg butted in, 'you could always find a Bulldog behind the counter, but not anymore. It's the same with the restaurants and take-aways, Chows and Pekinese have taken over the lot.'

'Don't forget the Poodles, trying to get in on the football,' Bruno added.

'I know, but they'll never beat us German Shepherds at football or anything else.'

At that moment, he pulled up at some road works.

'Look at these lads, Irish Bloodhounds. Ask them to dig a hole and it becomes a railway tunnel; good workers though.'

Meg stared at him. 'Your mother was Irish, but I never saw her do any work.'

'She was a bitch, that might have had something to do with it.' He gave her a smug look.

'Rubbish! Anyway, I am not arguing in front of Emma, she'll wonder what's going on.'

'So what!'

'Oh, shut up Bruno, your mother was a lazy sod.'

'Like I said, she was a bitch, what do you expect?'

'Stop the van! I'm getting out!'

'Okay, calm down, no need to get upset.'

'You make it sound as though I do nothing. Why did you send me in the store? Get my pipe tobacco, get the zomb food, don't forget the biscuits. Something wrong with your legs?'

At that moment, he suddenly swerved into the drive of a farm.

Pebbles flew in every direction as he accelerated then braked.

Emma couldn't stop herself from laughing and had the impression that once inside the house, the second part of the argument was to come.

Bruno couldn't get out of the van fast enough and went storming into the house.

Meg grabbed the zomb by his arm. 'Come on Robert, take no notice of him; he's a nasty piece of excrement.'

She looked at Emma, 'Sorry about all that; we don't argue all the time, just between meals.' She threw the chair in the back and took the zomb out of the passenger door.

Ken had slid to the floor when they turned up the drive, but he didn't awaken. Emma shook him; he jumped up, suddenly alert, drawing his gun at the same time.

She pointed two fingers at him, gun-fashion. 'Too late you're dead.'

'I've never been so tired. Planet-hopping plays havoc with your time clock. I've not slept in my own bed more than twice in a month. Are you okay Emma?'

'Absolutely. I'm fascinated by this couple; they're hilarious; they make everything they say seem like the best joke you ever heard.'

'Yes, but I know them well, they are serious business people. Right let's go see Gavin.'

When they left the van, Meg was talking to a pregnant young lady who was tending the roses in the garden. 'Hello, Louise.' She patted her and stroked her hair. 'Good zomb, looking after the garden are we?'

'She's extremely good looking for a zomb, Ken said.'

Emma smiled. 'Yes, and about eight months pregnant, I'd say.'

'In two month's time, she'll be one month pregnant again, it's her job.'

'Truly?'

'I'm not joking, you'll see.'

Bruno came outside. 'Meg, show Robert to number two flat, next to Sue's, we can't put them together yet, not until he settles in.'

One of their grown-up pups came running through the door. 'Can I take him out?'

'Not yet Petra, but you can take Gavin for a walk. This is Emma she's come to visit him; she'll go with you. Just a quick walk, it's nearly teatime,' Meg said.

Petra had a big grin on her face. 'Hello, Emma, what lovely hair, you're beautiful, can I touch you?'

Emma smiled. 'Go ahead, I won't bite.'

Petra played with her hair, tickled her under the chin, and then tickled her belly. 'I think you like that don't you?'

Emma chuckled inside. 'That was nice.' She felt herself wanting to do the same back, but it didn't seem right.

'We do that to the zombs, they all like it, but you aren't a zomb, I didn't think you'd let me touch you.'

'Let's say you got lucky, I'm not a snappy type of a person.'

'I wish you'd stay. We could have a new breed, person-zombs. They'd sell like warm bunny rabbits.'

Ken intervened. 'She won't be staying.'

'Pity.' Petra took them to a pen at the back of the farm. 'I'll just get his lead, be back in a sec.'

Ken put his hand on Emma's shoulder. 'Prepare yourself for a shock; you're about to see an example of what they can do with the mind-discs. They take out what they want and put in whatever, depending on the crimes committed on Earth.'

'Really?'

'Yes, really… and I need to have a few words with Bruno. You'll be okay with Petra, she'll answer any questions. I'll catch you up shortly, might bring Robert.'

Petra came running back with the lead. Emma stared hard at the lead. *Similar to the one I used for Pal,* she thought.

Petra gave her a puzzled look. 'Do you like it?'

'Yes, sort of.'

She smiled and opened the pen gate.

Emma thought, *Petra would make a nice dog if you took away the human bits. Even a nice human if you took away the dog bits, but I don't like the mix, and the clothes hang funny, but her smile makes up for everything.*

Petra put two fingers in her mouth and whistled. Gavin came bounding on all fours, out of a large hut in the corner of the pen. 'Don't worry Emma he won't bite if you're with me.' She slipped the lead on him. 'Let him smell you first and then you can pat him.'

Gavin licked her ankles, sat on his hind legs and gave her a sheepish look.

With open mouth and tears welling up in her eyes, Emma turned away covering her face with her hands.

'He likes you Emma, don't be frightened.'

'I'm okay, he just reminds me of a bad experience I once had.' She wiped her eyes with her handkerchief.

Petra gave him a chocolate as they walked along a lane, then she took him off the lead and let him run freely.

At that point, Ken and Robert came up behind them. 'Can you take him? We need to use Robert's flat, Louise has gone into labour.' He handed Robert to Petra and rushed off back.

'Oh, dear, and the labour ward's being refurbished.'

She held his hand. 'Hello Robert, I wanted to take you for a walk in the first place.'

'Hello,' he said.

She burst out laughing. 'You just spoke! Stud zombs can't talk!'

She held out a chocolate. 'Can you say please?'

'Please.'

'Clever zomb.' She gave him the chocolate. 'What else can you say?'

'Thank you.'

She let go of his hand and bent over double, laughing. 'You'll be a star, wait until my dad finds out; nobody's ever heard a stud zomb talk.'

'Another chocolate please.'

'Sorry, dad will go mad if he thinks I've given you chocolate. You're on special zomb food for breeders.' She gave one to Emma and stuffed the last one in her mouth.

'Thanks, nice chocolate, but what do you mean, *breeders?*'

'Zomb breeders, it's a stud farm. Sue is our prize female zomb. Her babies fetch good money. I think Robert will make top quality babies with her.'

'Can she talk?'

'No, she groans like the rest, that's all they ever do, grunt and groan. The males grunt and the females groan. Even so, mum and dad will be so pleased when they find out Robert can talk; the babies will fetch a fortune.'

Emma scratched her head. 'They'll be having babies, without first being introduced?'

Petra burst out laughing again. 'They're not like us; there's no preliminaries, it's a stud farm, not exactly a place for romance, they just get stuck in. He's the new stud zomb. Apart from Sue and Louise, there'll be other zombs to service; he'll be doing nothing else.'

'Supposing he doesn't like the servicing idea, I mean, he might not get on with it?'

'Makes no difference, mum and dad will make sure he gets on with it, he won't have a choice.'

'You mean they'll be watching!'

'It's their job, how else would they know if they'd done it right.' With Louis, it's easy; we always know when the stud has done a good job. However, some female zombs just lie there as if nothing has happened.'

'Really.'

'Yes, and people are paying good money for you to service their zombs.'

'What do you think about your mum and dad doing that for a living?'

'Nothing, I will be doing it when I leave university.'

Emma looked across the field at Gavin chasing a rabbit.

Petra shook her head. 'He won't catch the rabbit, it'll be a first if he does.'

'What does he do at the farm?'

'Nothing much, we picked him up to use as a stud; he was a normal upright zomb, but we found out he was firing blanks. Dad complained to Fort Locks. They reprogrammed him, said he'd have to be a guard zomb, he's been on four legs ever since and barks now and again.'

A tear rolled down Emma cheek. 'Poor Gavin… still, I suppose he keeps the burglars away.'

'That's the thing; we don't have burglars on this island or on Conking. Yet, if you own a farm, they make you keep a guard zomb as if there were burglaries every night. It's to do with the star point system.'

'How does that work?'

'Everyone that keeps a pet zomb has to have a zomb licence and fill out a report every month, but because we are in business, we have to keep a daily log; they use the feedback to work out the zombs star ranking. Robert must be on his last year and heading for Ungad; they've given him some speech back.'

As they turned back towards the farm, two chimpanzees were walking towards them with a pram. *Just a gentle stroll in the late afternoon sun,* Emma thought, *and why not, everything else is happening around here.*

Petra waved. 'Here comes George and Elsie, looks like they have a baby zomb.'

'Hi, Elsie, where did you find that, it's so cute, can I hold it?'

'It's sleeping, better not,' Elsie replied, 'we got it at the SPCZ home; nobody wanted it, they were going to put it down next week. Some dogs just don't know how to look after zombs.'

'Chimps dump them as well,' Petra replied.

Elsie put her hand over her mouth. 'Slip of the tongue, sorry.'

Petra pointed to the far corner of the field. 'Gavin almost caught a rabbit then.'

George puffed on a large cigar in the corner of his mouth and stamped his foot. 'Damn, he missed it… rabbits take great pleasure in pinching all our lettuces and yet they say they are not vermin anymore.'

Elsie shook her head. 'They are persistent little brats, I know that much.'

'You know our feelings about rabbits,' Petra said, 'they should never be a protected species; the government is not doing enough. I mean, we all like to eat rabbits more than anything, why don't they let us shoot the stupid things?'

'I agree,' George said, 'we like the young bunnies, we just nip their heads off and eat them while they are still warm, I cannot think of a better meal. Now, they say it is cruel and illegal.'

'He won't eat them from the microwave you know,' Elsie said.

'No way, nor warmed up in the oven,' George added.

'He looks a fine zomb you have with you, Petra. When did he come along?' Elsie eyed him up and down. 'You'll get some good stock off him.'

'This is his first day at the farm.'

'He is in for a shock, doesn't look like an Extungadling zomb to me.'

'When dad picked him up, the nurse said he was an Ungadling type, for some reason he missed out. Mum and dad think he will make a top stud.'

George gave her an odd look. 'Not if he is an Ungadling type, they don't mix too well with our lot.'

'How do I get to Ungad?' Robert asked.

At that, both chimps stood back in shock.

Elsie gave a big frown. 'He can talk, oh dear, he is an Ungadling.'

George gave him a sympathetic look. 'Well, it's too late now son.'

Listening to their conversation and watching their facial expressions, had Emma struggling to hold back her laughter.

Just then, a tall Spider monkey came along carrying a ladder and bucket.

'Afternoon, George, Elsie, I've done your windows, I'm off to clean the farm.'

'Hang on, we'll pay you for ours,' Elsie said. 'Pay him George.'

'No money, you'll have to get your purse out.'

Reluctantly, she rummaged about in the pram. Eventually, she found the purse and gave the monkey a five pound note. 'Hope you made a good job.'

'Thanks, Elsie, I'll come back if they aren't right.' He whistled his way down the lane.

'Seems a nice window cleaner,' Emma said, trying to join in the conversation.

'He is the best window cleaner we have had around here, and always leaves a note if we are out. Trouble is, it nearly always rains after he's done them.' Elsie said.

'He's okay, but sometimes he doesn't use his ladder, swings from one window to the next in total silence; he's caught us naked, hasn't he Elsie?'

She burst out laughing. 'When I was in the bath with the curtains open, remember?'

George gave her a dirty look. 'Yes, you didn't know I was on the landing by the open bathroom door.'

'Okay, okay, I only asked through the open window if he wanted to wash his cloth out in the bath water.'

'And he said, "Yes please". That's when I ran in, pulled the plug and told him to get to the bottom of the downspout before the bath emptied.'

'At least, he shouted "Thanks". Anyway, what would I want with a spider monkey in my bath?'

'Quite, that's what I wanted to know, but you wouldn't tell me.'

'He's a nice lad, and a good little mover.'

'Also a good plumber,' George added, 'mended our boiler when it broke down.'

'Now and again he comes in handy with his bucket at the stud,' Petra said.

'To split up the zombs you mean!' Elsie screwed her face. 'Ugh! It'll be filthy water.'

'They are such a nice couple,' Petra said, as they left. 'They cannot have chimps of their own. I'm glad they've got a zomb.'

Emma thought, *I can't believe this, and you certainly couldn't dream something like this.*

Petra put two fingers in her mouth and whistled for Gavin; he came bounding over. Emma avoided looking at him; she'd already seen enough.

At the farm, Ken was checking over his jeep. 'Hi Emma, just had it delivered, seems okay. You ready to go?'

'Please.'

'Oh, stay for tea,' Petra said.

'Sorry, must go.' Emma climbed in the jeep.

'I'll call in tomorrow to check on Robert,' Ken started the engine and pulled out of the farm gates. 'What did you make of Gavin?'

'I feel awful, that was worse than any jail.'

'He's in a good place, the best on my round. Gavin has free run of the fields every day, and they look after him well. A couple of his friends, James and John C, are on the other island, chained up all the time.'

'James and John C, what are they doing?'

'Guard zombs like Gavin, but I'm constantly checking up to make sure they're fed, watered and kept reasonably clean. The gorillas are a bit too rough with zombs, but you daren't say too much to them or they go mad, and that's the last thing you want.'

'Will Gavin be like that for the rest of his life?'

'What you must remember is that all the zombs have committed terrible crimes on Earth. They can't become part of our society until they've paid for their crimes. If I had my way they would stay zombs, but they are slowly upgraded.'

'So Gavin won't always be like that?'

'In six months, he'll be upright, in another six months he'll have some speech, within two years he'll be off the island and fending for himself on the mainland. If he keeps clear of his old ways, he can gain star points and be on Ungad within five years. Then supposing he keeps up the good work, he could be knocking on your door on Duplico.'

Emma shivered at the thought. 'So zombs could commit the exact same crime again.'

'Precisely, but, thankfully, by then they'll be fully reformed and no further threat, plus we still keep an eye on them.'

After they'd left the boat, the armed guards escorted them to the shuttle station. 'Pointless me going to Duplico and Thrastdale, but I'll log you on. Make sure you stand in the circle.'

'Do me a favour Ken, tell Big John about me and where I'm living.'

'No worries, I'll contact him today. In the meantime, you need to win over a friendly aristocrat.' He gave her a broad smile. 'Shouldn't be much of a problem, not with your looks. Then it's just a matter of them doing a search for Alistair; you'll be in his arms in no time.'

'I hope so.'

'One other thing, Homer has all the right equipment to receive calls from here; if you ring him at say five o'clock each day he'll give you any news we may have on Alistair.'

'Really?'

'I can't promise, but I think Big John might do a bit of research for you, seeing that you are friends.'

'Thanks, that would be great.'

When Emma materialized at Thrastdale, Katie was standing next to her. 'Well, how did it go then?'

'What an awful place, I'll tell you when I get my head back.'

At the farm, they found Zoe sitting at the patio table, eagerly awaiting the news. Emma sank into a chair and shook her head. 'What a day I've had, you'll say I've dreamt it when I tell you.'

'A good dream or a bad one?' Zoe asked.

'More of a nightmare, and no, I didn't find Alistair.'

Emma told them everything that had happened that day.

Katie hugged her, then held her hand and smiled. 'At least, you've acquired some good info, especially the three mind-disc grades, and maybe some help from Big John.'

'When you're at Sark Hall on Wednesday you'll be brushing shoulders with aristocrats, especially Lord and Lady Verona.'

'I know, and I can't wait to get there.'

⁓

The following morning after breakfast, Pal was restless and kept trying to nudge Emma to the front door.

She looked out of the window and saw Zoe playing with the rabbits. 'Okay, okay, it's only Zoe.' He shook his head in defiance and nudged her nearer the door. She opened the door and let him run out.

He ignored Zoe, ran straight to the caravan and started pawing the door.

Suddenly, the door opened and Ian jumped out. Zoe put the rabbits down, ran over to him and kissed him. 'How long you been here?' she asked.

'An hour, I came on the eight o'clock shuttle.'

'Did Katie see you?' Emma asked.'

'Yep, told her why I was here. She was really pleased.'

Zoe lowered her eyebrows. 'Pleased about what?'

'I told my new boss all about you and the Bram Sol thing. I was so proud. I told him we were to be engaged.'

'What did he say to that?'

'He knew about Verona's global cosmetics industry here. Said you were in for a meteoric rise if you win the contract.'

'Yes, we already know that,' Emma said.

'He told me to take the week off and sort out the engagement, otherwise I might not see you again.'

Zoe sighed. 'Oh, the rotten sod… but good of him anyway.'

Emma nodded. 'Well, you are going to be whisked here there and everywhere; a hectic work schedule, with late-night appearances at virtually every party.'

'Yes, I'm dreading that bit now.'

'My boss said,' Ian continued, 'if I could get him a bottle of the new Bram Sol perfume for his wife, I could take two weeks off.'

'No problem…' Emma gave him a serious look. 'What happened with the mind-disc search?'

'It said access blocked, diverted to closest match available. Within half an hour of me logging the details for Alistair, they sent this security guy to interview me. They thought I was a villain, until they checked me out.'

'The security guy, was he called Ken?'

'Yes, came back to see me last night — and guess what? Big John works for Fort Locks and knows all about your visit to Extungad. He knows we are living here.'

'I know, I told Ken to tell him.'

'This… sorts out our engagement,' Zoe butted in, 'We need a ring now.'

Ian grinned. 'We'll go and choose one today at Arimloch.'

Zoe, a startled expression on her face, blew out a long whistle and said, 'How much money you got on your card?'

He scratched his head. 'Enough, I think.'

She grabbed his hand. 'Let's go then.'

Later that day, Emma had dinner with Katie at the Swan. 'Do you fancy coming to Stark Hall, Katie?'

'I'd love to, but can't get the time off work, and Captain Richard is taking me for a meal tomorrow night, can't turn that down.'

'You could come at the weekend and bring Ian.'

'Richard might have something lined up.'

'Bring him along if you like.'

'Sounds okay, I'll put it to him.'

When they left the dining room, Homer and Jodie were chatting at the bar. 'Good luck for tomorrow Emma,' Homer said.

'Thanks, and hope the wedding goes okay for you both on Saturday, sorry I can't be there.'

'No worries, it's just a quiet ceremony at Arimlock town hall.'

At that moment, Ian and Zoe walked in. Zoe held up her finger. 'Look what Ian bought me, isn't it the most fantastic ring you've ever seen?'

22 Wednesday morning Emma went to meet Zoe at the Sedan park. She looked round the Sedans and found one with the door wide open. She stepped inside to find Zoe fast asleep on one of the settees. Careful not to wake her, she quietly closed the door.

Then she remembered that they had to use Zoe's card to log on to Charlene. She searched Zoe's bag for her card, scratching her head as she went through all the stuff: two bars of chocolate, matches, Swiss army knife, small torch, compass. *What the hell's all this for,* she thought.

A zip pocket finally gave up the card along with other private things, but she found nothing in the bag that you'd expect a girl to have, not to mention one about to take up modelling.

She inserted the card in the pad and logged in, Charlene 0364. *Right, I may as well have a nod,* she said to herself, and lay on the other settee as the Sedan roared off on its own.

Emma woke with a startle to a bleeping sound. Zoe was snoring away. A light flashed on the computer screen. *Destination in five minutes,* a message on the screen read.

She woke Zoe. 'Come on girl scout we arrive in five minutes.'

'Girl scout?'

'Yes, I had to go in your bag for the card.'

'When away from home always be prepared, you never know what might happen.'

'Well, you had me baffled.'

In the Sedan park, they pulled up alongside a posh Sedan with a fancy motif on the front. A young woman stood next to the open door.

'Hello, Emma and Zoe, I'm Charlene, I'll be looking after you for the week.' She spoke in a sharp voice, as though she was in a hurry and beckoned them inside.

'Jesus, this is upmarket,' Zoe whispered as they sat together on a three-seat leather settee.

'Absolutely, and complete with cocktail bar and coffee machine. Pity about the chaperone,' she whispered back.

Charlene sat in a swivel chair at the computer desk, with her back to them. 'Help yourselves to a drink, but it's such a short journey you'll hardly have time to finish it.'

'No matter, we'll try two coffees,' Emma said.

'Very wise, there's a huge party tonight. The launch of the new Bram Sol perfume will be phenomenal. Are you prepared for it Zoe?'

'Depends; if it's all a bit snobbish I might disappear.'

'Oh, you think so? Well, put it this way, there won't be any farmers at the party, and you won't be disappearing. You're working for the Verona global cosmetics industry now.'

'Right. I'll probably earn more in a day than some earn in a year.'

Charlene didn't reply.

There was a long embarrassing silence.

Emma broke in. 'Zoe, just go with the flow.'

The Sedan slowed to a crawl behind half a dozen other Sedans that were turning right. 'Media traffic, they started arriving here yesterday.' Charlene plugged a strange-looking gadget into the computer. 'Manual control, I hate these things. We travel everywhere on auto at seventy without ever a crash. Now it becomes more like a game, you half expect to crash; people just aren't used to driving on manual. Of course, on manual the cars are programmed at twenty miles an hour, but you still see them zigzagging towards you.'

Their voices faded to nothing as Emma took in the surroundings.

They drove past a church and half a dozen quaint little cottages, then over a cattle grid and between two lodges at the entrance to the grounds. The road meandered by a small lake, through glades and open fields where racehorses grazed.

At the hall, peacocks roamed among the Sedans on the forecourt. Emma spilt her coffee. She turned to Charlene. 'How long have you worked here?'

'Since Lord and Lady Verona had the place specially re-built to their liking eleven years ago.' She turned from the computer. 'You can leave your luggage, the porter will sort it.'

Zoe jumped out of the Sedan first. 'Not a cameraman in sight!'

'They aren't allowed on the forecourt, restricted to the tradesmen's park around the back… Don't worry, when the party starts you'll be tripping over them.'

A butler met them at the entrance. 'Lovely morning girls… Where are they staying Charlene?'

'The Paddock Suite… This is Emma, who turned down the new perfume contract, and Zoe, one of the short-listed five hoping to win the contract.'

'The Paddock Suite?'

'Yes, Edward, those are my instructions and before you ask, I've checked it out; it's definitely booked for Emma and Zoe.'

'Just making sure, that's all.'

'Okay, but that's my job, I wish you'd stop trying to go above your station.'

'Sorry, madam.'

'Good… come on girls.' She set off at a pace before Emma and Zoe had time to move.

Zoe smiled at Edward. 'I think you were right to make sure.'

Emma patted his shoulder. 'Absolutely.'

'Thank you girls, I appreciate your kind words.'

'Jesus, this is posh… You okay, Emma? You're shaking.'

'I know, I feel weak at the knees.'

Charlene came back towards them with a key dangling from her hand. 'I'm really busy, can we move on please?'

'Is the ballroom still at the end of the long passage leading from the great hall,' Emma asked.

'The ballroom hasn't moved anywhere that I know of.'

'In that case, you can give me the keys, I know my way around.'

'Stayed here before then? That makes my job a lot easier. Why didn't you say?' She handed over the keys. 'Must rush, catch up with you later.' She rushed off as if she were bursting for the loo.

'Brilliant, you conned her good and proper. How did you guess the layout?'

'No con, Zoe, and no guess; this place is identical to Lockstock Hall where I spent most of my time on Earth. I'll give you a tour of the place, but first, I'd like a word with Edward, a couple of things I'm unsure about.'

Edward was still at the entrance, and puffing away on a cigarette. He immediately stubbed it out in a sand tray.

Zoe gave him a naughty look. 'You're the first person I've seen smoking.'

'Not many of us left madam.'

Emma smiled. 'Tell me Edward; have you always worked here?'

'No, I worked for Lady Verona's great-great grandfather, Earl Verona, at Stock Lock Hall near Rombley; he booted me out. Lady Verona contacted me nine years ago; apparently, a couple of hundred builders had perfectly transformed the old hall here into what you see now. Would you like a drink, ladies?'

Emma nodded. 'Fresh orange, please.'

'I'll have the same.'

'In the lounge or the Rainbow Room?'

'The Rainbow Room's fine,' Emma said.

In the Rainbow Room, the floor was wall-to-wall, thick plate-glass. Underneath, tropical fish swam through weed beds and over pebbles. A fountain sprang from the centre and small waterfalls cascaded over rocks in each corner. Three ornate bronze benches with marble-topped tables lined each side among exotic plants.

'You're still trembling,' Zoe said as they sat down.

'Yes, inside and out, I should have ordered an Indiana. I'm convinced that Lord and Lady Verona are Alistair's parents, murdered on Earth, about eleven years ago. At the time, they owned Lockstock Hall, and they've made this place exactly the same.'

Edward brought in their drinks and went through a sort of ritual, as if the orange was some unknown Oriental pleasure.

Zoe winked at Emma. 'We've changed our minds, we want two brandies instead.'

He began reversing the ritual. .

'She's joking, orange is fine, Edward.'

Zoe pointed to the door opposite. 'What's through that door?'

'The swimming pool.'

Zoe went over and opened the door. 'Dead right and it's full size. Give me the keys to our suite, Emma, I fancy a swim.'

Emma took one of the keys off the ring. 'Take the passageway apposite this door and keep going, it's the door at the very far end after you pass the billiard room. Ring me if you get lost.'

Zoe gave her a funny look, and dashed off.

Emma chuckled to herself. *Well, it's not so funny if you do get lost with over a mile of passageways to go through.*

She sipped her orange and pondered over Homer's message that she expected at five o'clock. *God, that's five hours away, lunch at one, say an hour and a half, a walk around the grounds, talk to the horses and the peacocks, that's another two.*

Just then, Zoe returned, breathless. 'Nice digs, two double bedrooms, two bathrooms and a fabulous lounge with a fully-stocked cocktail bar.'

'Good… I think I'll go have an Indiana and a read. Don't forget lunch is at one and you need time to dry your hair.'

Later that afternoon, Emma gave Zoe a tour of the grounds, with thirty photographers in tow.

'We are just a couple of housemaids, can't you tell,' Zoe said, while doing a tantalising twirl for them. This drew calls of, 'Come on Miss Bram Sol, a bit more flesh, undo a couple of buttons.' Zoe spent the next half an hour posing, and enjoying every minute.

Emma dragged her away. 'We'll see you later.'

In the suite lounge, Zoe went behind the cocktail bar. 'Oooh, I feel glamorous, think I'll have a large cocktail. How do you make them?'

'There's a menu on the shelf,' Emma joined her. 'I'll do it if you like.'

Just then, there was a knock on the door; it was Edward.

'A message for you two. A couple of Verona directors want to see Zoe in the office, I'll show you the way Zoe. Emma, Charlene wants to see you in the ballroom.'

Emma, curious to see if the place really was identical to Lockstock, decided to go the long way, via the swimming pool. She entered the poolside changing room. *Well, not much changed here, she thought.* She combed her hair in the mirror. *And I can see myself clearly.* But it made her shiver and she turned away.

She left the changing room and went along the passageway to the great hall, which was identical to the one on Earth. It was empty, apart from staff setting up tables for the evening event. She flicked back her hair and strutted across the polished oak floor, sending echoes around the huge room.

She stepped from the hall into a long passage, a short passage led off to where she expected to see an old nursery.

She walked towards the nursery and opened the door. She froze on the spot. Far from looking old and unused, it was ready for use; everything looked brand-new. She gave her head a good shake, wondering if she was seeing things.

As she passed the study, she heard the door open behind her. A warm finger trickled down her back and a voice whispered in her ear. 'What is the thing women most desire?'

'Alistair!' she screamed. She turned, threw her arms around him and gave him a long kiss. 'In my case I'd say a good husband, two boys and two girls.' She smiled. 'And I'm no longer married or waiting for the right man to come along.'

'The nursery is ready; I need someone to help me fill it.'

'Really, what sort of a person you looking for?'

He didn't reply, and for a moment seemed deep in thought, then he stroked her hair, her neck, her shoulders; his smouldering eyes touching her very soul.

He pulled her close, she felt his firm body against hers; a wonderful feeling took over her whole being.

At that moment, a cleaner came in the passage and without noticing them, pushed a plug into a wall socket. Then she suddenly looked up and saw them, immediately pulled out the plug and retreated.

'Sorry about that, they always leave this passage until last.'

Reluctantly, she pulled away from him. 'Always?'

There was a short pause.

'Yes, most days.'

Emma raised her eyebrows and gave him a cheeky smile. 'Can we talk somewhere? I've a few questions that I'd like answering.'

They went in the study. Alistair sat in a big, authoritative-looking leather armchair at one side of a desk, leaving her the informal chair facing him. She stood next to the chair, feeling that he would be asking the questions if she sat down.

He locked his eyes on hers and smiled.

She stood spellbound; he had the same charming smile, the same deep blue eyes that turned her on, and the same flowing jet-black hair that resembled a swash-buckling pirate. His physique was exactly as she remembered it on Earth — tailor-made for a woman's pleasure.

Feeling her legs go to jelly, she sat down.

He grinned and shrugged his shoulders. 'Something worrying you?'

'Yes; who killed you on Earth?'

He held his chin in thought, his eyes opened wide. 'Gavin shot me, and from reliable inside information, John C and James the butler killed mum, dad, Trish and Amy. By the way, I've seen Amy, she confirmed my info on their shootings.'

'Amy, where is she?'

He came to her side of the table and stood behind her, massaging her shoulders. 'She's here, she's my secretary,' he whispered in her ear.

'My sister Katie rang here. They said they'd never heard of you.'

His hands slowed to a halt. 'Yes, sorry about that.'

'Alistair! I've been everywhere looking for you.'

'That is not my name anymore; it's Bram Sol.'

She gave him a startled look. 'Bram Sol … what a great name, it suits you … but—'

'Remember Big John?' he cut in, 'my gamekeeper on Earth? Well, he works for Fort Locks on Ungad. He also controls the security for Verona Cosmetics.' He continued with the shoulder massage.

'Verona is your company then?'

'My family owns the business.'

'Big John, have you seen him?'

'He's fine, told me to give you his regards; he'll see you at the party tonight.'

'Oh, great.'

She inspected her fingernails, then placed her hands on his and held them still. 'Sit where I can see your face Alistair.'

He gave her bum a quick squeeze, and went to the other side of the table. Resting his chin on both hands, he looked into her eyes, grinning. 'Well, I'm here, but the table's in the way, don't you think?'

She shook her head, forced back a smile and tried to hide her feelings, which were getting hotter by the minute. 'How did Big John know you'd be meeting me?'

His eyes roamed her body then back to her eyes. He smiled in such a way that she melted in the chair. 'Very intelligent guy, he found everybody that matters to me, including Pal, at the Hill top Inn, on his first day at Fort Locks.'

'You rotten sod! You've known where I lived all along!'

'Yes, and I dearly wanted to reveal myself, but I needed time for important preparations.'

'Preparations, what for?'

'The new Bram Sol perfume, the launch revolved around you being the model.'

'Why?'

He moved to her side of the table, put his arms around her and gave her a lingering kiss. 'Because, I had it made especially for you.'

His words thrilled her as much as the kiss. A tear rolled down her cheek. 'That's incredible, what a lovely gesture.'

He sat back in his chair. 'Of course, we needed a new model to go with the new perfume hence the interviews, but I'd already made my mind up, and then you go and turn it down. I'm glad you did though.'

'You mean you were the judge and the jury?'

'Yes, in the next room watching you on screen. Well, it's my name behind the perfume, and I've been around the modelling scene. I guess I know a good model when I see one.'

'In that case, you already know who's won the contract.'

'Certainly do; your friend Zoe has everything and more besides, a vibrant personality that talks to the camera, and such an exotic body.'

'Yes, well, as long as you don't try to sample it.'

'I already have, I haven't changed that much.'

'Bram!'

'I mean I still like a good perfume.'

'Great, let's keep it that way shall we?'

'I promise. Until death tries to part us again.'

'Good one. By the way, how deep is Loch Ness!'

'I don't know and I don't care, but I remember having to leave you naked on the bed. I've never stopped thinking about it.'

She cast her mind back to the moment when she was ready to take him, when he suddenly left and she never saw him again. 'Think what it did to *me!*'

He gave her a flirty look, left his seat, stood behind her and began a sensual massage. 'Okay if we begin where we left off? No... let's start over; an action replay from the beginning. All the props are ready, and the scenery is practically the same.'

'Yes I noticed, how did that come about?'

'Oh, the house... Just mum and dad trying to make me feel at home; they knew I'd arrive here one day. They just didn't expect me so soon, now they're buggering off somewhere else. Good isn't it?'

'Yes, well, they probably think you're old enough to look after yourself. Tell me something Bram, do you believe in the afterlife now?'

He kissed her, picked her up in his arms and carried her out of the study. 'I certainly do, and I definitely think it's a big improvement on the other one.'

Emma smiled. 'Good, so do I. Six hundred years to get to know each other.'

He put her down at the bottom of the stairs. His eyes penetrated hers. 'No, no, we'll know everything there is to know about each other within the next eight hours.'

She gave him a furtive smile, ran her hands over his silk shirt, and undid a couple of the buttons. 'You mean to say you've got it on a mind-disc?'

'Emma, I like your sense of humour; just keep unfastening the buttons. There's two bottles of champagne on ice in the bedroom and one next to the Jacuzzi, we'll start in the Jacuzzi.'

She opened his shirt and slipped it over his shoulders to halfway down his arms, trapping them by his side. She now felt in control and ran her fingers playfully over his chest. 'Are you being serious?'

'I've never been more serious, let's play it out exactly as it was.'

'Well, I don't feel nervous, and I hated it at the time; you want me to act that way?'

'If you can, and when we get to were I left, that's when the action starts, because I'll still be here.'

She played her fingers over his chest. 'I like your style and I get where you're coming from, but supposing I decide to walk off the set at the last minute?'

'If you leave it until the last minute, I don't think you'll want to leave the set.'

He led her upstairs to his bedroom and the adjoining Jacuzzi room. He poured two glasses of champagne. Then he began kissing her on the outside of her clothes, undoing her top buttons at the same time.

She emptied her glass. 'I'm feeling slightly nervous Alistair. Pour me another glass please, while I go and get my dressing gown.'

'Is that necessary?'

'No, but it's in the script.'

'Oh, yes, the script; we'd better keep to the script.'

It was twenty minutes to six when she put on her dressing gown and headed back, her heart pounding, her breath coming in gasps.

At that moment, her mobile rang in her dressing gown pocket.

'Hello.'

'It's me, where are you?' said Zoe.

'On my way upstairs.'

'On your way upstairs … have you phoned Homer?'

'Blast, I forgot.'

'I can't believe you forgot, but it's okay, I rang him, and guess what, Alistair's living in this house, but he's not called Alistair anymore.'

'Oh, right, go on then.'

'He's called Bram Sol… you know, the man behind the new Bram Sol perfume. Interesting isn't it?'

'Very interesting… look, Zoe, I'll catch you up later at the party, when I've finished my meeting with Bram Sol.'

'Oooh! Well, my oh my.'

When she entered the bedroom, he was naked and drying himself off. His well-formed body was as she remembered it, but this time she would have a chance to touch it, stroke it, and run her fingers over every part of it.

He passed her a glass of champagne.

The glass rattled against her teeth as she half emptied it. She let her dressing gown slip to the floor, lay naked on the bed, and closed her eyes.

A whiff of something exotic filled the air. Oil dripped on her hard nipples, in tune with the grandfather clock striking six downstairs, his other hand ran freely over her body.

This time the oil carried on dripping long after the chimes had stopped.

Printed in the United Kingdom
by Lightning Source UK Ltd.
115656UKS00001B/262-300